DICEY'S SONG

Books by Cynthia Voigt

THE BAD GIRLS SERIES

Bad Girls
Bad, Badder, Baddest
It's Not Easy Being Bad
Bad Girls in Love
Bad Girls, Bad Girls, Whatcha Gonna Do?

THE TILLERMAN SERIES

Homecoming
Dicey's Song
A Solitary Blue
The Runner
Come a Stranger
Sons from Afar
Seventeen Against the Dealer

THE KINGDOM SERIES

Jackaroo
On Fortune's Wheel
The Wings of a Falcon
Elske

OTHER BOOKS

Building Blocks
The Callender Papers
David and Jonathan
Izzy, Willy-Nilly
Orfe
Tell Me if the Lovers Are Losers
Tree by Leaf
The Vandemark Mummy
When She Hollers

DICEY'S SONG

CYNTHIA VOIGT

ATHENEUM BOOKS FOR YOUNG READERS
New York London Toronto Sydney New Delhi

ATHENEUM BOOKS FOR YOUNG READERS
An imprint of Simon & Schuster Children's Publishing Division
1230 Avenue of the Americas, New York, New York 10020
This book is a work of fiction. Any references to historical events, real people, or real locales are used fictitiously. Other names, characters, places, and incidents are products of the author's imagination, and any resemblance to actual events or locales or persons, living or dead, is entirely coincidental.

For information about special discounts for bulk purchases, please contact Simon & Schuster Special Sales at 1-866-506-1949 or business@simonandschuster.com.
The Simon & Schuster Speakers Bureau can bring authors to your live event. For more information or to book an event, contact the Simon & Schuster Speakers Bureau at 1-866-248-3049 or visit our website at www.simonspeakers.com.
Also available in an Atheneum Books for Young Readers hardcover edition
Book design by Debra Sfetsios-Conover
The text for this book is set in Baskerville.
Manufactured in the United States of America
This Atheneum Books for Young Readers paperback edition March 2012
10 9
The Library of Congress has cataloged the hardcover edition as follows:
Voigt, Cynthia.
Dicey's song.
Summary: Now that the four abandoned Tillerman children are settled in with their grandmother, Dicey finds that their new beginnings require love, trust, humor, and courage.
ISBN 978-0-689-30944-1
[1. Brothers and sisters—Fiction. 2. Family Life—Fiction] I. Title.
PZ7.V874Di
[Fic] 82-3882
ISBN 978-1-4424-5060-8 (hc)
ISBN 978-1-4424-2879-9 (pbk)
ISBN 978-0-689-84798-1 (eBook)

To Duffle

What a day, Dicey thought. What a summer, for that matter, but especially, What a day. She stood alone in the big old barn, in a patch of moonlight; stood looking at the sailboat resting on its sawhorse cradle, a darker patch among shadows. Behind her, the wind blew off the water, bringing the faint smell of salt and the rich, moist smell of the marshes.

You never knew where a road would end, Dicey thought, the breeze curling around her ears, you just knew that roads ended. Not like water, which always kept moving. Not like the stars, tossed out across the sky—the stars had made that light millions of years ago and already they were burning with new light. And the moon too, the moon would swell and dwindle, go dark and swell again. But the Tillermans traveled on a road, and roads ended. Dicey's road, and James's, Maybeth's, Sammy's, had ended here. The Tillermans' road had rolled up against Gram's house, and they had tumbled off it into Gram's—Dicey grinned. Not exactly into Gram's arms, maybe not into her lap. Certainly into her life.

So. So they were going to live here, on the rundown farm, with Gram—Dicey's heart danced again, inside her, to say it to herself like that. Home. *Home with their momma's momma, who was also a Tillerman. Home: a home with plenty of room for the four children in the shabby farmhouse, room inside, room outside, and the kind of room within Gram too—Dicey had seen Gram and how she listened when Maybeth sang, how she talked with James, how her eyes smiled at the things Sammy said and did—the kind of room that was what they really needed. One of the lessons the long summer had taught Dicey was how to figure out what they really needed.*

Dicey studied her sneakers, gray with old grime, the places where her toes had worn through pockets of darkness. When she wiggled her toes in the moonlight's shadows, she couldn't see anything moving. Home for Dicey, too, with the Bay—the Chesapeake Bay, quiet with little waves and long tides—the Bay just out of sight, with this grandmother whose character had sharp corners and unexpected turns, with the sailboat waiting here in the barn.

She stepped into the darkness and placed both her hands flat against the rough hull of the boat. Imagining how it would feel when the little boat rode on the water; how it would respond to the wind in its sails, to the waves sliding by, to her hand on the tiller. She leaned her forehead against the wood, feeling the solid curve of the hull against her skin. Unexpectedly, she found herself yawning, a huge, hollow yawn that stretched her diaphragm up against her heart and cracked the hinges of her jaw.

Dicey smiled to herself. Here it was, probably the most exciting day of her life, certainly one of the best, and all she felt was tired. As if all the walking and worrying, all the hunger and hope of the long summer, all hit her at once. Her bones sagged and her brain couldn't grab onto any ideas. The muscles that held her bones in working order ached, but not a hurting ache, kind of a contented throb.

Dicey yawned again. She guessed she'd better get to bed, but she guessed she knew why she didn't want to: this happiness blew through her like wind, buoyed her up like water, and she wanted to float along on it. But the summer had worn her out, like it had worn out her sneakers; and tomorrow she'd have to start school, but on the weekend she'd get the boat into the water and learn how to sail it; the long summer stretched behind them, they'd made it through, made it home.

CHAPTER 1

And they lived happily ever after.

Not the Tillermans. Dicey thought. That wasn't the way things went for the Tillermans, ever. She wasn't about to let that get her down. She couldn't let it get her down—that was what had happened to Momma.

Dicey lay on her back under the wide-branched paper mulberry tree. She opened her eyes and looked up. The paper mulberry had broad leaves that made a pool of shade in which she lay. Thick roots spread around her, making a kind of chair for her to lean on. She wore only shorts in the hot midday air. Her arms and chest were spattered and streaked with red paint, and the barn was completely painted, top to bottom, all four sides, patched and painted and looking good. The paint and sweat were drying on Dicey's body. She could hear the buzzing of insects and nothing else. For once she was alone, but she knew where everybody was.

Gram had taken James downtown in the motorboat. Gram was going to get groceries and James was going to the library to find some books for Dicey, on repairing and maintaining wooden boats. Maybeth was up in her room, doing some of the many extra assignments her teacher gave her, so she could catch up with the rest of the third graders and not be kept back again. Sammy was out back, on the other side of the old farmhouse, spading up fallow land to increase the size of the vegetable garden. Gram had said, right off, that they would have to do more planting next spring than she'd done for years, with four more people to feed. Dicey suspected that Gram hadn't been sure how the children would feel about the work.

Well, Gram would learn about them. And they would learn about Gram. There would be some surprises for everyone, Dicey guessed. She knew Gram had already been surprised: at Dicey's reaction when her sailboat—the one she had hoped over and dreamed over—sank into the shallow water by Gram's dock. Even James was surprised by how calm she stayed, maybe because he had seen Dicey's face as they hauled it down the quarter-mile path through the marsh, seen her strain and pull and check to be sure the wheels they'd removed from a wagon and fixed to the legs of the sawhorse cradle didn't fall off, seen how much it mattered to her.

Dicey had watched the water pouring in through the leaks where the boards had shrunk apart with all those years of drying out. She had watched—they had all stood and watched, as the little boat filled up with water and settled quietly down onto the sandy bottom of the Chesapeake Bay.

"I should have remembered," Gram had said. "I knew, if only I remembered."

"You can't sail in that," Sammy declared.

Dicey had stared down at the chipped paint on the gunwales of the boat, which still showed above the water. The boat was her lucky charm, her rabbit's foot, her horseshoe, her pot of gold, it was the prize she'd set for herself for leading them from nowhere to somewhere. Okay, she said to herself, thinking about what needed to be done. They'd have to bail it before they could get it out of the water. Then they'd have to take it back to the barn. She told James to find something to bail with. They'd have to slide the cradle back into the water, it would probably take all four children to do that.

"You don't rest a minute, do you," Gram had said. Dicey shook her head; she had already gotten used to her grandmother's way of asking questions without question marks. "But you'd do better to let it sit out here a day or so," Gram had advised. "Let the wood soak up water, to swell up again. I knew that once, but I forgot. I'm sorry, girl," she said.

Dicey hadn't answered, just looked at Gram where she stood on the dock with the wind blowing her curly gray hair around her face.

"Dicey doesn't mind, as long as she knows what to do about things," Maybeth told Gram.

"Is that right," Gram asked Dicey.

"I guess so," Dicey said.

"What do you do when there's nothing you *can* do," Gram said.

"I dunno, I do something else," Dicey said.

"That doesn't make sense," James pointed out. "That's illogical."

Gram looked around at all of them.

"Which one of your sons built this boat?" Dicey asked, but Gram had turned away to go back to the house and didn't answer.

Remembering that scene, Dicey reminded herself that they all had a lot of learning to do. The boat was back in the barn and she had to begin scraping off the old layers of paint. But not quite yet. Gram and James would be back soon, and they'd have lunch, and then Dicey wanted to go downtown to see about a job. She'd been thinking about what kind of job she could get, all those long first three days of school. There wasn't much else to think about in school. As far as she was concerned, about all school was good for was using up your days. Dicey hadn't talked to anyone, except to answer teachers' questions. That was okay with her, because she had important things to think about. Getting a job, to bring in some money was one. Tillermans always needed more money, because there were so many of them to feed. Dicey knew Gram worried about that. For that matter, Dicey worried about that too, and had worried all her life, because at thirteen, she was the oldest. That worry about food had been her single biggest worry all summer long, when they had traveled down here, after Momma disappeared. The other worries—about what James was thinking, because what James thought in his head told him what to do; about whether or not Maybeth was retarded as people claimed, or only shy, slow, and frightened, which was what Dicey thought; about why Sammy was so angry he hit out and didn't mind how much the person he fought with hurt him;—those worries, and worries about how much Dicey should give up for her brothers and sisters in order to have any kind of home together—or if she was driving them too hard; about how many miles they had covered and where they were ever going—all the other worries had come and gone. The worry about food had haunted her all summer long, and maybe it always would.

There were still things to worry about here, but nothing crucial. James said everything was all right now, now they could live with Gram. James was smart, but he wanted everything to be all right so badly that he couldn't see—

Couldn't see what? Dicey asked herself. She hunkered up, resting her back against the tree.

Couldn't see how big troubles had little beginnings, just like little troubles.

Dicey heard voices approaching the house from behind. Nobody ever came up the front driveway. Gram didn't have a car and couldn't drive. She always went downtown in the motorboat. So except for the children's bicycles, the overgrown tracks that led off from the front of the house, through a stand of pines and between two long barren fields to the road, were unmarked. The voices came clearer.

Lazily, Dicey stood up and went around to help carry in bags of groceries. When she got around back, Sammy had taken the extra bag in his grubby arms. His face appeared at the top, streaked with dirt. Dicey looked at him and grinned, and made a mental note to tell Gram that he was having his seventh birthday next week. James trailed up through the garden, carrying another bag.

"You two are a mess," Gram announced, before she even went up the back steps. She looked at Dicey and hesitated, as if deciding whether or not to say what she was thinking. "You're too old to go around half-naked," she announced.

"What do you mean?" Dicey demanded. "I am not." Gram was already in the kitchen. "Am I, James?" Dicey asked.

"You know, Dicey," he said. His eyes shifted away from hers. At ten he was old enough to be embarrassed. He hurried after Gram.

Well, she guessed she did know. She guessed she had noticed when she had stripped off her T-shirt that her breasts seemed to be pointing out—maybe. But she had convinced herself that wasn't true. Dicey shrugged. There wasn't much she could do about getting a bosom, but she didn't have to like it.

Gram made a plate of peanut butter and jelly sandwiches for lunch, and she had put out a bowl of apples. Dicey had washed off most of the paint with turpentine. Then she and Sammy rinsed off with a quick swim, and she had put her shirt on. Sammy's yellow hair was slicked down.

James was on his third sandwich and Maybeth was still nibbling at her first. "How did it go?" Gram asked. "How many pages did you get read?"

"Four," Maybeth answered softly, without looking up. "That's not enough," she added.

Gram looked at Dicey, and Dicey sighed. "Is the book too hard?" Dicey asked her sister's bent head. Maybeth's hair was as bright as sunlight, and she'd tied it back with a red ribbon. "Where'd you find the ribbon?" Dicey asked.

"Gram got it for me," Maybeth said. She looked up at Dicey then, with a little smile. Dicey liked the way Maybeth looked, like an angel, a Christmas angel. It was partly her wide, hazel eyes and her soft hair that curled gently at the ends; but more, it was the quiet ways she had. "I think it's pretty."

"It is," Dicey assured her. She, herself, like James, had their father's straight brown hair. Which was about all they had of their father, that and the narrow face; Maybeth and Sammy looked like Momma—round and fair. But Dicey and James were mixes: Yet all the Tillermans had hazel eyes. She couldn't remember the color of their father's eyes, or exactly what he looked like; just his voice. Not surprising since she was seven the last time she saw him. "Was the book too hard?" she asked again.

Maybeth shook her head. "I have to keep working, Mrs. Jackson said," she told Dicey. "Only I can't remember what the words are, so I have to go back and memorize the lists again. If I work, Mrs. Jackson says, everything will be all right."

Dicey wanted to cooperate with this Mrs. Jackson. "We'll do fractions after dinner," she promised Maybeth, who nodded with no more enthusiasm than Dicey felt. "Is it okay if I go downtown this afternoon?" she asked her grandmother. "The barn is finished," she added, to distract her grandmother from any question about what Dicey wanted to do in town.

Gram looked as if she knew Dicey wanted to distract her. But she didn't know why. She decided not to ask. "I'm pleased it's done," she said.

"You don't sound pleased," Sammy pointed out.

"Appearances," Gram declared, "can be deceiving."

Sammy thought about that. "Why?" he asked.

Gram snorted. "Because you can't judge a book by its cover."

"Why not?" Sammy wondered.

Dicey had decided to ask Millie Tydings, who owned the little grocery store down by the water at the foot of the one main street, if she had a job open. The store wasn't ever busy, at least not ever when Dicey was in there. She wondered if anybody besides Gram shopped there, and she couldn't blame them. Millie didn't keep the windows or floors particularly clean. Dust gathered on the cans and boxes on unwashed shelves. The meat and fish counter, behind which Millie worked most of the time, got wiped down every day, Dicey guessed from the way the white enamel gleamed. Millie might be lazy, she might just be too tired (and Dicey guessed if she had to tote that body around every day, all day long, she'd get tired too), or she might just not care. Whatever the reason, Dicey figured there was a lot of work she could do in Millie's store.

Dicey leaned her bike up against the grimy plate glass window and entered the dim little store. Millie was at the back, leaning against the top of the meat counter. "What can I do for you today?" she asked. "Your grandmother forget something?" Her little blue eyes rested lazily on Dicey. She had gray hair that she braided into circles around her head.

"No," Dicey answered. "I came to ask you if you might give me a job."

"A job? Why? Why should I do that? I don't make enough to keep myself in comfortable shoes," Millie told her.

"But if I kept the place cleaner, more people would want to come and shop," Dicey argued. "If I washed the windows and the floors and dusted off the shelves and the cans and the boxes."

"My Herbie used to do that," Millie said, "before he died. Business isn't good," she told Dicey.

Dicey made herself be patient. She'd just been talking about that, and how to make it better. "But it should be," she argued. She'd thought about this all the long bike ride into town. "I mean, you have the only grocery store right downtown, the only store that people can walk to. The supermarkets are way out on the edge of town, and people have to drive there. It would be more convenient for people to come to you. If your store looked nicer they would want to."

Millie seemed to be thinking about this. "Business used to be better," she finally said.

Dicey stared at the woman, at the heavy mottled flesh of her face. She thought maybe Millie wasn't very smart at all. She'd never thought of that before. If that was the case, how would she go about convincing Millie to give her a job?

"I think business could be better, if the store looked better," she said.

Millie's eyes moved slowly around, studying the narrow aisles. "It's dirty," she said. "But not back here," she added. "I've always passed the health department inspection."

"You're a good butcher," Dicey said, trying a little flattery. "Gram says so."

"Really?" Millie smiled at this. "Did she really?" Dicey nodded, it was the truth. "Ab always was smart and quick. You know, we all—all of us in school—hankered after John Tillerman. He was so handsome and dignified, you know?" Dicey nodded, even though she didn't know. "But it was Ab he courted. There were some tears shed over that, I can tell you." Millie nodded her big head wisely.

Dicey didn't know how to get the conversation back on the

track she wanted. "Gram says your husband taught you how to be a butcher."

"When we got married, that's right. I wasn't so fat then," she said. "We never did have any children." She relapsed into silence.

"If I worked here," Dicey said finally, "there's lots I could do."

"Aren't you supposed to be in school?"

"I mean, maybe after school for an hour, maybe Saturdays in the mornings."

"That wouldn't be very long. So it wouldn't cost me very much. I'd like the company," Millie said. "How much were you thinking of me paying?"

"A dollar an hour," Dicey said. She was under age, so she couldn't charge much.

Millie thought about this, her fat sausage-shaped fingers working on the countertop.

"I thought, if I worked four days a week after school, and then three hours on Saturday," Dicey said.

The fingers moved. "That would be seven dollars a week," Millie announced. Dicey nodded. She figured, with seven dollars, she could give each of the little kids an allowance of a dollar a week and the rest to Gram. Except—now she changed that plan—she'd give herself an allowance too. They'd never had allowances. Momma never had any extra money at all to be able to count on to give them. So when they wanted paper or pencils for school, or shoelaces, they had to ask her, and her face got all worried until she figured out where to find the extra money.

"I don't know," Millie said.

"We could try it," Dicey offered. "I could work for three weeks on trial. Then, if your business wasn't getting better, you could fire me."

"I never fired anybody, I don't know how," Millie objected.

"You see," Dicey spoke urgently, "my theory is that your

business will get better, and so instead of costing you money, I'd be making you money."

"Do you think so?" Millie asked.

Dicey bit her lip and nodded. This was like talking to a bowl of Jell-O. Everything you said slipped in and jiggled the Jell-O, but it didn't make any dents.

"So you think it might work out that way?"

Dicey nodded. Like a bowl of strawberry Jell-O, her least favorite kind.

"Then maybe I should."

"I'll start on Monday," Dicey said quickly. "I'll come in after school on Monday, so that'll be about three fifteen I'll be here."

"All right," Millie said.

Dicey left before the woman could change her mind. Maybe it would work, maybe it wouldn't; her guess was that it would. In any case, she had the next three weeks taken care of. She was satisfied, she thought, riding seven miles back over flat, curving roads to her grandmother's house. To our house, she corrected herself. But when she said *our house* she couldn't help thinking about the cabin in Provincetown, up against the windy dunes; even though she knew that wasn't their house any more.

At dinner, she told everyone about her job. She looked mostly at Gram while she was telling, and thought the woman approved. "But aren't you under age?" Gram asked her.

"Yes, but Millie didn't seem to mind. She didn't even ask," Dicey said.

"That's because she never had a thought in her head that somebody else didn't put there for her," Gram said.

"You mean she's stupid?" Sammy asked. He shoveled spaghetti into his mouth in long strands, because he was too hungry to practice winding it on a fork. He had spaghetti sauce all over his face.

"You might say that," Gram agreed. "What about school?" she asked Dicey.

"School's easy," Dicey told her. "I won't have any trouble in school." At least, she wouldn't have any trouble passing, unless it got so bad in the stupid home ec course they made her sign up for that she started cutting classes. "I thought"—she looked at James's admiring face, and Sammy's spaghetti decorated one, and Maybeth's quiet one—"we should have allowances. A dollar a week," she announced, pleased with herself.

"Even me?" Sammy demanded.

"Even you," Dicey agreed.

"Good-o," Sammy said. "Even Gram?"

Dicey met her grandmother's eyes. She couldn't tell, from the expressionless face, whether Gram was amused, or angry, or insulted. "Gram too, but Gram gets more. It's only seven dollars a week, all together," she apologized. "That would be only three dollars a week. And if her business doesn't get better, after three weeks I'll have to find something else."

"You could get some shoes," Sammy told his grandmother. "You need to wear shoes when the weather gets cold."

Gram's expression resolved itself into amusement.

"Well, you do," Sammy pressed on. Gram always wore bare feet, unless she was going into town, bare feet and a long skirt, with a blouse loose over it. She wore her clothes for comfort, she told the children.

"I have shoes I wear in cold weather," she told Sammy. "How do you think I lived so long? Not by going barefoot in cold weather."

"I didn't know that," Sammy complained. "How could I know? I thought it was a good idea."

"It was," Dicey assured him. "So it's all right?" she asked her grandmother.

"If you've made the arrangements, it'll have to be," Gram said. "But I always thought, if you were a family, you talked over your plans first."

"And got permission," James reminded Dicey.

"Not permission," Gram said, "just to check in."

Dicey bit back anger. She thought, she said to herself, she was doing something pretty smart and to help out too. Nobody said thank you, or anything.

"I'm proud of Dicey," Maybeth said softly.

"Oh, so am I," Gram said. "I think Dicey knows that. You get things done, girl, I've got to give you that."

"So do I," Sammy said.

"It's what Tillermans do," Dicey said, feeling better.

"And I had something to talk over too," Gram told them. "I've got an appointment downtown next week, about getting welfare money," she said, as if the words tasted bitter. Then she added, "I thought I might as well talk to a lawyer and get advice and ask about adoption. If that's what you want."

"But what about Momma?" Sammy asked.

"Momma's sick, you know that," Dicey said quickly. "She can't take care of us. She might get better, and she might not."

"The doctors think she won't," James added.

Sammy had stopped eating. "Because she's crazy sick?" he asked.

Dicey nodded.

"But how does she eat?" he demanded. "If she doesn't eat she'll die."

Dicey looked helplessly at her grandmother. "They have ways of feeding people, with tubes and special liquids," Gram said. You could see Sammy thinking about this.

"But if you adopted us and Momma came back—" he said to Gram.

"Then we would put you and James into one bedroom, and your momma would sleep where you're sleeping," Gram answered quickly, "because that was her room when she lived at home." Dicey could have gotten up and hugged her grandmother, except that they never did that kind of thing, the Tillermans, hugging and kissing. "Or," Gram said, "we might turn the dining room into a bedroom. We never use it and she would have more privacy." Gram waited a minute for more questions, then nodded briskly. "That's all taken care of then," she said.

"If you wanted to adopt us," Dicey said, "I'd like that."

"And me," Maybeth said. The boys, too, agreed.

"It would be safer for us," James explained. "We'd have legal status, and rights. But what about you?" he asked his grandmother.

"Might be safer for me, too," Gram said sharply. James looked at her, with sudden intensity, as if he wondered what she was thinking and suspected that it might be very interesting. But he didn't say anything.

Dicey and Maybeth washed up the dishes. Dicey hurried through them, but Maybeth lingered, humming. It was Momma's song, about giving her love a cherry without any stone, and Dicey joined in. She was drying the forks and putting them away while Maybeth scrubbed down the wooden table. "How can there be a baby with no cry-ing," they sang. All of a sudden, Dicey remembered how the words to the last verse answered that question, and the other impossible questions the song asked. "That's funny," she said.

"What is?"

"The song. You just look at things another way and it all makes sense. When a chicken's an egg, it doesn't have bones. Isn't that funny?"

"I think it's sad," Maybeth said. "Anyway, the music is. Momma sang it sad."

Dicey didn't know what to say, so she started the last verse.

They worked at fractions. Maybeth's class had done them last year, in second grade. Mrs. Jackson had told Maybeth she should understand fractions from one half to one eighth. Dicey figured that would be pretty simple. She took an apple and a knife and cut the apple in half. Then she cut it into quarters, then halved the quarters. Maybeth watched with big eyes. When Dicey wrote down the fractions and showed Maybeth the numbers one fourth and one eighth and asked her which was bigger, Maybeth pointed to one eighth.

Dicey tried to explain. "That *one* up there doesn't mean anything. I mean, it's called the numerator and it tells you how many of the eight parts are there."

"I know," Maybeth said, studying the numbers seriously. "Since the *one* is the same, the fraction with *eight* is bigger."

Dicey showed her on the apple pieces, but since she had to combine two of the eighths to make a quarter, Maybeth said the *two* was bigger than the *one* now.

Dicey tried another approach. "In fractions, the bigger the number in the denominator—that's at the bottom—the smaller the fraction is."

"But how can that be?" Maybeth wondered.

"Because you're talking about parts, not the whole number. It's different from the whole numbers." Dicey felt frustrated. It was so clear in her own mind, and Maybeth just sat and looked at her, or at the apple pieces, or at the paper. Her eyes got bigger.

"I don't understand," she whispered.

Dicey didn't know what to do. "That's okay," she said. "They aren't important."

"I'm supposed to know them," Maybeth said.

"We'll try again," Dicey said. "Some other time. I am going to eat an eighth," she announced, popping the crisp apple slice into her mouth. She had done it wrong and she didn't know how to do it right. She tried not to look as discouraged as she felt.

Maybeth smiled at her. "And I'm eating a half," she said, eating another eighth, one that had been set beside its equal to make a quarter.

The rest of the family was in the living room. They had opened the windows to catch any suggestion of a breeze. Outside, the sun was setting and splashing the sky with colors. Maybeth went right to the battered upright piano and picked out the tune she had been singing in the kitchen. She searched for notes that harmonized with the melody lines. Dicey watched her for a while, trying to figure out how to explain about fractions. Maybeth's back was straight. Her face was serious as she watched her fingers on the piano keys. After a while, she tried to add more harmony with notes played by her left hand.

Gram and Sammy sat playing checkers, both of them barefooted, both concentrating on the board. They sneaked looks at one another's faces, as if trying to see what the opponent was thinking of for his next move. When Sammy was doing something tricky, it showed on his face. His eyes danced while he waited for his grandmother to fall into his trap, as if he could barely keep his cleverness inside. Gram gave herself away by her mouth, Dicey decided, because it would get all stiff and straight. That way, you could tell she was hiding something, and all you had to do was look at the board to figure out what her scheme was. Dicey thought she'd like to play a game of checkers with Gram. She thought she could probably beat her.

"King me," Sammy ordered. Gram pointed out that he was still one move from the end of the board. "Momma used to,"

Sammy argued. He was losing the game. His voice quivered.

"If you're going to play with me, you're going to play by the rules," Gram said. "You're big enough, aren't you, to play by the real rules."

Sammy didn't want to say yes and he didn't want to say no. When he saw the way Gram looked across at him, he didn't say anything.

Dicey went to stand behind James, who sat at the big wooden desk reading a thick book. He looked up over his shoulder at her and marked his place on the small print with a finger. "How long do you think it'll take to get the boat fixed up?" Dicey asked him.

"Not now, Dicey, I'm reading."

"What're you reading?"

"The Bible."

"Why?"

James sighed. "Mr. Thomas said every educated man should. He said it's one of the underpinnings of western civilization." His face lit up. "Isn't that an idea? Underpinnings of civilization? As if—civilization were a big building, you know? Besides, there are some good stories in the Bible."

"And besides," Gram added in, "it was the fattest book on the shelves and James always likes to read the fattest ones."

"That's not true," James said.

"Isn't it," Gram answered.

"And besides," James said, "if you have a big idea, you have to write it down in a big book, otherwise you won't be able to explain all the complicated parts."

"Didn't say there was anything wrong with what you were doing," Gram remarked.

The piano behind them played on, softly, through all this, as if Maybeth knew that everything was all right in the room.

"And look at this, Dicey," James said quietly. He turned the heavy pages back to the beginning. There was a long list of names and dates, in different handwritings. Some of the ink was so old it had turned brown. The list went all the way down one page and partway down the next.

James's finger pointed to an entry on the second page. *John Tillerman md. Abigail, 1936,* she read. Then there were three names, in a row, in the same handwriting, with dates of birth beside them: John Tillerman, Elizabeth Tillerman, Samuel Tillerman. By Samuel there were two dates, and the last date had been put in later, by a different hand. The same hand that put in a date of death for the first John Tillerman. Dicey touched Momma's name there in the ink and pointed at Samuel's name. "That's Bullet, our uncle."

"He was only nineteen," James pointed out. They were talking almost in a whisper.

"It was a war," Dicey explained.

"Even so," James said, "that's still young. He was only six years older than you. Only nine older than me."

We should be written down too, Dicey thought. But maybe Gram didn't want that.

"I can hear what you're thinking, girl," her grandmother said. Dicey looked up, alarmed. "And you're right," Gram said. She got up, took James's place at the desk, and pulled an old fountain pen out of the drawer. Slowly, she wrote down their names: Dicey Tillerman. James Tillerman. Maybeth Tillerman. Samuel Tillerman.

They all looked at the names there. At last, Gram said, "That's settled too." She gave James back his seat.

None of the children said anything. Dicey guessed that, like her, they couldn't think of how to say all the things they were thinking. Finally, Sammy found words. "Good-o," he declared.

Gram smiled to herself and agreed to play another game of

checkers with him. James went back to his reading, Maybeth back to the piano. For a while, Dicey watched them all.

Then she wandered out of the room. She had nothing to do. Her homework she had finished quickly after school on Friday, just some math, and memorizing for science. There weren't any chores she could think of. She decided to go outside.

Outside was better than inside, Dicey always thought that. In Provincetown, where they had lived with their momma, they were always outside, on the dunes and down by the rushing water. Summertimes they would go out early in the morning and stay all day. The rooms in their little cabin were awfully small, especially with four children and one of them Sammy, so they had spent all the time they could outside. But even here, in Gram's house, with its big, boxy rooms, Dicey preferred outside. She liked the water. She liked the stretch of water leading before her and she liked the stretch of sky overhead.

Dicey crossed the lawn at the back, went through the garden, and then headed down the narrow path through the tall marsh grasses. Overhead, the growing darkness turned the sky to the color of blueberries, and long clouds floated gray. The only movement Dicey could see in the Bay, when she sat dangling her feet over the end of the dock, was the turgid, slow sweeping of tide. She wiped sweat off her forehead. She looked out across the flat water. Just a band of burning orange was left from the sunset, but the water caught that and transformed it, lying before Dicey like a field of gold. Like cloth of gold.

Dicey was feeling edgy and not really like herself. Probably, she told herself, it was all these changes that were permanent. The new home and the new school and Gram. But Dicey didn't mind changes, she'd gotten used to them over the summer. For a minute, she unrolled the adventures of the summer out, like ribbons. The ribbons unrolled back until Dicey saw her momma's face. But it wasn't her momma's own face she saw, it was the photograph the police in Bridgeport had shown her for identification, that faraway face lying back against a white pillow, with the golden hair cut short all around it.

The sadness of Momma lost to them, maybe forever, was something Dicey carried around deep inside her all the time, and maybe that explained her edginess. Dicey wasn't used to carrying sadness around. She was used to seeing trouble and doing something about it. She just didn't know anything to do about Momma.

What Dicey was used to, she realized, was things being simple, like a song. You sang the words and the melody straight through. That was the way she had brought her family down here to Crisfield, singing straight through.

Gram probably knew something about carrying sorrow around. However she acted, Dicey knew Gram had cared about her three children who all left her and never came back. She wondered how Gram carried her sorrows. Maybe someday, when they had all got used to one another, she would ask.

The first pale stars were coming out. It was the dark of the moon, so the stars burned brighter, especially the evening star, hanging just over the horizon. Dicey knew she should get back inside and send Maybeth and Sammy up to bed. But she didn't want to and maybe she wouldn't.

She lay on her back along the dock and looked up at the stars. The sky was turning black and the stars burned out there, unchanging. All those stars, and those dark millions of light years . . . Dicey wondered if the space between was to push the stars apart or hold them together.

She jumped up impatiently. That was James's kind of idea,

and when she started having ideas like that it was time to get back inside.

When she returned to the house, only James was still in the living room. "Where are the little kids?" Dicey asked.

"They went to bed, half an hour ago. They're asleep; Gram tucked them in and went up to check later."

"You should have called me."

"Gram said maybe you wanted to be off on your own. She said you put in a long, hard summer with all of us, and we should remember that you might want to get away once in a while."

Dicey didn't know what to answer. She was surprised to hear that Gram understood that, but still—she almost wished Sammy and Maybeth hadn't wanted to go to bed without saying good night to her.

James had his face back in the book. "Am I bothering you?" Dicey asked. He shook his head, but his eyes were asking her questions. "Is something wrong?"

He put his eyes back on the page. "I'm just wondering how things are going to go for us this year. And for me. I mean, it's not as if we were her real children—and at school too. What if it doesn't work out?"

"She's going to adopt us, you heard her. She wants to, she likes us," Dicey said. "She put us down in the Bible."

"I know," James said. "But, Dicey? You never understand, because it's always so easy for you, you just go ahead and do what you want. And Sammy, too, and everybody likes Maybeth. And I think Sammy must remind her of our uncle Bullet."

"What are you talking about?" Dicey demanded.

"But I never fit in, not at Provincetown, or coming down here if you think about it. I think about it."

"But you did, we did it together," Dicey pointed out. The trouble with James was he thought too much about things.

"Some people, they're always outsiders, wherever they are."

"So am I," Dicey told him, finally understanding what he was worrying about.

"Yeah, but you don't care," James said.

Dicey couldn't argue with him about that. "I wouldn't worry about it, James," she advised.

"Why not?" he asked.

"Because it won't do any good," Dicey snapped.

He didn't believe her, she could tell. She didn't let that bother her. She just picked up one of the books on boat building and went up to read in bed.

During the next week, Dicey settled herself into a routine. She rode her bike to school (the little kids took the bus, which stopped for them right by Gram's mailbox), sat through classes, and spent an hour exactly in Millie's store. Except for the windows, the difference Dicey's work made didn't show much the first week. But after she'd spent three hours on Saturday morning washing down the floors, the store really did look cleaner, more like a place where you would like to buy food.

Dicey had planned out her work at the store, what to do first, second, third, during the long, slow school days, going from science to math to social studies to gym to English to home ec. The only class she couldn't think in was home ec, because there you had to do things. Stupid things, Dicey reported to James. They were starting with sewing, buttons first. It wasn't interesting, but you had to watch what you were doing or you attracted Miss Eversleigh's attention and she would come stand behind you at the long table, explaining over again all the boring things you had already listened to, how to thread a needle and tie the knot, how to position the button and lock it in place, boring-boring-boring. Dicey had more important things to think about. Miss Eversleigh might care about that stuff, that was her business, and

Dicey guessed the tall, bony, white-haired woman didn't have anything better to do. But Dicey had much better things to do. She had her own routine.

When she rode home from her job, Dicey would work for an hour on the boat, scraping off the old layers of paint, before going inside to help Gram with supper or some other housework. After supper, she would listen to Maybeth read for a while and help her review the lists of words. Then she would dash off the busy work her teachers gave as homework and spend an hour studying the boat books.

On Sunday, Gram asked Dicey to give her some advice about the papers and pamphlets she had been given at the welfare Office and by the lawyer. "I can't figure these forms out," Gram said, irritated. She had them all spread in front of her, covering half the long kitchen table. "So you're going to have to put your nose into them and help me, girl."

If Gram needed her help, that was fine with Dicey. And if she couldn't figure things out, she could always enlist James's aid. "Between us," she promised Gram, "we can do anything."

"Humph," Gram said. "I hope you're not counting on that."

Dicey met her grandmother's eyes, across the table. "You do it too, don't you?" she asked. "Worrying," she explained.

"Doesn't hurt to be prepared," Gram said. "I've never taken charity, never wanted to. I don't expect to enjoy the experience, don't expect it to be easy. I like to be prepared for the worst. It saves trouble."

Dicey remembered that the next Wednesday, when Maybeth came home from school with a note. As Dicey walked over from putting her bike away in the barn, she saw Gram shucking the last ears of corn from the garden. Gram sat on the back steps with her toes dug into the sun-warmed dirt. "Something on the table you should look at," Gram told her.

Dicey knew what it was before she picked it up. A note from Maybeth's teacher. Maybeth was always coming home with notes from her teacher, saying could they please have a conference, not saying what they wanted to confer about. In Dicey's experience, what they wanted to talk about was what to do about Maybeth being so slow, about how they wanted to put her back a grade, which wasn't doing anything as far as Dicey could tell. Only the nun at the day camp in Bridgeport that summer had talked about really *doing* something. But what she wanted to do was send Maybeth to a special school for retarded people. Dicey didn't believe Maybeth was retarded, not the way she could learn music, the melodies and the words. But Dicey couldn't be sure; how could she be sure? She made herself pick up the piece of paper from the table.

She took the folded paper outside to sit beside Gram while she read it. It was from Maybeth's music teacher, asking Gram to come in for a meeting, the next day, at three fifteen, as soon as school let out. "But Maybeth can sing," Dicey protested. "She never had a note from her music teacher before," Dicey told Gram.

"I don't know," Gram said. Her fingers pulled the long protective leaves from the ears of corn. This late in the season, half of the ears in her pile were too wormy to eat. Those she tossed into a mound on a brown paper bag. "I don't know what this young man is in such a hurry for."

"I'm sorry," Dicey said. "I'll go in and see him before work."

"I'll go," Gram told her quickly. "I was planning to. I'm the one who should, anyway, I'm the name that's on their thousands of forms."

Dicey was so relieved she didn't know what to say. Instead, she picked up an ear and started pulling off the leaves. "I'm sorry," she said again.

"You don't look it," Gram observed.

Dicey looked up at her grandmother's face. Gram rewarded her with a sudden smile and spoke briskly. "You're not the only one responsible, girl. You've been responsible a long time and done a good job. Take a rest now."

Dicey nodded her head and that was that. She finished the corn and dropped the husks into the garbage can on her way out to work on the sailboat.

CHAPTER 2

Dicey swallowed back a yawn and looked out the window. It was close and hot in the classroom, just like every other classroom she had ever been in. The windows were open, the temperature was almost ninety, the grass on the front lawn of the old brick school building was dry and brown. The building, which housed all the grades from seven through twelve, had been built like a double decker U; from her window Dicey could see the front entrance, the long sidewalk, and the empty street. No breeze stirred the leaves on the big oaks that marked the front of the schoolyard. Their leaves drooped down, dispirited by the heat, and hung there. Like dogs' tongues, Dicey thought, and pictured the tree panting with many tiny tongues, maybe even dripping saliva the way a dog's would. She felt a smile wash over her face.

Lazily, she brought her eyes back into the classroom. Like every classroom she had ever been in, it had long, many-paned windows and a wall of green chalkboard at the front. At the back was a wall of bulletin board, so close behind her she could reach back and touch it if she wanted to. The students' desks made a square, six by six, and Dicey was sitting where she always did, back in the far left-hand corner, next to the windows. Her desk had a kind of tray attached to it, to write on, and a rack under the seat for her books. She had an English textbook open in front of her and the teacher, Mr. Chappelle, was introducing the next unit of study. They'd spent the first three weeks on diagramming and now they were going to read some stories. Dicey was sorry the diagramming was finished. She liked the precision of it. Besides, it was easy.

"Conflict," was written on the board in Mr. Chappelle's square printing. He couldn't write on a straight line. He was young and skinny and had carroty red hair that he kept trying to brush flat with his hands, but it always popped back up. He always wore a suit and tie. He had a pale face: pale blue eyes, pale skin, even his freckles were pale brown. He was one of those teachers who taught standing up, but he didn't move around much, just stood in front of the chalkboard. He had pushed the big teacher's desk over to the side of the room, so there was a clear space in front of the board. He always rolled a piece of chalk in his fingers. On the first day of class, he had introduced himself as the English and drama teacher. In Dicey's opinion, he wasn't very dramatic.

"If we define conflict as requiring two opposing forces, what might we look for?" he asked the class. "For how conflict might appear," he added. "In what forms," he added. "In a story," he added.

There were always a couple of people who put their hands up right away, usually girls, usually from the town kids who dressed up for school. They sat in the front of every class, boys and girls together. Then, the blacks sat together, some of them at the front and some right behind. The country kids, which included the watermen's families, as far as Dicey could tell from overhead conversations about the crab catchers and the fishing season and oyster beds, sat in the middle and back.

Nobody sat near Dicey, who sat alone. She scratched at the shoulder of her T-shirt and waited to hear how stupid the answers to the question would be. There was only one other person in the class who thought of interesting answers, and that was a black girl who sat in the front row, diagonally across from Dicey. This girl usually waited until all the stupid guesses had been made before she raised her hand. Dicey never raised her hand, but if Mr. Chappelle asked her she'd answer.

The black girl looked about eighteen, with a full bosom and long muscular legs and round hips. She wore a denim jumper, the kind some of the town girls wore, and different blouses, and stockings with low-heeled shoes. Her hair was a short afro and her face looked lively. The eyes especially, dark brown and liquid, but also her mouth, which was always moving, since she had a lot of friends. Most often she was talking, or laughing. Wilhemina was her name.

Every now and then, this Wilhemina would catch Dicey's eye in class (they had three classes together, English and home ec and science) and Dicey wondered what she was thinking then. Wondered if she wasn't thinking something interesting.

Dicey leaned back and waited to see what the answers to Mr. Chappelle's question would be. Vaguely, she thought about the scraping of the boat she planned to accomplish that afternoon.

"Conflict between two men," the answers began. Mr. Chappelle wrote *two men* on the board. Since it was correct, a whole lot of hands went up. "A woman and a woman." "A man and a woman?" "A boy and a boy?" "A girl and a girl." The predictable list went on. Mr. Chappelle wrote everything on the board. Dicey made her own list, inside her head, because you could have conflict between someone with power and someone without any, between someone honest and a liar. The voices petered out around her as she continued with her own thoughts. You could even, she realized, have a conflict between somebody and himself: and that *was* an interesting idea. Like Gram, Gram was like that.

Wilhemina had her hand up, and Mr. Chappelle was waiting until the rest of the class settled down ("A man and his dog?") to call on her. "Yes, Wilhemina?"

The rich voice spoke out. "What about conflict between an individual and the society he lives in?"

Dicey usually kept her eyes down on the fake wood surface of her desk, but this caused her to swivel her head up. She tried to think out what it might mean. There were questions she would have liked to ask the black girl. She caught Wilhemina's eyes on her face, as if the girl were aware of Dicey's reaction. Mr. Chappelle wrote out the letters on the board, slowly, as if he was thinking.

"What do you mean by that, Wilhemina?" Mr. Chappelle asked.

"Well," the girl began. Dicey couldn't stop herself from leaning forward in her seat. "A lot of the time, conflicts are between one person and the people he lives with. Or she lives with. If the society thinks one way and the person thinks another."

Mr. Chappelle was listening carefully, you could tell. Dicey figured, from the way he wrote down everything everybody said, even when it repeated the same basic idea, that his brain didn't work very fast. "Can you give us any examples?"

The rest of the class shifted in their seats, getting bored. Too bad for them, Dicey thought to herself.

"Jesus, for one," the girl answered quickly, "and St. Paul, and John the Baptist. St. Joan, maybe. And even Moses, if you think about it."

"We know your daddy's the minister," somebody muttered, and Wilhemina turned around and smiled, not taking offense.

"Then what about the suffragettes?" she suggested. "Everybody laughed at them, and they went to jail and had food pumped into their stomach when they refused to eat and a lot of them were disowned by their families. Or Louis Pasteur, everybody thought he was crazy. Or the people who ran the underground railways."

Mr. Chappelle seemed to be thinking about all this, maybe trying to figure out what he should say.

"Yeah, but yours are all the good guys," a boy from the town section called over.

"That's right, Wilhemina," Mr. Chappelle agreed. "Is society always wrong and the individual always right?"

"John Wilkes Booth," Wilhelmina announced triumphantly. Dicey felt herself fill with laughter. Nobody else seemed to find it particularly funny. Mr. Chappelle harrumphed and turned his attention to the class.

"Dicey," he inquired. "Do you have anything to add?"

Dicey chewed on her bottom lip, and why did he have to notice her. "Between someone and himself," she said, not bothering to keep the anger at his intrusion out of her voice.

Mr. Chappelle kind of stared at her.

"I mean," Dicey sat back, to show it couldn't mean less to her what anybody thought of her idea, "sometimes you want one thing and the opposite at the same time. Or you say one thing when you really mean the opposite. Or there's something you want to do and something you have to do." She was getting warmed up, and she liked her idea.

One of the town girls interrupted. "Like there are two boys and you like them both," she said, then giggled.

Dicey closed her eyes briefly, then turned her attention back outside. If she hadn't, just then, she would have missed seeing the straight-backed figure emerge from the main doors with a clumsy purse over its shoulder. Gram. Dicey couldn't mistake that high carriage of the chin, or the unkempt curly gray hair. But her meeting about Maybeth wasn't until three fifteen. What was Gram doing at Dicey's school?

Mr. Chappelle, figuring (Dicey guessed) that the argument about whether or not you could like two boys best at the same time had gone on long enough, called on them to open their textbooks and start reading aloud the story that would be their homework. He told them which questions at the end they were supposed to write answers to, and then called on someone to read, one of the worst readers in the class, who stumbled over any word more than two syllables long and made sentences sound senseless because he never paid any attention to punctuation. People groaned and muttered to one another. Dicey looked quickly at the clock behind her. Only ten more minutes. Only one more class after this.

The bike rack was out behind the school building, by the parking lot. Dicey hurried out as soon as the bell released her from home ec class. (Who *cared* about the right way to pin up a hem, and she didn't have any skirts anyway.) She was one of the first out. But not *the* first. A boy sat on the low concrete wall playing a guitar. He had black hair and wore a blue workshirt with its sleeves rolled up. He was playing a melody Dicey didn't know. Dicey had never seen this boy before. He looked like an upperclassman, maybe a junior or senior. She stopped for a minute, to listen, because it sounded so good to her.

His fingers continued playing the song even though he sensed Dicey and looked up at her. He had wide gray eyes and dark, straight eyebrows, and a straight mouth. His thin face had a light tan. His eyes questioned Dicey.

"I never heard that song," she said, to explain why she was standing staring.

He started to sing, in a thin, soft voice. "When first unto this country, a stranger I came. And I cour"—his voice held the note high and round, for three beats—"ted a young girl, and Nancy was her name." He kept singing, and Dicey kept listening, trying to memorize the melody, while the song told the story of how the man was rejected by the girl and arrested and put in jail and had "a coat of many colors." What did that mean, a coat of many colors? Dicey hummed the melody inside her head, concentrating on it.

When he finished, he strummed a couple of chords. "Have a sit, kid."

Dicey shook her head and turned away. She heard the guitar begin another melody as she unlocked her bike and rode off downtown.

That day, Dicey began on the shelves. She'd done a quick surface dusting, just so things wouldn't look so *old*, the week before. Now, she took a bucket of warm water and a sponge and began washing down the long shelves. Millie was behind the meat counter, cutting up a side of beef that had been delivered that morning. When Dicey said hello, she saw the huge knives and cleavers, the thick-bladed saw, all laid out on the butcher block table. Millie had wrapped a bloodstained apron around her. When she cut into the beef, she leaned all her weight against the knife and the muscles worked in her arms.

Millie's cuts were sure and straight. Even when she hacked at a bone with the cleaver, she always hit the same spot. Dicey would have liked to stay and watch her, but she had money to earn.

Often, as she methodically moved cans of soup off the shelf, washed down the bottom and sides and back, then replaced the cans, washing each one off with a damp sponge. Dicey heard someone come in and interrupt Millie at her work. The store owner would give the customer what she or he wanted, then plod down to the counter and patiently add up the bill. Nobody said how much better the store looked and smelled. But Dicey figured maybe her plan was working out the way she hoped.

When she finished her hour she was about halfway down the long shelf. She replaced the unwashed cans, making a mental note that she should begin the next day at chicken noodle soup. She went back to the meat counter to say she was leaving.

There, she lingered for a few minutes. Millie was cutting out a roast with what looked like rib bones in it. She used a thick, cutlass-shaped knife to go through the meat between two ribs, then whacked once with the cleaver before taking the saw and cutting through bone with five strong strokes. Then she took a short, slim knife and cut off large pieces of fat, tossing them without looking into a lined trash barrel beside her. All of her movements were confident. Her little eyes concentrated on what she was doing. It was like watching somebody good play a sport, Dicey decided. A couple of odd scraps of meat went onto a growing pile beside the carcass. Stew beef?

"I'm off now," Dicey said.

"Is it an hour already?" Millie asked. She turned over a fat wrist to look at her watch. "I'm being awful slow with this."

"You had interruptions," Dicey reminded her.

"That's right." Millie sounded surprised. She couldn't have forgotten, Dicey knew. She'd heard her employer talking with the customers, about the weather and the hog market. "That would slow me down back here, wouldn't it," Millie asked, as if she had just realized the connection.

It was getting on to five when Dicey rode her bike up the overgrown driveway. She decided she didn't have time for a snack, not if she wanted to get some scraping done on the boat. She dropped her books on the desk in the living room and asked James, who sat reading the Bible again, if he didn't have homework. "Some, not much," he told her. Maybeth was in the kitchen with Gram, reading a list of vocabulary words aloud while Gram listened and peeled potatoes for supper. Sammy she saw spading fiercely at the garden.

Dicey pulled the barn doors wide, for maximum light, and settled down to work. For scraping the old paint off she had a special tool Gram found for her, a kind of spatula with its tip bent back. It was slow work. The first couple of strokes over a place were the easiest, then you had to scrape away at old paint layers that had been smoothed down by the first couple of scrapes and were, thus, harder to get off. From this tedious point of view, the twelve-foot boat didn't look so little to Dicey.

Sammy wandered in behind her. Dicey greeted him. He was carrying the shovel and he cleaned it off with his hands before setting it back in its place against the dark wall. Dicey, leaning her weight into her work, trying to find just the right amount of pressure so that she would scrape off the paint without gouging the wood beneath, forgot he was there. Until he spoke into her ear.

"I could help."

Dicey grunted and shook her head.

"Why not?"

"There's no tool." Dicey gave the first excuse she could think of. Sammy went to the workbench and began rummaging around.

After a while he came up to her again, holding a rat-tailed chisel. "What's this for?" Dicey didn't answer. "Dicey, do you know?"

"Nope," Dicey said. "Better put it back."

She heard him rummaging around behind her. With an angry sigh, she turned to see what he was doing. He was pulling out the little drawers from the miniature cupboard where Gram stored nails and screws of different sizes. "Better not mess around with that."

"Why not?" Sammy demanded, ready for a fight. And dropped one of the little drawers, scattering thin nails along the surface of the bench and onto the dirt floor.

"Oh, Sammy," Dicey said. She only had a little time for this work, and she didn't want to have to interrupt it to help him pick up after himself.

"I'll *fix* it," Sammy told her. He bent down and began to pick up the nails from the floor.

"Don't get dirt or straw mixed in there," Dicey warned him.

"I *won't*," Sammy said. "I said I'd pick it up."

Dicey turned her attention back to the job. But she couldn't concentrate, because she was waiting for the sounds Sammy would make putting the little drawer back in, so she could take a quick look to be sure he cleaned off all the nails before replacing them.

Sammy seemed to understand that, because he brought the little drawer over for her to check it. She nodded and he went away again. She heard him climbing around.

"What are you doing?" she demanded.

"Bet you can't see me," he answered.

Dicey looked around quickly, and she couldn't. "C'mon, Sammy," she pleaded.

"I told you," he said, pleased with himself.

Dicey felt anger spurt up her spine. "Wherever you are, get back where I can see you," she said, tossing the scraper into the ground like a jackknife. "I've about had it, you hear me? There's almost no time for me to work on the boat, and you're interrupting me. You know the lofts aren't safe to play in."

Sammy stepped out of the shadows beside an old stall. He looked chastened and sulky. "We don't know that. We just haven't checked them yet. You said you'd check them," he reminded her.

"I will," Dicey told him, bending down to fetch the scraper, wiping it clean on her pants. "I will. But not right now, please, Sammy?" She felt desperate.

Sammy went back to the workbench and began to fiddle with the paintbrush soaking in its can of turpentine.

Dicey gave up. "Okay," she said, feeling in him the kind of unused energy her frustration was giving her. "Tell me about school today. How was it?"

"I already told Gram."

"So tell me. I wasn't there, remember?"

"It's boring," Sammy said.

"All right," Dicey said. "Suit yourself."

He watched her work.

"Why won't you let me help?" he asked.

He was too little, he wouldn't be sure to do it right, and Dicey wanted some time at least to herself. She wanted the boat to herself. But she couldn't say that, so instead she asked him, "Do you know fractions yet?"

"Naw, not until spring."

"Tell me something, Sammy," Dicey began.

He sat down. Contented now.

"If you had an apple and you cut it up, what would be bigger, the half or the quarter?"

"The half, a'course," he said. "Why?"

"And if you cut the quarter in half, what would you have?"

This he had to think about. "An eighth?"

Dicey nodded. "If you cut the half into eighths, how many pieces would you have?"

"You mean, if I had half an apple?"

Dicey nodded.

"I think four. Why?"

"No reason, I was just wondering. You already understand fractions," Dicey said.

"Then why doesn't Maybeth?" Sammy asked.

"I don't know," Dicey answered.

After supper, they did homework. James was usually finished first, but that night he worked as long as Dicey, doodling on a piece of lined paper. He had a report to do, on the pilgrims, and he was trying to pick a subject, he told Dicey. He didn't want any help, he had lots of ideas, it was just a matter of finding the right one. What did he mean the right one, Dicey asked. James explained that he wanted one the other kids would enjoy, because they were going to read them out loud in front of the class. He wanted them to like his. Dicey said she thought the kids in his special class were all smart. "They're okay," James said.

Dicey looked up into his narrow, thoughtful face. She could hear Gram and Maybeth working in the kitchen. It sounded like Maybeth was stumbling through the same list of words she'd been reading that afternoon.

"I thought they were smart," Dicey insisted. "Like you."

He shook his head. "Not like me," he said. "I thought they might be, but they aren't. They're okay," he repeated. His eyes slid away from hers and back to the boxes he was drawing on his paper.

When Gram and Maybeth came into the living room, Dicey asked Gram if she'd ever heard the song the guitarist had played that day. Gram said she hadn't. Dicey hummed the tune, and Maybeth hummed it with her. So Dicey taught Maybeth the first verse, which was the only one she could remember.

"I like it," Maybeth said. Her eyes had little bags under them, and no wonder, Dicey thought, since she spent most of her days bending her face over one book or another. Trying to catch up and keep up. They sang the verse together, twice. Maybeth went to the piano to pick out the tune. Dicey made a mental note to find out the rest of the words, if she could see that boy again. "It has something about a coat of many colors," she told her family, who were kind of half-listening, the way families do.

"Joseph's coat," James said. "Right, Gram?"

Gram agreed, and told how Joseph's father had given him that coat because he was the favorite of twelve sons, in Israel.

"But this was about a man who went to jail," Dicey said. "It sounded American."

"There's gotta be a book, somewhere, where somebody's written down these songs," James remarked. "I bet there is."

Gram cleared her throat. "I have a question to ask you all. Maybeth? You too," she called.

They waited.

"I went to see Maybeth's teacher today," Gram began. James caught Dicey's eye. "Her music teacher, a Mr. Lingerle," Gram said. "A pleasant young man. Well—he wouldn't seem young to you. He told me—are you all listening? Sammy?—he told me that he thought Maybeth should have lessons."

"She doesn't need lessons," Dicey said hotly.

"Take it easy, girl," Gram said. Her eyes were laughing at Dicey. "The kind of lessons he was talking about were special lessons."

The children were puzzled, and she let them sit in their puzzlement for a long minute.

"Lessons for someone who is talented."

Dicey felt a smile begin and she looked at Maybeth. Maybeth's face hadn't changed, as if she hadn't yet understood that this teacher note was different from all the other ones she had carried home.

"Piano lessons are what he suggested," Gram said.

"Can I too?" Sammy asked.

Gram shook her head at him. "Just Maybeth. What do we think of that?"

"Terrific," Dicey said.

"But how can we pay for them?" James asked.

"Do you think I can?" Maybeth asked Dicey.

"Do you want to? It would mean even more work, practicing. You have to practice piano, don't you, Gram?" Dicey asked.

"Mr. Lingerle said he would be happy to give Maybeth the lessons, once a week, after school, and he would drive her home afterward," Gram announced. "He said he would charge five dollars a lesson, which isn't unreasonable in my opinion." She sat back then to let them think about that.

Maybeth was on the piano bench, her hands clasped tight together, not looking at anyone.

"He said," Gram added, "that in over ten years of teaching, Maybeth is the most exciting student he has ever had."

"If, instead of having allowances, I'm earning seven dollars a week at Millie's and it looks like I'll be able to keep the job—" Dicey rushed out the words because she was so glad for Maybeth and because, if she rushed them out and committed herself to them, it wouldn't do any good to think about how she was going to be able to buy caulking material and paint, if she ever got through the job of scraping the boat.

"But I want an allowance," Sammy protested. "You *said.*"

Dicey could have throttled him.

"There'll still be two dollars left," Gram told him. She didn't even sound angry. "You could each have fifty cents."

"I wouldn't need any," Maybeth spoke softly.

At fifty cents, it would take twice as long to save up, Dicey thought. "But then we couldn't give any to you," she told Gram.

"Let me worry about that," Gram said.

Dicey was willing to go along with that.

"Maybeth, do you want to take piano lessons?" Gram asked. "Even if it means another lot of work for you?"

"Yes, please," Maybeth answered quickly. "If it was all right with everybody. If Dicey doesn't mind and Sammy can still have an allowance."

"That's decided then," Gram decided.

"You talked to a lawyer too, today, didn't you?" Dicey asked.

"It was a busy day," Gram agreed.

"Anything else?" Dicey asked. Gram shook her head.

Dicey guessed that whatever it was that took her to Dicey's school, she wasn't going to say anything about it.

James was looking a Dicey curiously, as if he suspected there was something she was thinking about. "I have a report due in three weeks," he told Gram. "Something on the pilgrims. So Mr. Thomas will have something to show parents at the conferences."

"What conferences?" Gram asked, startled. "What parents?"

"You don't have to come in," James assured her. "There are conferences when we've finished six weeks of school, so the teachers can talk about how the kids are doing, and the parents can meet the teachers. Lots of classes have special projects due just before then, so the parents have something to look at."

"We're going to make a bulletin board with poems on it," Sammy said. "Poems," he repeated, without pleasure. "We're going to vote," he added, with more enthusiasm.

Dicey could figure out what he meant, probably vote on the poems to be put up on the bulletin board. "I bet you can write poems all right," she told Sammy. He shrugged.

"I'd like to write something the kids in my class will be interested in," James said. Dicey wasn't sure who he was talking to, and what he wanted to be answered.

"I'd think you'd want to write something *you* would be interested in," Gram said.

"I wanna play checkers," Sammy announced.

James shrugged his shoulders. Gram began setting out checkers on the board. "I would," Gram said to James.

"Yeah, but you—" James started to say, then didn't finish.

Dicey knew what he was thinking, that Gram wasn't like other people, she was different, an oddball. A lot of people in town thought she was just plain crazy. Dicey had found that out the first day they arrived in Crisfield, before she even walked out to her grandmother's farm. It was what Millie said. But Millie didn't seem to really think that. At least, not now, not any more.

James was squirming in his chair. Gram just looked at him, waiting, and didn't say a word. "Let's *play,*" Sammy demanded.

Dicey thought maybe James and Gram should have this conversation. "I'll play with you, Sammy," she said.

"No, her, she's more fun anyway." He rejected Dicey's offer without a thought.

"Then I can hear Maybeth read," Dicey said.

"I already did that," Gram told her, ignoring James. So all Dicey had to do in the time before the little kids went up to bed was sit with Maybeth on the piano bench and sing. That was okay with her. James came over to join in, and she could hear Sammy's voice sometimes too.

That Friday, when the science teacher announced that they would need partners for the next two weeks, which would be laboratory work classifying rocks, Dicey felt a moment of unease. There were thirty-seven kids in the class, so probably one person wouldn't have a partner, and probably that would be her. That was okay, she liked working alone, she was used to it; but she wanted to be sure everybody knew that she didn't care about not having a partner. She stared down at the notebook opened before her on the high table, pretending to read what was in it, to show she wasn't interested in the babbling of voices. When she felt someone standing beside her, she thought probably it was the teacher and didn't look up, as if she was too engrossed to notice.

"Wanna work together?" A ringing voice spoke.

It was Wilhemina. Dicey was too surprised to do anything

but nod. The big black girl put her notebook and textbook down beside Dicey's. She dropped a half-dozen pens and pencils beside it. She hoisted herself up onto the stool beside Dicey. "I'm Wilhemina Smiths, Smiths with an *s* at both ends," she told Dicey. "My friends call me Mina. You're Dicey Tillerman."

Dicey nodded and stared. She was pleased to have this girl for a partner, but she wondered at the buzzings of conversation around them, and she wondered if Mina had felt sorry for her, the new kid, and that was why she chose Dicey.

"We're the smartest ones in here," Mina said, lowering her voice so that nobody would hear. She smiled at Dicey, and her teeth flashed white and her round cheeks got rounder. Her skin was smooth and milk-chocolate brown. Her hands, arranging things on the table top, were large and quick.

"How do you know that?" Dicey asked.

"I know about me," Mina answered, "and I've been keeping an eye on you. Don't worry, I won't eat you," she told Dicey, grinning.

Dicey looked at the girl, grinned back at her. Did she think that just because Dicey was scrawny and small, and she was so large and strong-looking, that Dicey would be scared of her?

"I'm not worried," Dicey said. If Mina knew the kind of things Dicey had done all her life and especially last summer, she wouldn't think Dicey could be scared. The teacher called the class to attention and began to dictate the background information.

At the end of that day, Dicey came home to see three boys' shirts lying on the kitchen table. They didn't look new. When Gram and Sammy came in, Dicey asked about them: "Where'd you get these?"

"From the attic," Gram said. Dicey drank a glass of cold milk and picked up the top shirt. It was plain white cotton, with a collar that buttoned down.

"I didn't know you had an attic," she remarked.

"They're for you; I altered them to fit," Gram said. "You're too old for T-shirts, and it may be weeks before we see any money from the Welfare Office."

"I didn't know you could sew," Dicey said. For her? She unfolded the shirt and touched the material. It had been worn down soft. She could see tucks along the sides, where it had been recently stitched.

"I've got an old treadle machine in my room," Gram said. "Aren't you going to try it on?"

Dicey peeled off her T-shirt and put on the boy's shirt. She buttoned it up, until the top button, which she left open. She pulled the sleeves straight and buttoned the wrists. It felt good, cool and cottony, freshly ironed. Gram watched her and nodded her head. Dicey tucked the shirt in at the waist of her cutoffs. Looking down, she saw that her bosom pushed the front of the shirt out a little. She quickly pulled it out again, so it would hang loose.

"Thank you," she said. There was a white shirt and two blue ones. She didn't know what more she was supposed to say, although she felt like there was more to say. She wanted to ask whose shirts these had been.

"It suits you," Gram said.

James agreed, when he came in later. "Much better than the T-shirts," he approved. "Is the attic that trap door upstairs in the ceiling?"

Gram nodded.

"What's up there?" James asked.

"Nothing much."

James stared at his grandmother. Then he decided not to pester her. "I got a job," he announced.

"You what? How did you do that?" Dicey demanded. She had never thought of James getting a job.

"There's a kid in my class, he had a newspaper route for Baltimore and Annapolis papers. He was griping about it and I said I'd do it. It gets him twelve dollars a month," James said.

He looked at Dicey and then at Gram. Neither of them said anything.

"It's okay," he explained to Gram. "I haven't told him yes for sure yet, I said I had to check with my family."

James was always the one who did things right, Dicey thought. She wished that he would make some mistakes, just once or twice. He did make mistakes, she knew that, but he always seemed to be the one the grown-ups approved of.

Sammy came bowling into the room and ran smack into Dicey. She wheeled around, ready to yell at him. His eyes were already angry, she noticed, and his color was high.

"I rode a mile as fast as I could, all the way," he declared. "I'm not even tired. So I'll help James." Gram smiled at him and kept herself from laughing.

They were all turning away from her, Dicey thought. When this had happened before, at Cousin Eunice's house in Bridgeport, it had been bad for the little kids. But here, with Gram, on the farm, with a home, it wasn't bad for them. She wasn't sure James was old enough for a job, or reliable enough for it in how much he knew about hard work (and carrying newspapers around, even on a bicycle, was hard work). Sammy hadn't been in any fights at school, and that was good; but she didn't understand why he got weepy when he was losing at checkers or Parcheesi. Maybeth seemed contented, and pleased with her first piano lesson. Maybeth didn't seem to mind all the schoolwork.

Anyway, nobody was talking to Dicey, so she guessed they were doing all right without her.

"I'm going out to the barn for a while, if that's okay," she said. Nobody answered her. Maybe they didn't even hear her. She put her glass into the sink and went on out. It was a relief, in a way, not to have all that responsibility. It felt pretty good to be able to do things without worrying about the little kids. And if Sammy was going to be Gram's favorite, and James was going to do everything right, and Maybeth was going to get caught up in school, so everybody could be proud of her, and with piano lessons too, why should Dicey mind?

CHAPTER 3

On the days when Sammy rode along behind James on the paper route, Dicey picked up the mail on her way home. It was early in October when Gram got an answer to her letter to the hospital in Boston where Momma was. Dicey found the letter among a pile of advertising circulars in the mailbox. She stuffed all the mail into her science notebook.

Dicey would have liked to just leave the circulars or to have returned them to the senders, but Gram said they'd use them to start fires when the weather got cold. Dicey doubted that it ever got cold here in southern Maryland. By October on the Cape, back home, the air was crisp and the leaves were turning colors, and the sand had lost all of its summer warmth. Here, all that happened so far was the water in the Bay turned clear and you could see to the shallow sandy bottom. And the leaves on the paper mulberry were turning a yellowy green. The nights were chilly, but the days were warm enough for the children's shorts to be comfortable. But Gram promised Dicey there would be cold weather coming.

Gram already had Sammy at work chopping up kindling with a small ax. She had forewarned Dicey that they were going to need to take the big, two-handled saw to a couple of fallen trees one of these weekends. Dicey had groaned at this, knowing that the time would have to be taken from the slow work on the boat.

At the rate she was going, it would never be ready for the water next spring. But she had groaned silently.

Dicey showed the Boston letter to Gram, who was making bread at the kitchen table. Gram looked at it out of the side of her eyes, grunted and continued kneading. Dicey ate an apple and waited. When they sat down together, Gram looked at Dicey before she opened the envelope. "I hope you're not expecting good news," she said.

"I'm not expecting anything," Dicey answered impatiently. "I just want to know what it says."

"I'm not expecting good news," Gram said. She opened the envelope carefully with steady fingers.

It was a long letter, typed, three pages. Gram read it once quickly, then again slowly. She didn't show Dicey the pages she was finished with. Dicey bit her lip with impatience and tried not to fidget. When Gram finished the second reading, she folded the papers back into the envelope and then folded her fingers tightly together.

Dicey waited. Gram's mouth was straight and her eyes stared vacantly at the envelope.

Dicey waited.

"I need a cup of tea," Gram announced. She went to the stove to heat water. When her back was to Dicey, she said, "No change."

"None at all?" Dicey asked. She kept her voice level, hiding her own disappointment. She spoke as matter-of-factly as Gram did.

"So we'll go ahead with the adoption," Gram said. Dicey stared at her, at the strong back under the loose clothing, at her tanned legs and bare feet. "We can get to work on those forms, now we know."

"What did they say?" Dicey asked.

"I told you once, girl, no change. Are you listening?"

But the letter was three pages long. It didn't take three pages to write *no change.* "What if we went to see her?" Dicey asked.

"Do you know how much that would cost?"

Whatever it cost it would be too much.

Gram dunked the teabag in her cup, then set it aside to be used again. She turned and looked at Dicey. "Life is a hard business," she remarked.

"Was it bad news?" Dicey asked, even though she knew she shouldn't.

"Don't you listen?" Gram demanded. There was anger in her voice and in her dark hazel eyes.

"It doesn't take three pages to say *no change,*" Dicey answered, her own anger rising. But *she* was angry because she was worried and frightened.

Gram snorted. "For doctors it does," she said. "I don't want you making the mistake of thinking life isn't going to be hard," she said again.

"I know that," Dicey said.

"I guess you do. I'm a natural fool," Gram said. "I keep trying to count on things. And Sammy's too young for that long bike ride. Maybe," Gram said.

Dicey knew what the woman was thinking, how the connections were made behind her eyes. But she was glad nobody was there to hear how Gram's mind jumped around.

"I'm going to the barn, if that's all right," Dicey said. She waited for her grandmother to answer. If Gram wanted Dicey to stay, for company, Dicey would like that. But Gram just said, "Suit yourself." Dicey shrugged and went out to get a little work done on the boat, and she did not let herself wonder what it was Gram had been counting on. Because Gram said the letter said no change.

October went on. The children were settling in, just as fall was settling in, over the farm and the water, into shades of brown: the harrowed soil, the dried summer grasses, the broken stalks of corn, and the long golden bars of sunlight from a sun setting closer to seven now than eight. Gram had filed all of her forms, with the lawyer's help. Now they awaited action on the fat folders filled with copies of the children's birth certificates and school records, with government papers in triplicate, saying everything that could be written down in numbers about Gram and the farm, about Momma and the kids.

Sammy mostly left Dicey alone with the boat, and when he did come bother her (she had one side more than half done by then) seemed interested only in asking questions, about how the Indians scalped people and whether there were ghosts, about the ragged bottom of the big barn doors. "Do you think someone did that on purpose?" he asked, fingering the broken-off boards. "Dicey? If you hit at it with a bat, or a sledge hammer."

"How's school?" Dicey asked.

"Fine I guess," Sammy told her, not interested in the subject. Well, at least he wasn't coming home with black eyes and bruises and ripped clothes, the way he had from school in Provincetown and from summer camp in Bridgeport. As long as Sammy wasn't fighting, Dicey wasn't going to worry about him.

James worked hard, reading and taking notes for his report. He'd decided on a topic, "Why the Pilgrims came to America." "It's interesting," he said, but he didn't want to talk about it. "It's nice to have something to do again," he told them.

Maybeth came home from school one day with an invitation to a birthday party. "You can ride your bike and I'll ride mine to pick you up," Dicey said, because it would be getting dark when the party was over. "What'll you do about a present?" Dicey didn't know what a guest at a birthday party was supposed to do.

"I thought I'd make something," Maybeth told her. "With pine cones. Gram will help. Will you help, Gram?"

"Of course, I will. But you can't wear your shorts and T-shirt."

All the children's clothes had to be practical. They had shorts and shirts, that was all. "That doesn't matter," Maybeth said.

"Maybe it really doesn't," James said to his grandmother. "Do you know who else is invited, Maybeth? Is it the whole class?"

"Just some of us," she told him. "The cake's going to have pink frosting."

Maybeth was making friends, and Sammy seemed not to be getting into trouble, and James was working hard. Dicey herself had what might be called a friend in Mina. They'd gotten A's on their rock classification project, and Mina always greeted Dicey at school, whenever she saw her. "Hey, Dicey, how you doing." Dicey always answered, "Pretty good and you," the way you were supposed to. Then she beat a fast path to her desk, or the next class. She didn't want anybody to think she was trying to have friends.

She had seen the guitar-playing boy a couple of times. The first time, she had walked right up and asked him the words for that song about the coat of many colors. He remembered her. After a while, she saw him every day it wasn't raining. He was sitting in the same place, playing his guitar when she rushed out to get on her bike and go to work. He told her his name, Jeff, and asked her hers. "Dicey Tillerman," she said, and waited for what he would say next.

"You related to that old lady with the farm?" he asked. Dicey nodded, her chin high. "What are you, a grandchild?" Dicey nodded again. "Listen, you can sing the melody of that song?" he asked her. "I want to try a harmony." Dicey could and did, listening to his voice as he made a harmony line with what she was singing, sometimes blending, sometimes moving in contrast. She thought he was fancying it up too much, but she didn't say so. And she liked singing that song, even though she didn't understand the story of it. "You sing pretty well," Jeff remarked.

"Not particularly," Dicey told him. "Just better than you. My sister is the one who can really sing. You should hear her sing this song."

"I'd like to," he said, his face friendly. What did he expect her to do, invite him to her house or something? There was something he expected, or wanted, Dicey could see that.

"I gotta go now," she said.

"Why?" he asked. "I've got another song you might like."

"I gotta go," Dicey insisted and turned away to get her bike out of the rack and ride away.

Millie never minded if Dicey was a few minutes late. She didn't seem to notice. The business continued to improve, Dicey thought; Millie never said anything, as if she had forgotten the terms of their deal. The third week came and went without a word from Millie. And the fourth week. The only thing Millie said about business to Dicey happened when Dicey came in to find her at the checkout counter studying a long printout. Behind her, all over one of the aisles, boxes of dried cereal were spread around. Millie was reading down the sheet, her lips moving silently, her fingers moving along under the words.

"Want me to put those up on display?" Dicey offered.

"I dunno where they came from," Millie said. "I dunno where they'll fit."

"You didn't order them?"

Millie shook her head. Dicey looked around for what to do. The windows could wait another day or two, or they could be washed right away. The floor—needed a damp mopping she decided. The windows would wait.

"Oh no," Millie spoke behind her. "Look what I did. Sometimes I'm so *stupid.* Just look at that."

Dicey looked over her shoulder. The page was the distributor's order sheet. Millie had filled it out in pencil, changing her mind many times, as Dicey could tell by the erasures and crossings out. "I meant to order corn chips and I ordered corn flakes. I'll never sell all these boxes. What'll I do?"

"Can't you send them back?"

"But the corn chips are for people who want them. I always have them."

"Or have a special sale on corn flakes," Dicey suggested. How could Millie have mistaken those two words?

"I hate the ordering, I always make mistakes, and I have to check it all the time. Herbie—he tried to teach me how to do it, but he gave up."

The sheet looked pretty simple to Dicey. You just found the items you wanted and put the number you wanted in a little box beside the name and then figured out how much it cost and copied that down. "How can you make mistakes on this?" she asked.

"Because I never learned how to read, not properly. I can't even read a newspaper. You didn't know that, did you. You didn't know what a stupid old woman you were working for."

"But you went to school," Dicey told her. "You said you went to school with Gram."

Millie laughed, but it wasn't a happy sound. "They kept me back some, when I was littler. Then, I got so big it was embarrassing to them, and I always behaved myself. So they'd just pass me on. I never graduated, didn't Ab tell you? No, she's no gossip. It doesn't matter and it didn't then, because I was going to get married. Herbie didn't care. He liked me the way I was. You wouldn't understand, you're one of those smart kids."

"You can't read?" Dicey was amazed.

"Of course, I can read," Millie said patiently. "I just take so long at it, and the words all look alike. I don't know, maybe now with all the machines they have for teaching, maybe now I could have learned. But it's too late for me."

Dicey didn't know what to say. "If you told me what you wanted I could fill out the order sheets," she finally offered.

Millie's face showed hope. "Do you think so? You're awfully young."

"Sure," Dicey answered. "I don't have any idea of what you should stock in, but I can read names and numbers."

"That would be a load off my mind," Millie said. "It's gotten so, since Herbie died, the distributor won't let me return things any more if I make a mistake. And then," she confided, "I get so nervous about making a mistake I go over it again and again, and it takes so long, and I can't think properly about it. Sometimes I cross out what I wanted to order and order the wrong things. As if I *wanted* to do it wrong."

Dicey nodded and kept her face expressionless. "Then you do want me to stay on," she said.

"Stay on? Here? Of course," Millie said, "what made you think I didn't? I can't handle all this business alone."

"I was just making sure," Dicey said quickly.

Dicey rode home to Gram's house these October days through sunlight turning golden and red, stopped by the mailbox (wondering each time why Gram had said nothing to the little kids about that letter from the doctor in Boston) and put in a quick half-hour's work on the boat. She had accepted the slowness with which she was going to make progress. She kept herself from being impatient, just as she kept herself private at school.

After supper these days, and before she dashed through her own homework, she read with Maybeth for a half hour or so, the two of them at the kitchen table. Maybeth had lists of words she was supposed to memorize, vocabulary sheets. In the reading book, these words appeared in the stories. Mrs. Jackson had told Maybeth that if she stumbled on a word in a story, then she should go back and memorize the list again. So most of the time poor Maybeth was guessing her way through a list of twenty words, and Dicey would stop her when she made a mistake and Maybeth would go back to the top of the list and start again. Maybeth didn't seem discouraged, but Dicey sure was.

She thought about Maybeth and Millie; and she didn't want Maybeth to be like Millie when she grew up. It wasn't that Dicey didn't like Millie, because she did. It was all right, working for Millie. Dicey was learning a lot about how to run a grocery store, and she hoped that sometime Millie might show her how to butcher the sides of meat. But it wasn't interesting, not like other people she had worked for, when she had conversations with them. She felt pretty sorry for Millie, so big and slow-witted. She wanted something better than Millie's life for Maybeth.

Maybeth plugged along, reading, math, social studies. She never practiced her piano until everything else was done.

At the piano, at least, Maybeth moved fast. The scales had given way to rhythmic exercises and to real pieces, with chords. James, studying the music in one of the books Mr. Lingerle loaned Maybeth, said he couldn't figure out how she could read the notes off onto the piano keys. Maybeth said it wasn't hard. James said he thought it looked harder than reading words. Maybeth shook her head, no, and went back to the piece she was playing.

Gram took an old blouse of hers, with tiny flowers printed on it, and cut it down to make a dress for Maybeth to wear to the birthday party. It took her a week, every night, to finish it. It wasn't a great dress, but Maybeth looked pretty in it. She was so excited, she whirled around the living room, letting the skirt swirl out.

James showed Dicey his report on the pilgrims. Dicey only read it because he wanted her to so badly, but once she'd started she found herself really interested. James had written about *all* the reasons why the Mayflower people wanted to come to America. He had found out who they all were and where they'd come from, and what had happened to them once they got to Plymouth. Dicey was surprised at what he was saying. Only some of the people came over for religious reasons, and even those (as James pointed out) hadn't come because of a belief in religious freedom. They came over to practice their own religion, which was a very different thing from what Dicey had always heard. Some of the people came because they weren't welcome in the society of England, because they were sort of rotten apples there. Some came because they had to, like wives, children, and indentured servants. Some came because they wanted to live and work in a land that civilization hadn't already polished and divided, because they loved wildness, because they wanted to match themselves up against the wilderness and see how they did. Dicey could understand that feeling. Some of the settlers were looking for easy money, gold or furs, to get rich quick.

"It's really good," she said to James when she finished reading. He was standing anxiously behind her.

"You think so?"

"It's interesting," Dicey said. "I bet it's the best report anybody does—I bet it's miles better than any other report in your class. I'll tell you," she said, overwhelmed into honesty by the impression it made on her, "I don't think I could write one this good."

James tried not to look as pleased as he felt. "You think Gram would like to read it?" he asked.

At about that time, Mr. Chappelle assigned Dicey's class a

paper. He wanted them to write a character sketch, he said, about a real character they had met, someone they knew. He wanted them to show the conflict in a real person's life. As soon as he said that, the complaints and questions began. Dicey stopped paying attention. She knew who she'd like to write about, she knew a whole lot of people. Momma, for one; but she couldn't, because that wasn't any of his business. Will Hawkins was another. She'd like writing about him. Not about the way he'd been a good friend to the children, taken them along with his circus and driven them down to Crisfield; and not even about what it was like to live with a circus, although that would be interesting. Dicey would write about the way Will was so honest with his friends, yet tricked the people who came to see his shows. Because the circus was like that, full of tricks that you didn't know about until, like the four children, you had lived in it. Probably the people who came to see the shows didn't care, but it wasn't what the people wanted that interested Dicey. She wanted to write about those two opposite sides of Will. Maybe, if she wrote about him, she could figure out how he fit those two sides together in his life; maybe he did it by keeping them entirely separate, his friends and his work. She thought about him, traveling now around the country with his circus. He'd promised to come see them when the circus came back to the area, and she believed he would.

And there was Cousin Eunice, back in Bridgeport. In Dicey's opinion, Cousin Eunice was a boring person, but she had conflicts too. She too had taken the children in. But she had only done it because she wanted people to think she'd done the right thing. What she really wanted to do was live the life she'd planned for herself before the Tillermans turned up. She didn't want the children, they were nothing but trouble to her, trouble and expense; but she'd made herself change all her plans.

Dicey might just write something as good as James, she thought, the ideas tumbling around in her head. Then she corrected herself: almost as good as James. James was just too smart for her to keep up with.

Maybe she *could* write about Momma. If she called her Mrs. Liza, then Mr. Chappelle wouldn't ever guess who she really was. If she just didn't say certain things.

After class, Mina waited for Dicey by the door. "This essay might be fun," Mina said. "I've got an idea."

Dicey didn't know why Mina wanted to talk to her. They hurried on through the crowded halls to home ec.

"I'd like to talk to you about it," Mina said.

"Sure," Dicey said. She usually liked Mina's ideas.

"How about after school?"

"Can't," Dicey said. Mina waited for her to say more, but Dicey didn't. She wasn't sure why she didn't, except that the more anybody knew about her . . . they had a kind of hold on her. She wasn't sure, anyway, how Mina would feel about Dicey having a job, if Mina would feel sorry for her.

"You want to come by my house?" Mina asked.

"Can't," Dicey said.

Mina looked at her and Dicey looked right back. Contradictory expressions were on Mina's face, a little confusion and some anger and some laughter. Mina chose to laugh. "You sure are a hard person to be friends with, Dicey Tillerman."

Was that what Mina was doing? Dicey was so surprised, because Mina had lots of friends already, she didn't even answer. They entered the horrible home ec class, where they were supposed to be making work aprons, using everything they had learned about cutting and sewing, hems and buttons. Dicey had figured out a way to avoid most of the button troubles, a pretty clever way, she thought. The rules were you had to have two buttons on it and a hem and a tie around the neck. Dicey was following the rules, but in her own way.

It had gotten so she could almost count on seeing Jeff after school, over by the bike racks. He'd call out to her, "Hey, Dicey."

She would saunter over. "You ever hear this one?" he'd ask, and play her a song. Some of them, a lot of them, she already knew. Once, because it was in her mind for some reason, she asked him to play one of Momma's favorites, "The water is wide, I cannot go o'er." He didn't know it, said he'd never heard it, but a couple of days later he had it ready for her.

Usually, Dicey would stay and sing with him, because she liked singing. A couple of times, he asked her about her sister who could sing so well, but Dicey never told him much. She thought, though, Maybeth would like Jeff. He was in tenth grade, he said, and he reminded Dicey that she was in eighth. "I know that," Dicey answered.

"So do I," he said, peering up at her from where he sat bent over his guitar. The conversation was stupid, but she smiled. He smiled back, but she had to get to work so she didn't bother finding out whether he thought it was stupid too.

One day, when Dicey came up to the back porch under a gray sky, her hands and shorts flecked with some of the paint she had scraped, she heard the piano playing a rolling, rippling melody, one that you couldn't ever sing along with. There were no words that could keep up with the notes that swept from bass up through tenor to soprano. The piano was the only voice that could manage to sing that song. She stopped and listened, dumbfounded. How had Maybeth gotten so very good all at once?

She stepped into the kitchen and saw Maybeth sitting down at the table with Gram. Their heads were bent down over a reading book. Beside them was one of the word lists Mrs. Jackson never ran out of. Maybeth read aloud, word by stumbling word. You could hear her guessing. Dicey followed the music down the hall.

A man sat at the piano. He was so fat that his fanny hung down over the back of the bench. He was fat like a cartoon fat person. For a minute, Dicey saw nothing but fatness, then looked at the details. The back of his head had a bald spot, a pink circle with a few stray hairs carefully combed over it, as if he were trying to hide it. Like trying to hide a basketball under three shoelaces, Dicey thought. His eyes and nose and mouth were all buried in the flesh of his face, and his double chins hung down. His hands, despite looking thick and clumsy at the ends of huge arms, danced over the piano keys. He was concentrating so hard—adjusting his position on the bench as the chords took him up and down the keyboard, staring down at the keys under his fingers—that sweat ran down by his ear and his shirt was stained under the armpits. His mouth was open as if he was panting. And the music poured out of the piano like a stream pouring down the side of a mountain, or like the wind pouring over the bending branches of trees.

Dicey stood, listening.

After a while, the music ended. He sat in the silence, smiling to himself. He pushed his glasses back up his nose. Then he seemed to sense Dicey, silent in the doorway. He turned and looked at her.

"Who are you?" Dicey asked. "Are you the music teacher?"

"Isaac Lingerle," he said. He watched her watching him. "You must be Dicey."

"I didn't see any car," Dicey said.

"It's parked out front, under a big tree."

"What are you doing here?"

"I brought Maybeth home, and I want to ask your grandmother a question. But she said first Maybeth had to do some reading. That couldn't wait, she said. Your grandmother's not the woman to argue with."

At that, Dicey smiled. He smiled back at her.

"Maybeth has to work awfully hard," Dicey explained. "It's important for her."

"What about you, do you have to work hard?"

"Not at school," Dicey told him. "They'll be through pretty soon. I've gotta wash my hands to help get supper."

He turned back to the piano. His hands, poised above the keys, as if he was thinking about what to play. He was as massive as a mountain, Dicey thought. Or at least a big hill.

She was coming back downstairs, having dusted off her shorts and her shirt as well as washed her hands, when she met Gram. The woman went into the living room and waited for the music to break off.

Mr. Lingerle turned to face her and stood up. "Beethoven," he said, as if she'd asked him something.

"You're not married," Gram told him.

He looked puzzled, then his face turned a little pink. "As you see," he said.

"Then you'll stay for supper," Gram told him.

Dicey almost protested: they would never have enough food to fill that huge body.

"I don't know," he said. He looked uneasy, as if he didn't trust Gram.

"I've got no time to talk now, but after supper while Dicey does the dishes," Gram told him. She turned and left the room.

Dicey was laughing inside her head at the effect Gram always had on people. Mr. Lingerle stood looking at the place where Gram's bare feet had stood.

"How'd she know I wasn't married?" he demanded.

"She was asking you," Dicey said.

"That was a question?" He shook his head. "What a family," he remarked.

Dicey closed her mouth over her response and left him alone there.

They had crabs for dinner and baked potatoes. Gram told the boys to empty every crab they had into the bushel basket, and by the size of the mound of cooked crabs on the center of the table, Dicey could tell that Gram shared her estimate of Mr. Lingerle's appetite. James looked at their guest once, and then kept his eyes off him. Sammy tried not to stare and didn't succeed. Maybeth, looking tiny next to him, kept up a kind of chatter about school. Sometimes, if Mr. Lingerle asked him a direct question, Sammy talked too. Mr. Lingerle seemed to know Sammy. Mr. Lingerle ate only four crabs after all, just like Dicey, and he picked out the littlest potato when the plate came to him, and he had only a couple of slices of tomato.

Finally, Sammy couldn't keep his mouth shut any longer. "You don't eat very much," he accused the guest.

Mr. Lingerle flushed again. Dicey wondered about this, because he was entirely grown up and not even that young any more, not even a young grown-up. He took a deep breath and answered Sammy, and all the rest of them. "Let's just acknowledge that I'm fat."

"Nobody said anything," Gram snapped.

Mr. Lingerle drew back. "I just think it's better to say," he apologized.

"Well, you're right," she snapped. "On both counts."

Dicey giggled. She thought her grandmother was pretty funny sometimes. Dicey enjoyed her grandmother, and the way her grandmother's mind worked. Mr. Lingerle gave Dicey a curious look, then he gave Gram a curious look, and his eyes became less wary. "You Tillermans certainly take some getting used to," he remarked.

"Maybeth has been surprise enough. I'm a simple man," he said, with a smile that creased the flesh around his mouth. "I'm planning to relax and enjoy myself, unless you object?"

"We want you to," Maybeth told him.

"*Did* you eat enough?" Sammy asked.

James tried to shush him, without success.

"Frankly, no. But here's what I'll do. When I get home, I'll stuff myself with something. I'm always nervous, the first time people meet me, and I'm never hungry when I'm nervous. Does that answer your question?"

"You count your blessings, young man," Gram said to Sammy; but her eyes were twinkling.

"Yes, Gram," he answered. "Next time I won't say anything."

"Good." Then Gram sent the little kids into the living room to do their homework. Dicey rolled up the crab shells in newspaper, washed and dried the dishes and glassware. She heard Mr. Lingerle ask Gram if Maybeth couldn't have two lessons a week instead of one. She heard Gram say no.

"Listen to me for a minute," Mr. Lingerle pleaded. "I'm not saying Maybeth is a genius, or anything like it. But she *is* one of those people, one of those lucky people, who will always have music in their lives. People who can always find pleasure in music, no matter what else—hurts them, or goes wrong. I'd like to give her as much music as I can, because—because I want to. It's a pleasure for me. And then"—his chair creaked as he leaned forward—"when I hear what the other teachers say about her—and when I see how hard she works—at the piano she has success. Don't you want her to be successful, somewhere?"

"Of course, we do," Gram snapped. Dicey, polishing plates dry, knew what was bothering Gram. Money. But Gram wasn't going to admit that. Dicey admired her pride, but she thought Gram was wrong not to tell Mr. Lingerle.

"I know what you're thinking, girl," Gram said. Dicey came to stand beside her.

"I'm right," Dicey said.

"You always think you're right," Gram said.

Dicey just went back to the sink. She could have been finished five minutes ago, but she wanted to listen in.

Gram was silent, then said, "We don't have the money."

"I wasn't asking for money," Mr. Lingerle cried, exasperated. "Did I mention money?"

Dicey turned around to catch the end of Gram's quick smile. "If you can afford it," Gram said.

"I can't afford not to," Mr. Lingerle told her. "I guess you can't know—how exhilarating it is to teach someone like Maybeth. So, we're agreed?"

"Entirely," Gram said.

Before he left, Mr. Lingerle played them all a couple of pieces on the piano. Then he asked them to sing for him, because Maybeth had told him they liked to sing, so they sang "Amazing Grace." Mr. Lingerle joined in with a rich bass harmony. Gram asked them to sing "Who Will Sing for Me," and they did. Then Sammy wanted to sing "The Old Lady Who Swallowed a Fly." When they had sung themselves out, Mr. Lingerle thanked them for a pleasant evening and left, getting himself, somehow, into a little Volkswagen that jounced off down the driveway, following its thin beams of light. They turned back to homework.

When Dicey was saying good night to Sammy, her brother said to her: "I didn't know he was like that."

"Like what?"

"Nice."

"What did you think he was like?"

"Funny." Sammy rolled over and looked at her with hazel eyes. "The kids all laugh at him."

"Because he's fat?"

He nodded.

"Do you?"

Sammy shrugged. "I've never been in trouble yet," he said.

Dicey finished her work apron the earliest of anyone in the home ec class. She spent the rest of the days assigned to this project pretending she still had work to do (so that Miss Eversleigh would keep off her back) and getting her other homework finished. On the day the project was due, Miss Eversleigh told every girl to put on her apron. Dicey stuck a marker in the story she was reading for English and jerked her apron over her head. She sat down again and opened her book.

But everybody had to stand up. Dicey wasn't sorry she'd done as bad a job as she'd done, but she wished she didn't have to stand up so everybody else could see. She made her face stony.

There was silence for a few minutes, while everybody looked at what everybody else had made (everybody except Dicey, who kept on reading), and Miss Eversleigh went around to everyone, like a general reviewing the troops, Dicey thought, acting as if the aprons mattered. When the first ripple of laughter began, Dicey looked up.

They were looking at her, at her apron. Well, she knew the hem rippled up and down, and the neckband pulled one side of the bib up to her shoulder, and the two big red buttons she'd used for decoration on the bib sat at just the wrong places. She knew that and she didn't care. She glared at the laughing faces, her chin high. Wilhemina was trying not to laugh, but her cheeks puffed out with holding it in, and her eyes glistened. Dicey just stared at her. The only other angry person in the room was Miss Eversleigh, and she was staring anger at Dicey. Dicey was thinking of what to say, and she kept her chin up high like Gram's, when the bell rang. Ending class.

Dicey whipped her apron up over her head and rolled it into a ball. She grabbed her books, fast, because Miss Eversleigh was moving toward her. She rushed out of the room, slamming the apron into the trash basket by the door.

In the hall she collided with Mina. "What do *you* want," she demanded.

"It *was* funny-looking," Mina said.

"I wanted to take mechanical drawing," Dicey said. "If I were a boy, they'd have found room for me in that class." She heard the anger in her own voice.

"Don't take it out on me," Mina said, angry herself now. "Boy. I thought I could count on you not to be—ordinary."

"I never asked you to count on me for anything," Dicey said. She stormed down the hall, riding the waves of her own anger. At least it was Friday and she wouldn't have to go to school again until two days later.

When Dicey got home on Fridays, she usually had the house to herself for a few minutes. Gram picked Sammy up at school, and they did grocery shopping before returning together in the outboard. James was off delivering papers. Maybeth had her second piano lesson on Fridays.

Dicey slammed around the house, taking her books up to her room, pouring a glass of milk. She swept out the downstairs with quick strokes of the broom. She began to feel all right again. She was about to go out to the barn and get down to work, when Sammy and Gram arrived; so she went down through the marsh to the boat, to get the last bags of groceries.

"We're having steak tonight," Sammy announced. "Gram got it."

"Got the steak, and a check from welfare," Gram said. Her

mouth was tight. "They paid us everything from the time we first filed. So I thought—something to celebrate. If it deserves celebration."

Gram didn't like taking charity, Dicey knew that because Gram said so. For that matter, neither did she. But Gram had said, when she finally agreed to take them in, that that might be what they had to do.

"I must say," Gram said, moving from table to refrigerator, "I've never gotten money back on taxes before. It ought to feel good."

Dicey finished the sentence for her: But it doesn't. She felt like she ought to apologize to Gram. After all, it had been her idea to come down here and see if they could stay. The words *I'm sorry* started to form themselves on her lips. But nobody made Gram do things. If she didn't want the children, all she had to do was say so.

"Steak'll be good," was all Dicey said.

"It better be," Gram answered.

"I wanna play catch," Sammy said. "Dicey?"

She shook her head.

"Please?"

"James'll be home in a while. Ask him."

"Gram? Will you?"

"Not today." Gram was slamming around the kitchen. Dicey guessed she knew about how her grandmother felt.

"I'm gonna go meet James," Sammy decided. He ran out the door, letting it slam behind him. Gram had taken off her shoes and was putting eggs and butter out on the table. She hauled down her big mixing bowl. "What are you making?" Dicey asked.

"Chocolate cake and I don't want any help, nor need it," Gram said.

The last time they had Gram's chocolate cake was for Sammy's birthday; but then Gram seemed happy about making it.

Dicey went out to the barn. While she scraped, she thought about the English assignment. She'd show them she could write something good. She began thinking of how she would write about Momma, how to say enough for it to tell what had happened, but not as if she was talking about her own mother. After a while, she put down the scraper and went upstairs to the desk in her bedroom. She had thought of a way to begin that would give her a good ending too. She began to write.

Downstairs, she heard the boys come in, with raised voices as if they were quarreling. Vaguely, she wondered what they could be quarreling about. Gram would settle it. Dicey continued writing, until a question that had been hovering around the back of her head, away behind her ideas, sneaked around to the front: wasn't Maybeth supposed to be home by now?

Outside, the sun was going down. Time to get to the kitchen, probably past time. Clouds crowded the sky, heavy and dark. The marsh lay under a pale mist, and in the distance, the Bay was dark purple.

James and Sammy sat over a game of checkers. Dicey said hello before turning down the hall to the kitchen. "I'd steer clear," James advised her. "Something's eating Gram."

"She got a welfare check today," Dicey explained.

"I don't know," James said.

Gram had set the table and put out glasses on the counter. She had put potatoes into the oven to bake. She had a stick of butter ready on the table. The cake she had made stood on the sideboard, tall and frosted. The steak waited beside a huge iron frying pan, beside the stove. Gram sat at the head of the table, in her usual place. Under the yellow kitchen light, her face looked pale and tired.

"And what do *you* want?" Gram demanded.

"I was going to set the table," Dicey said. Why was Gram angry at her? "Where's Maybeth?"

"Late," Gram said. Her face closed off.

"What were Sammy and James fighting about?" Dicey asked.

"The place of a perfectionist in this world," Gram said. Whatever that meant. "Ask 'em yourself."

Dicey went back down to the living room. "What *were* you two quarreling about?" she demanded.

"Are you angry?" Sammy asked. "Why is everyone angry at me?"

"Nothing really," James told her. His hazel eyes were worried. "We shouldn't have bothered Gram. Sammy just said I wasn't being careful where I threw the papers, it wasn't even important."

"Were you?" Dicey asked him.

James shook his head.

"I told him," Sammy said.

"Do you think something's happened to Maybeth?" James asked.

"What could happen to Maybeth," Dicey said to soothe him. But, of course, anything could happen to Maybeth, or any of them, or anyone. James was too smart to be fooled about that, but he let himself believe her. She could see in his eyes how he was making himself believe her, and her tone of voice.

"Is that why Gram's angry?" Sammy asked.

Dicey began to understand. She looked out the front windows, past the wide porch and down to where the driveway disappeared into the narrow stand of pines. Nothing except growing darkness. "She really is late."

"I'm hungry," Sammy said.

Dicey wandered back down to the kitchen. Worry was like

the mist along the marsh, it rose up from the floors of the house.

"What time does she usually get in?" Dicey asked Gram.

"An hour and more," Gram answered, "If you haven't got anything to do in here, why don't you just leave me alone."

Dicey obeyed. She was halfway down the hall when she met James and Sammy coming at her, both running. "The car's here!" Sammy called, as if Dicey were miles away.

Maybeth had burst into the kitchen and was explaining. Gram had a smile on her face that didn't flash away the way her smiles usually did. Mr. Lingerle climbed heavily up the steps and waited in the doorway, with the darkness behind him. He had a bandage on his right hand.

". . . a flat tire," Maybeth was saying.

"That's all right," Gram said.

"And the jack slipped, and it caught his fingers, and somebody stopped to help us. We went to the Emergency Room."

Gram looked up. "Come on in, what's this Maybeth's telling me?"

"I'm so sorry, Mrs. Tillerman, I know you must have been worried. I tried to call from the hospital—"

"I don't have a phone," Gram told him.

"It wasn't even that serious, only a couple of stitches," he apologized.

"I don't have a phone and I should. With children in the house it's irresponsible not to have a phone," Gram said angrily.

"It's all right, Gram," Maybeth said. Gram reached out and hugged Maybeth close. Then she let her go and took a deep breath.

"Yes, it is, and I'll get a phone put in. You'll stay for supper," she asked. "We're having steak."

"Gram," Sammy protested. *"Gram."*

She ignored him and waited for Mr. Lingerle's answer. Dicey understood, just then, and wished she didn't, just what the Tillermans had done to Gram by coming to live with her. Because she did love them, and that meant not only the good parts, but also the worry and fear. Until the children came along, nothing could hurt Gram. And now . . . but Gram must have known that, she'd had children of her own, she must have known that when she said they could live with her. Dicey wished she didn't understand. She wished she could still be like Sammy, concerned only about whether or not he'd have as much steak as he wanted, already forgetting the worry since everything was all right again.

"Thank you, I'd enjoy that," Mr. Lingerle said.

"Good," Gram said, with a quick glance at Sammy.

Sammy looked up at Mr. Lingerle. "Are you still nervous when you eat here?" he asked. His eyes shone hopefully.

Mr. Lingerle burst out laughing, and the Tillermans joined him.

CHAPTER 4

The day that Gram had to go in for conferences was also Halloween, and a Wednesday, and the day Dicey's English paper was due. She hadn't told any of her family what she was doing; she wanted to astound them, when it was handed back. She was the only one going to school that day. Because of the conferences, the little kids had a day off and were staying home, under James's care. Dicey offered to stay home and look out for them, but Gram refused, saying it would only be for three hours or so. She looked like there was something else she wanted to say, so Dicey waited. But Gram didn't say anything. Dicey, too, didn't say what she was thinking, that she was worried about giving James all the responsibility.

When she got home after a day at school and an hour working with Millie on the distributor's order sheets, Gram was alone at the kitchen table. Dicey didn't hear any noise from anywhere.

"Where are they?" she asked.

"In their rooms," Gram said. "James is riding his route."

"What did their teachers say?" Dicey asked.

"We'll talk about it later."

Dicey looked at her grandmother. Gram did not look back at her. Dicey shrugged, took a banana, and went out to the barn.

James's bike was gone, but the others were there. She hoped Sammy would stay up in his room, that he wouldn't come hang around her. Now that they were back on Eastern Standard Time, she couldn't even get an hour's work in. And she was just getting to the end of the first half of the boat.

The Tillermans weren't celebrating Halloween. They never had, in fact. Their house in Provincetown was set way away, so no kids came to the door. Nobody ever came, anyway. That was lucky, Momma always said, because they couldn't afford to buy a bowl of candy. A couple of those years they had all, even Momma, gotten into costumes (sheets for ghosts, or paper-bag armor) and had their own party, making popcorn on the gas stove, bobbing for apples in the dishpan. They ended up, as they usually did, singing.

Dicey sighed—for what, she didn't know. Maybeth had been asked to a Halloween party, but she said she didn't want to go. Dicey hadn't asked her why not, because they couldn't have gone to get her when the party was over. The girl lived inland, not on the water, and too far away for a late bike ride.

James walked his bicycle into the barn and set it against the side of an empty stall. He stood behind Dicey, watching.

"Did she tell you?"

"Tell me what? Who?"

"We're in trouble."

Dicey turned to look at him. "What do you mean? James, what happened?"

"We went up in the attic," he told her, daring her to be angry with him.

"And?" What was the matter with going up in the attic?

"And she came home. Gram. She said we had no business. She sent us to our rooms. She only let me come out for my paper route."

Dicey thought about that. "She's right, we hadn't asked."

"I thought we lived here," James complained.

"We do," Dicey said, "but—"

James waited for her to finish her sentence.

"That wasn't a very smart thing to do, James."

"I know. I was just curious. We apologized and told her we wouldn't do it again. Maybeth cried. Sammy didn't."

It all seemed fair enough to Dicey.

"We weren't even up there long enough to really look around," James said. "There are boxes of stuff and trunks and a couple of old toys. And a cradle. Do you ever wonder, Dicey, why she doesn't have any pictures of her children?"

Dicey shook her head.

"And she doesn't talk about anything before," James went on. "And we know where Momma is, and that Bullet is dead, but there was a third name, remember? Don't you wonder?"

"Nope," Dicey said.

"I do," James finished unnecessarily. "I wonder about Momma, what she was like then. I promised we wouldn't go up there again, but I wish I hadn't. I bet there's an album up there."

"Momma never had one," Dicey argued.

"Gram could have afforded it," James argued back. It was a stupid argument and Dicey didn't continue with it.

"Did you get your report on the pilgrims back?"

"He kept them to show the parents. But he said I got an A. The kids thought it was super, they said so." James smiled at the memory.

Dicey envied him. But it was getting too dark to work any more, and her bare legs were chilly, and she was going to have to go inside and see if she could straighten out things between Gram and the little kids.

It turned out that Gram didn't think anything needed straightening out. She looked around the dinner table at the three subdued faces and the one wary one. "I believe in closing the book on things," she announced.

"Does that mean you aren't angry any more?" Sammy asked.

Gram nodded.

Sammy smiled and looked relieved. "Good-o," he said. "I didn't like being in trouble."

"Neither did I," Gram agreed.

"And if we do it again—" Sammy went on.

Gram interrupted. "If you do it again—I'll take your hands and sew them over your ears."

Sammy giggled. "How could I eat?"

"We'll get you a dog dish," Dicey offered. "We'll put it on the floor and your food will be all mushed together, so that you can get it out with your tongue."

"Ugh," Sammy said happily.

"What about the conferences?" James asked. Maybeth looked down at her plate.

Gram put down her fork and waited until they were all, even Maybeth, looking at her. "About the conferences," she said. "I want to wait to talk about them until I've talked to Dicey."

Dicey looked up, surprised. What was wrong now?

"When, tomorrow?" James insisted.

Gram shook her head. "I have a plan. This Saturday, Dicey and I are going to take a day away."

"What about me?" asked Sammy.

"You and Maybeth and James are going to stay home. I called Mr. Lingerle, to give him our number." The black telephone had been sitting on the living room desk for two days by then. Nobody had used it to call them, although the little kids had all dialed the weather and time. "And I asked him if he would come out to take care of you."

The three faces went down to the three plates again. "We're sorry, Gram," Maybeth said softly.

"I know you are and I know you won't do it again, but—" She

hesitated, then went on. "There was a lesson for me in this. I'd forgotten that when you leave children alone they have a natural tendency to get into trouble."

"Did your children do that?" James asked.

"I also spoke to Millie, who said you could take the morning off," Gram said to Dicey.

"But—" Dicey said.

"No buts, girl," Gram said. "Besides, it won't be much fun. We're going shopping. I don't know if you have noticed the cold coming on, but I have. While we've got the money from this welfare check, there are things you have to have, things I can't make myself. So Dicey and I will have a day off, after which we will talk about the conferences."

"Were they bad?" Maybeth asked.

"There were good things and bad things," Gram acknowledged. "But there was nothing that made me regret you living here with me." The children exchanged pleased glances, and Sammy's face (Dicey noticed) was flushed with pleasure. "I was proud to go in and say, I'm Sammy Tillerman's grandmother or Maybeth's or James's."

Dicey bit on her lower lip. What Gram would say about Dicey's home ec grade—she was almost sorry she hadn't tried harder in the class, if it mattered to Gram.

"Is that all right with you, Dicey?" Gram said.

"Sure, if you want to," Dicey said.

"We'll take the bus up to Salisbury, where there's a mall," Gram said.

"I like bus rides," Sammy volunteered.

"Well, I don't," Gram said.

Apparently Dicey thought from her seat by the window that Saturday morning, Gram meant exactly what she said. Gram sat straight and stiff beside Dicey. She was wearing her blue suit and a white blouse, tucked in. She carried a purse and had put on her loafers, with stockings. Gram wasn't planning to enjoy herself. Dicey wore her shorts, as always. She thought about talking to her grandmother, but shrugged and looked out the window instead.

Because Dicey did like buses. She liked any means of transportation. She liked going places. They rode up a highway, past marshlands and farmlands. A brisk wind blew at the grasses and trees. For the first time, Dicey felt like it really was fall. The sky hung low and gray over fields. She could see smoke curling up out of chimneys in some of the houses they passed. It was one of those first fall days, that look colder than they really are.

But it really was cold. When they had stood waiting at the bus station, her legs got goose bumps from the wind. Mr. Lingerle drove them into town, and he said he'd come pick them up, too. Gram didn't want to take the ride, but he pointed out how large the waves would be under this wind, and that if they bought anything it would be soaked before they got home again. He said he liked to help.

Gram's chin went up when he said that, because she did *not* like to be helped. But he had insisted and insisted, saying that Saturday was usually a pretty long, lonely day for him, saying that he was going to try riding on Sammy's bike (Sammy bit his lip to keep from saying something about that), saying finally that he liked being welcome at their house, and he was only offering what family friends offered. So Gram gave in.

The bus entered the limits of the scraggly city. Dicey studied the shopping centers and the low office buildings, each surrounded by its own parking lot. Cars and trucks crowded the road. For a few minutes, Dicey found this exciting, all the people, all their different lives and faces. Then the grayness, the papers blowing on sidewalks, the sandy-colored sameness of the buildings diminished that excitement. Beside her, Gram stirred.

"Do you know where we're going?" Dicey asked.

"Yes," Gram answered.

The mall had an arched gateway leading to acres of parking lots. The bus stopped before an entrance to the long building. Dicey and Gram climbed down the steps and went in.

Gram went straight to a list of stores in the mall and began reading down it. Dicey planned to enjoy herself, if she could. She listened to the voices of the crowds of Saturday shoppers, she stared at families and couples, at gangs of girls and boys. Some of the people were hurrying on, as if they had a lot to do and not much time. Others were meandering about, stopping at store windows, as if they had a whole day to kill.

Gram joined Dicey. "When I was a girl," she said, looking about her, "Crisfield was the big town. The people from Salisbury came down to Crisfield." She took a breath and her chin went up. "Let's get going, girl, we've got a lot to do."

"But I thought we were going to talk," Dicey said.

"That too," Gram said, stepping briskly out.

Gram took Dicey first to a five-and-ten. They stood in front of a small table covered with wool, while Gram touched the skeins of yarn and made "hnm" sounds. At last she turned to Dicey. "You like any of these?"

Dicey studied the unnaturally bright colors, greens and reds and yellows. She tried to find one that wasn't as bad as the rest. "No," she said.

"Neither do I."

Gram marched out and on down the center walkway. When she found a little store with its windows crammed with pillows on which kittens had been embroidered, she entered. At the back of this store, there was a whole wall of wools. Gram started pulling down colors. Dicey looked around. There were a few women in the store, looking at instruction books or studying kits. The saleslady sat on a tall stool behind the counter, her hands busy with thread and canvas. She looked more like one of the summer residents of Provincetown than a saleslady in a mall, Dicey thought. She wore makeup on her eyes, lips, and skin. Her hair had every strand in a particular place. The woman looked up and caught Dicey's eye. "Can I help you?" she asked. Dicey shook her head and turned her attention back to Gram.

Gram had pulled down a dozen colors. She had spread them out on the table before her. Every now and then she would touch one and move it around to sit by itself.

"What are you doing?" Dicey asked.

"Sweaters," Gram answered. "Is there a color you like?"

"You're going to make us sweaters?"

"It's either that or buy them," Gram answered grimly.

"I didn't know you could knit."

Gram shrugged. She put her hand on a yellow the color of daffodils. "This looks like Maybeth to me. And a good blue for Sammy, but brown for James, don't you think."

"Isn't that an awful lot of work?"

"Come winter, I've got the time. What about you, what do you like?"

Dicey liked the brown, but Gram pulled out a kind of greeny-bluey skein, flecked with white. "Heather," she said.

Dicey liked that all right too, and she liked it more the more she looked at it.

"Feel it," Gram instructed. Dicey obeyed, and the wool was thick and soft under her fingers. "Heather's the one I like for you," Gram said.

"What about you?" Dicey asked.

"I've got plenty, I don't have to go out in public," Gram said.

Dicey, her mind on sweaters, thought that Gram should have one in a dusty rose, or maybe in black to set off the snap in her eyes. But Dicey couldn't knit. Gram paid; Dicey hefted the awkward bag of wool.

"Did your momma teach you to knit?" Gram asked Dicey.

"I can't do any of that stuff," Dicey mumbled.

"Oh well," Gram said.

They walked on, into a two-story Sears & Roebuck that occupied one end of the mall. There, Gram wound her way to the children's department. She picked out eight pairs of blue jeans, and they went to get in the line by the cash register.

"That's—thank you, Gram," Dicey said. Because their grandmother was buying them clothes.

"Children can't wear shorts all year round," Gram answered. "Maybeth's teacher is worried about her. She's not progressing, not to speak of. Mrs. Jackson says the school system has home tutors who are trained teachers and know the kind of work the class is doing. She says, we should get one. She says she doesn't think it will help, but she wants to try everything because Maybeth is such a sweet child. She says Maybeth is failing. She says, Maybeth gets along beautifully with her classmates and is very mature." Gram stopped as suddenly as she had begun.

Dicey felt as if Gram had been hitting at her, punch, punch, punch. "Millie can't read," she announced, following her own thoughts. "Not much, not like she should."

"She told you that? She'd never admit it to me. We were girls in school together."

"I know," Dicey said.

"Maybeth's not like Millie," Gram said.

How had Gram known that was a question in Dicey's mind. "Are you sure?"

"Sure," Gram told Dicey. "But—"

At that moment their turn to pay came, and Gram just said, "We'll talk about it over lunch. Think about it, meanwhile."

They had to go to another department for long-sleeved shirts for the little kids. Dicey already had all the made-over shirts she needed. Gram made quick selections, plain colors for Maybeth, and striped for the boys. They got into another line. "Sammy's work is all right," Gram reported. "She told me I was lucky to have such a quiet, well-behaved grandson, because boys could be such hellions. She said if only every boy in the class had Sammy's attitude."

"Well." Dicey was surprised. She was glad that was all right. "He hasn't always been that way," she told Gram, relieved.

"He still isn't," Gram said, then snapped her mouth shut.

Dicey felt her shoulders sag. It wasn't because they were tired, or she was tired. The bags they got were big, but not heavy. She thought she had a good idea what Gram was thinking. Sometimes she almost wished she didn't have any brothers and sisters. "How about James? Was James's teacher pleased with him?"

Gram had her purse open to pay, and she put bills into the salesclerk's hand before she answered. Dicey almost told Gram not to bother saying, unless it was something good.

"Oh yes. He says what we all—including James—know, that he's unusually intelligent. He says James's work was better at the beginning of the year, but the other kids caught up with him pretty quickly. He especially mentioned James report. He showed it to me."

"James got an A," Dicey said.

"It wasn't the same report he showed us," Gram said.

Dicey took the bag, jammed it into the bigger one that held the jeans and did not answer.

Back in the center of the mall, Gram looked about her.

"Lunch," she said. She led Dicey back, along the length of the building, to the other end, where there stood a two-story department store. There was a restaurant, too, right by the entrance, a real restaurant where there was a special waitress who asked how many you were and led you to a table.

"But Gram," Dicey protested. They had seen a couple of hamburger stands.

Gram ignored her. The waitress gave them a table by a window that looked out to the center of the mall. "Put those bags down," Gram instructed Dicey.

Dicey obeyed, jamming the bags up against the wall.

"This is my treat, for me," Gram said, looking around with satisfaction. She opened the menu and looked at it.

Dicey followed suit. She studied the prices. She found the three cheapest things and then looked to see what they were. When Gram asked her what she wanted, she said, "Spaghetti."

Gram stared at her over the top of the menu.

"I like spaghetti," Dicey said.

"My rule is, when you go to a restaurant, you have something you don't get at home," Gram announced. "I'm going to have a club sandwich and I advise you to do the same."

Dicey skimmed around for a club sandwich, to see how much it cost. "Why?" she asked, playing for time.

"Because it tastes good," Gram said, folding her menu firmly onto the table. "I know what you're thinking, girl, and with the amount of money we're spending today this little isn't going to make any difference." Then she smiled quickly. "Besides, I've handed you some problems you'll need food energy to work on."

"Okay," Dicey said. "I hope I like it."

"If you don't, I'll eat it," Gram said. She ordered them two club sandwiches on white toast with extra mayonnaise. For herself, she ordered a pot of tea. Dicey wanted a soda.

"Small, medium, or large?" the waitress asked.

"Small," Dicey said.

"Large," Gram corrected her.

Dicey just shook her head.

When their drinks were before them, Gram looked at Dicey and said, "What do you think?"

Dicey didn't know what she was talking about.

"About your family, girl. Snap out of it. You've had weeks and weeks without worrying, but the vacation is over now. You've got to help out."

But, Dicey thought, I am helping out, I have a job. And I haven't exactly not worried.

"I don't know," she said. Gram snorted impatiently. So Dicey tried. "If the teacher says Maybeth can get a real tutor, for nothing, that's not bad is it?" she asked.

Gram waited.

"And Sammy's all right. And James is doing well. So what's the problem?"

Gram waited. Dicey put the straw into her mouth and sipped at her soda. She looked out the window. Walking away from them, down the mall, were a boy and a girl. They had their arms around one another. The boy's arm was over the girl's shoulder and his hand was tucked into the rear pocket of her jeans. Her arm went across his back and into the pocket of his jeans. They leaned their heads toward one another, talking, as if there was nothing important in the world except what they had to say right then.

"When I was a girl," Gram said, "only engaged couples could spend an afternoon alone together. And even then, the most they would do in public was hold hands. People say things were easier then, and maybe they were."

Dicey followed the couple with her eyes. She didn't know

why Gram was talking like this, but she was interested in what Gram would say about what it was like when she was young.

"Things were surely simpler. But I guess we made them hard, because I don't remember anything simple, or easy, about it. I'd be inclined to think things are easier now, wouldn't you?"

Dicey looked back but didn't answer.

"I didn't say better, just easier," Gram told her.

Dicey nodded, to show she was listening. But she was wondering: how long was she going to have to spend worrying about her brothers and sisters?

"It's for as long as you live," Gram said, as if Dicey had spoken aloud. "That's something I learned, even though I didn't want to. For as long as you live, the attachments hold."

At that moment their sandwiches were put down in front of them. Dicey looked at hers, four triangles of toast layered with turkey and bacon, lettuce and tomato, like rock strata on cliffs. A pile of potato chips was in the center of the plate. Gram passed her a little glass of mayonnaise.

"So you've got to think," Gram said, "and I'd be grateful if you'd tell me what you think."

Reluctantly, Dicey agreed. Well, Gram was right, she'd had a nice long rest from it, longer than any she could remember ever before in her life. And she couldn't fool herself that her family didn't matter to her. She took a bite. "Okay," she said. "I think I know about James. But, Gram—this sandwich is good."

"I told you, didn't I?" Gram answered, pleased with herself.

"James never had friends, none of us did really, on account of Momma and where we lived, and a whole lot of things. But James always wanted them. I think—if he wrote another report—he did it because he didn't want to be too different. Because if you're too different people don't like you."

"But is he making friends?"

"I dunno," Dicey said. "I never asked. He told me the kids liked his report. The trouble is," she went on, "that if James doesn't have something to think about he gets bored and— because he doesn't like working the way I do, not physical work. Working with his mind, that's what James likes. So he needs to do a lot of thinking in school."

"Which he won't, because then he'd be too different," Gram pointed out. "So he will have to find something to think about at home."

"He reads those books," Dicey said.

"Your grandfather read books at home, alone."

"Was he like James? Is James like him?"

Gram didn't answer. "I don't know what to do," she said finally.

Neither did Dicey.

"And what about Sammy?" Gram demanded.

"He's just trying to be good."

"I appreciate that," Gram declared. "But he isn't good, you know. Not the way she thinks he is; he isn't her idea of good. But he's trying to be that. She said he sits quiet as a mouse, all day. It's no wonder he's got so much energy to burn off when he gets home. Did you ever think of that?"

Dicey hadn't.

"Well, think about it," Gram said. "See if you find it a pleasant thought."

"No," Dicey said, her voice low, "I don't. But, Gram? If he wants to be the kind of boy she likes, it's for you, and for me. For all of us."

Gram nodded grimly. She had finished her sandwich, and she poured out a cup of tea.

Dicey had a picture in her head of Sammy putting on a mask every morning, to wear all day long. It was a heavy iron mask, and he pulled it around his own face and bolted it closed.

"If I was just in the same school," Dicey wished.

"But you're not," Gram answered. "Do you remember when you were little in school?"

"Not much. I got in trouble, for fighting."

"What stopped you?"

"The other kids learned to steer clear."

Gram stared at Dicey for a minute and her eyes snapped as if she was either angry, or trying not to laugh. "But what were you fighting about?"

Dicey made herself meet Gram's dark, hazel eyes. "They'd say things—about Momma. About—our father being gone—about our not having his name—"

"I can guess," Gram cut her off.

"Sometimes, they'd laugh at me, I don't know why. I didn't like that. But Sammy doesn't mind being laughed at. He likes being a clown."

"Not the Sammy that woman's got sitting in her class. That Sammy—I don't know, he's not at all like our Sammy."

"Not the good ways or the bad ways," Dicey realized. "But what can we do?"

"That's what I thought we could talk about. That and Maybeth."

"Does she *have* to go to school?"

"You know better than that, girl. Be sensible."

The waitress came and took their plates away. She asked did they want some dessert. Gram said no, thank you, and the waitress went away.

Dicey leaned her elbows on the table. She didn't know what Gram was going to think of, what she was going to say next. "I don't think Maybeth is learning anything," she said.

"I agree," Gram said.

"When I was explaining fractions, she didn't learn anything,"

Dicey said. "But I had the feeling—if I could do it a different way, then she would." She stopped.

"Go on, keep telling me," Gram urged.

"Well I wonder—those lists of words she's supposed to memorize. I don't think she *can* learn them."

Gram was watching her so hard, Dicey felt like she was sitting too close to the fire. "So if she has a school tutor, wouldn't she teach Maybeth the same way?" she concluded.

Gram leaned back and smiled. "Exactly. I just wanted to see if I was the only one thinking that. Sometimes, I get crazy ideas, and I know how stubborn I am."

"But we can't afford another tutor, can we?" Dicey asked. "Because she shouldn't give up her piano lessons, because I won't let you do that."

"Who said I wanted to do that?" Gram demanded. "Give me some credit, girl. What did your momma do about Maybeth?"

"She'd pretend it wasn't happening."

Gram thought about that. "Now we know two ways that don't work," she said finally.

Dicey giggled. Gram gave Dicey one of her sudden smiles.

"We should have had James along," Dicey said. "He's the one with ideas."

"I needed just you for this today," Gram said. "We'll confer with James when we get home, but I wanted—besides, we never get to talk much, do we."

"You're kept pretty busy," Dicey said excusing her grandmother. "And I haven't been much help to you," she admitted.

"Well, I'll tell you, Dicey, I'd be happy not to bother you with this. You've already done a lot for your brothers and sister. I don't say that to you, but I think it." Dicey felt her face grow hot, and she looked down at her glass. She stirred the ice cubes around with her straw. What was she supposed to say?

Nothing, apparently, because Gram went right on. "But I'll tell you something else, too. Something I've learned, the hard way. I guess"—Gram laughed a little—"I'm the kind of person who has to learn the hard way. You've got to hold on. Hold on to people. They can get away from you. It's not always going to be fun, but if you don't—hold on—then you lose them. Now, let's get going."

Dicey wanted to stay, then, and ask Gram what she meant. Not about holding on, because Dicey could figure that out, but what she meant to be saying about herself. Did Gram wish she had held on to her own children? To Bullet and Momma—did Gram think that would have made any difference to Momma up in that hospital, or Bullet dead in Vietnam? And what about her son John, whoever he was, wherever he was?

But Gram wasn't waiting for any questions, she was walking on out to pay the bill. Dicey gathered up the bags and followed.

She thought Gram would go back to the bus stop then, but instead her grandmother went along the fancy department store, past purses and hats, past sweaters, past racks of dresses and mannequins leaning over in impossible poses. She went right into an area where nightgowns and robes hung out, and slips and bras and underpants and girdles. She went right up to a counter and turned, waiting for Dicey to join her. A saleslady came over, her hair brushed high and wavy and held in place by spray so thick it glistened. "May I help you?"

"My granddaughter needs a bra," Gram said.

Dicey looked away. She looked back at Gram, angry. She looked at the saleslady, who was staring at her. She glared at Gram. This was a trick, a rotten trick.

The saleslady took out a tape measure and measured Dicey. She made clicking noises. Dicey raised her chin, ignoring the woman. Gram pretended to be looking into a counter, but since the counter was filled with thick girdles laid out, like the steaks in

Millie's store, Dicey knew Gram was just pretending. She tried to think of how to get out of the situation. She could run away, she supposed. But she didn't have any money with her and how would she get home? She could start a fight with Gram right here—but Gram wasn't enjoying this any more than Dicey was. Dicey could tell that by the way she was pretending to be especially interested in a girdle that was black and lacy, that hooked up the front from your hips to your bosom.

The saleslady brought out a handful of bras and asked them to step back to the dressing room, to try them on. Gram wanted to refuse, Dicey saw that as clear as day. "I'll wait here," Gram said.

Dicey felt mean. "You better come with me," she said. Gram's chin went up, and she came along. If Dicey hadn't been so uncomfortable herself, she would have laughed.

They bought three bras, three little scraps of nylon at four dollars each. Dicey, who agreed to keep one on since it was either that or have a fight with both Gram and the saleslady at the same time, figured it served Gram right. If she was going to insist that Dicey wear a bra, then Dicey wasn't going to feel sorry at how much money it cost. If Dicey was going to have to go around feeling like a dog with a collar on, Gram could just pay for it, and Dicey wasn't going to apologize.

They left the lingerie department silently. Then Gram led Dicey up the escalator to the second floor. Dicey followed without any questions. Let Gram be angry at her. She didn't care, after that trick.

Gram went into a girls' section, where the mannequins were of teenagers wearing slacks or party dresses. They were in the same poses as the mannequins for ladies, which Dicey thought was pretty stupid. The dresses were pretty stupid-looking too. The slacks—well, anybody who would pay the price for those when they could wear jeans was stupid.

Gram went over to a rack and pulled out a denim jumper. "Come over here, girl, and put down those packages." She held the jumper up in front of Dicey. It was too short.

Yet another saleslady came over and asked if she could help. This one wore loops and loops of necklaces and loops and loops of bracelets. She jingled as she walked.

"Try one of these on," Gram instructed Dicey. "We don't know her size," she said to the lady.

The lady jingled around to measure Dicey with her eyes. She picked out a jumper and told Dicey to follow her. This time, Dicey didn't insist that Gram come too. It was going to be hard to keep on being angry.

The dressing room had mirrors and mirrors and mirrors. Dicey looked at herself, in her boy's shirt and shorts. She didn't look too terrific. Her sharp face was reflected back to her, from all angles, front and sides. She could see herself from the back. Her raggedy hair, her old shorts—at least the bra didn't show. The saleslady slipped the jumper over her head and marched Dicey out to show Gram.

"Looks all right," Gram said. She had sat down in a chair with something brown laid over the big bags beside her. "Do you like it?" she asked Dicey.

"But Gram—" Dicey started to protest.

"You going to answer my question?"

"Yes, of course, I do, you know that." Gram grunted. "But Gram—" How could she tell Gram not to spend the money when the saleslady was listening?

"I went to your school one day," Gram said.

"I saw you," Dicey answered.

"I didn't see anybody in shorts," Gram said. "I saw some in jeans, lots in skirts and dresses. I kind of liked the way these jumpers looked. They look sturdy."

Dicey tried to stop the smile that was about to take over her face. She kept her mouth still, but she had the feeling her eyes were giving her away.

"She'll need a couple of pairs of those high socks," Gram told the saleslady. "In blue. Will you try this on too?" she asked, holding out the brown thing.

It was a dark brown dress, made out of some soft material that looked like velvet but was thicker. The dress had a white knitted collar and matching cuffs; it had a brown belt that went with it.

"I don't need a dress," Dicey said.

"I just asked you to try it on," Gram insisted.

Dicey cooperated, mostly because she wanted to show Gram that she appreciated the jumper. The saleslady hung around while Dicey unbuttoned her shirt, then struggled into the long sleeves. The lady zipped Dicey up the back and watched her put the belt around her waist.

"Now that's more like it," the lady said.

Dicey looked in the mirrors. The dark brown of the dress was like the soil in Gram's garden, where Sammy had turned it over. The heavy-soft fabric hung close to her body. Her bosom showed a little, and the belt at her waist made her look curved. She looked unfamiliar to herself, the kind of plain that was really fancy. She stood, biting her lip, looking at the girl in the mirror.

"Go show your grandmother *that*," the saleslady said, obviously pleased.

Dicey walked out again, feeling foolish, feeling different.

Gram just nodded, as if she had expected to see exactly what she saw.

The saleslady waited for one of them to say something, then said it herself: "She's a pretty child."

Dicey looked up, alarmed.

"I don't know why they dress the way they do," the saleslady said to Gram, leaning confidentially over in an adult-to-adult position.

Gram looked up at her. "You don't? I do."

The lady's mouth tightened, and she jingled herself up straight again.

"Those shoes," Gram said to Dicey, her mouth twitching. "We'll have to see what we have at home. I like it, girl."

"Me too," Dicey said. She spread her hands down the soft fabric over her hips. "But—"

"We'll take the two, then," Gram said, "and the socks."

Dicey went back to change into her shorts and shirt. She felt utterly confused, but not displeased. She remembered to thank Gram, but her grandmother ignored that, except for a nod of the head. "I don't know when I'll wear it," Dicey said.

"That's all right," Gram answered. "You're not going to grow that fast any more. It'll wait."

They went down the escalator and back out into the mall. "Can we go home now?" Gram asked Dicey, as if Dicey were the one who had thought up these errands.

Dicey just grinned. Then, walking along beside her grandmother, she had an idea: "We can't tell James we know what he did, can we? Or why."

"I agree," Gram said. "And we *should* tell Sammy we know, but we have to do it . . ."

"Indirectly," Dicey finished.

"It's not as if we want him to go out and get into fights," Gram agreed.

They waited by the bus stop. The wind had gotten colder, like knives with edges. Dicey tried to ignore the cold in her legs. "What do we want to tell him?" she asked.

"That the way he is is all right, good and bad. That *Sammy* is who we want him to be, not some idea that teacher has of who he should be. I didn't much care for her. But I'm not known for liking many people. That he doesn't need to change himself for us to think he's all right."

That was it exactly, Dicey thought. "You know about us," she said to Gram.

The bus rolled up then, and they climbed into it. Dicey sat by the window again. She didn't interrupt her grandmother's thoughts until they were almost outside of the city limits. "Gram?"

Gram turned her face to Dicey.

"I understand what you mean about holding on. It *is* what I want to do," Dicey said.

"I think so," Gram remarked.

"And Gram?"

Her grandmother turned back again.

"We'll ask James what he thinks about Maybeth tonight. After the little kids are in bed. He'll have an idea."

"He'll have seven ideas, if I know him," Gram remarked. She turned away, leaving Dicey to her own thoughts. One of Dicey's thoughts was to wonder what it was that Gram was thinking so hard about. They were about halfway to Crisfield before she got the answer.

"There's one other thing we have to talk about, girl," Gram's voice spoke in her ear. Dicey jerked herself back from her mental picture of the little boat, newly painted, next summer.

"What's that?"

"You."

"I'm all right," Dicey said.

"You're on my list," Gram said, with a small smile. "It's not just the bra, Dicey."

Gram's cheeks were pink.

"The bra is just the beginning," Gram said.

Dicey understood. She grinned at her grandmother, who

opened her mouth to protest. ("I'm not joking, girl," that was what her grandmother was going to say, Dicey knew it.) "It's okay, Gram," she said, glad that she could make this at least easier for Gram. "I know about menstruating."

Gram nodded and shut her mouth. Then she took a deep breath and opened it again.

Dicey cut her off. "And I know about sex," she assured her grandmother.

Gram looked doubtful, hesitated, started to speak, stopped, started again.

"I'll tell you what I think," Dicey said, to help Gram. "You can decide if there's stuff I should know more about." She wasn't enjoying the conversation any more than Gram was. "I think that, even though I know how it works, sex—I don't know how it feels."

Then Dicey heard what she had just said, and she felt her face burn hot. Now Gram was smiling.

"I mean, how it feels to want to. I mean—I don't know—I'm much too young," Dicey wailed.

"That's all right then," Gram said. "You would ask if you had any questions."

Dicey nodded.

"Because I get the feeling you're not too pleased about growing up," Gram said.

Dicey looked out over the tall marsh grasses, blowing in the wind. If the wind blew, the grasses had to bend with it. She wondered how they felt about that. "It's just," she said to her grandmother, "I have the feeling that I know who I am, only I'm not anymore."

CHAPTER 5

Mr. Lingerle stayed to have supper with them, stayed for music after supper, stayed even after Sammy and Maybeth had gone upstairs to bed. Dicey regretted having built a fire, when she came back into the living room to see him sitting in front of it. He leaned toward the crackling logs with a dreamy expression on his face. Gram was coming out of the kitchen with another cup of coffee for the man. She looked at Dicey and shrugged her shoulders. What did that mean? Dicey wondered.

Mr. Lingerle took the cup and said, for about the tenth time, "I should be going."

"Have I thanked you properly?" Gram asked him.

"For what? For staying out here today? I enjoyed myself. Didn't I, James?"

"I think he did," James assured his grandmother. He and Dicey were playing a game of Parcheesi on the rug in front of the fire. Dicey's right side felt hot, and her left side felt cool, and that reminded her of every other time she had sat in front of fires. She kind of liked the way fires went to extremes: either it was too hot or too cold. It had been the same way with the big kerosene stove they used the heat their drafty cabin back up home, in Provincetown. She rattled the dice in her cup and let them roll out onto the board. James looked at her roll and then studied the board to see what moves her men might make.

"James," Gram spoke. He looked up. "Dicey and I were talking about Maybeth today, and we thought you might have some ideas."

Mr. Lingerle put down his cup, so fast the china clattered. "I'm sorry, I didn't realize," he said. He started to push himself up, out of the chair. "I've stayed too long, I was just too comfortable, I'd better be going."

Dicey knew she shouldn't have been surprised at his quick perception of what Gram was saying; but she was. She kept making the same mistake, she guessed, thinking that because he was heavy and clumsy in his body, he was the same way in his mind. She should have known better, from listening to his piano playing, if for no other reason, or the way he joined in with harmony when they sang. Or the way Maybeth trusted him, she reminded herself.

Gram answered Mr. Lingerle. "You might as well stay. You know Maybeth, so you might be able to help."

He hesitated, rocking up and back to get out of the chair, then sitting back, then lurching forward again.

"I thought about it, young man, before I brought up the subject."

"If you wanted me to leave, you'd say so, wouldn't you?" Mr. Lingerle asked. He answered himself. "Yes, you would. I don't know you well, but I know you that well."

Gram just waited for him to finish. "Now, about Maybeth," she began. She told them what Maybeth's teacher had said, and the notion she and Dicey shared about Maybeth not being able to learn the way this school taught reading.

While Gram was talking, James quietly picked up the pieces and dice, the cups and the board, and put them back into their box. Dicey didn't say a word. Neither did Mr. Lingerle.

"She said Maybeth is flunking?" James asked at last. "She said that?"

"Not exactly. She said, at this rate, Maybeth could never complete the work for third grade."

"It's only November," James protested. "How can she know? What's she like, anyway, this Mrs. Jackson?"

"She's perfectly ordinary. Except, she's one of those people who think that if you just work hard enough, everything will go your way," Gram said. "That's why Maybeth puzzles her. Upsets her."

"What's *wrong* with Maybeth, anyway?" James demanded.

Dicey thought she knew what he was thinking—that Maybeth was like Momma. "Nothing's wrong with her," she said quickly. "You know that and I know that, James."

"All right," he agreed, looking down at his hands. "It's just—besides, she's making friends, isn't she?"

"She's slow," Dicey said. "We've always known that. Slow at school."

"Because she's shy," he pointed out.

"Not only shy," Gram told him. "But that, too. What we want to know is, do you have any ideas?"

"Ideas?"

"About what to do about Maybeth," Gram repeated patiently.

"Oh sure, but nothing any good. She could go into a special school. Or, we could take her out of school and have tutors. It's only seven years until she can quit. We could work harder with her, helping her—but she works so hard already. Poor Maybeth," he said.

"You can do better than that, James," Gram snapped at him.

He looked up, hurt and surprised. He started to answer, then stopped himself. His eyes went back to the long shelf of books behind the desk. "You're right," he said. "I'm sorry. All right, let's think about it. The basic problem is reading, isn't it?"

"Right now, yes," Gram said.

"Maybeth isn't learning how to read. Now, what does that mean? It means—"

Dicey let out a gust of exasperated air. What was James doing now?

He looked at her and shook his head to stop her saying anything. "It means she reads slowly, can't remember what she has read, out loud or silently—because she hasn't understood the words—because of her mistakes, and because if you go so slowly— It must be like, if you try to walk in slow motion. You always lose your balance."

He stopped speaking then. He was staring hard at his hand spread out on the rug. The light from the flames made shadows that moved across his face. Gram got impatient: "Well?"

"I'm thinking," James said. "Let me think. Because what all that means—Maybeth sees the words with her eyes, but she doesn't connect them in her brain right away, the way I do. The question is, why the connection isn't made. So that, if we want to solve the problem, we have to work on the connection part of it." He raised his face and smiled at them all.

"I don't understand," Dicey said.

"Look. Maybeth can talk, can't she? So she knows the meanings. She can see, so she can see the words. But she doesn't make the connection."

When he put it that way, Dicey thought she could understand. But she didn't see that it helped them any.

"Okay," James said eagerly. "Now listen. The way Mrs. Jackson teaches, and I guess the whole school system, is to look at a whole word and recognize it. Maybe that's it, maybe that's what we should do."

"What do you mean?" Gram demanded.

"Well, Maybeth sees the whole word, but that doesn't make sense to her because she can't remember it, as a word. But we know she can remember the letters. Maybe she should be working on reading the letters, not the whole word."

"But she can read some whole words," Dicey protested. "I've heard her."

"Yes, but not as many as the other third-graders can. That's where the slowness comes in."

"Do you mean we should go back to the beginning with her?" Gram asked. "Do all the lists again?"

James shook his head, hard. "No. I mean we should try another way. I have to think more about it, I don't know anything about the subject, I'll have to go to the library. But that's what I think would work for Maybeth. Another way."

"I don't know," Gram said doubtfully.

Dicey had a sudden memory, of Millie reading *cornflakes* for *corn chips.* "You mean, what Maybeth does is sees—like the beginning of the word, and then she guesses?"

James nodded.

"And she's not a guesser by nature," Dicey went on. She didn't know exactly what James had meant, but she could see how it would work on Maybeth, this guessing. "It would make her nervous, and she'd always be waiting to be caught in a mistake, and she wouldn't hear what she was reading, so it would be hard for her to understand what she was reading. Maybeth likes—knowing how to do what she's doing. When she gets nervous, and scared—she can't think about things."

Gram looked over at Mr. Lingerle. "Do you have anything to add?"

"No." He shook his head. "Except to say that I never found Maybeth stupid. But you know that already."

"We do," Gram said, "but sometimes we get to doubting. It's good to hear. All right then, James, you'll do some reading on the subject. In a hurry."

"I'll do it when I can, as soon as I can. I've got my job and all," James said.

Dicey felt her mood of hopefulness fading as she remembered that James was good at ideas but not so good at following them through. She made a mental note to remind him.

The next day was Sunday, and Dicey had a whole afternoon to work on the boat. It was a cool afternoon, but in her new jeans she was warm enough. Sunlight came in through the opened doors, a broad beam of yellow light. Dust motes danced lazily up and down in the light. Dicey stood, pulling the scraper across the curved planks. She was singing to herself, "When first unto this country, a stranger I came." She wasn't thinking about anything in particular. She was wondering vaguely how long she should give James before she reminded him and wondering how long Mr. Chappelle would take correcting their essays, how long before she got her essay back. Sammy came in and stood beside her. She broke off the song, and her thoughts. She hoped he wouldn't stay too long, because she had been enjoying her mood.

"Gram's teaching Maybeth how to knit," he reported.

"Is she."

"I just said so," Sammy pointed out.

"Yes, you did," Dicey agreed.

"Can I help you?"

"Isn't there wood to cut?"

"Gram said Miss Tieds says I'm good."

"So I heard," Dicey said. She hadn't looked at him yet and she didn't plan to. He stayed for a few seconds, as if waiting for her to say something, or do something, then he turned sharply away. He turned so sharply, his shoulder shoved against Dicey's. The blade of the scraper dug into the wood.

"Sammy!" she yelled. "Watch out what you're doing!"

He was already by the barn doors, standing in the stream of

sunlight. He turned back to face her, and the sunlight glowed around him.

Sammy had gotten taller, in his legs especially, she thought. His hands were on his hips and his face was hard. It was as if he was daring her.

Daring her to do what? Start a fight, probably. She stared at him, and he stared at her.

Then Dicey began to remember. She remembered Sammy's sturdy brown legs walking, all that long summer long, keeping up with the bigger kids. And she remembered Sammy, memory going backward, like flipping through a photograph album, until she came to a vague picture of the little baby Momma brought home from the hospital. Their father had walked out by then, he'd left pretty soon after Momma told them that Sammy was coming. Because she was the oldest, Sammy was Dicey's responsibility. She was the one who changed his diapers and fed him cereal on a spoon when Momma was at work. She was the one who watched him sleeping in the night until Momma got home. She was the one he'd splashed water all over in his baths in the dishpan, slapping at the water with his chubby little hands, and his eyes laughed.

His hands looked strong now, and you could see the bones running from his wrist to his fingers. His eyes weren't laughing now, they were as flat as his mouth. Their colors didn't shine out at her.

No wonder, she said to herself, still looking back at his expressionless face, feeling for a minute as if she were Sammy and hearing the conversations they'd just had as he might have heard it. Or, she corrected herself, the conversation they hadn't just had.

"Can you find me some sandpaper?" she asked him.

"Why?" he asked, without moving. It was as if he wanted to stay angry.

"So I can sand this place smooth. And then"—Dicey thought fast and it seemed like a good plan—"if you really do want to help—"

"I do!" he cried, running back to the work bench. "I can!" he cried.

"The next thing, after scraping, is sanding. We'll have to sand it down about three times, three different times. The book said."

"Why so many?" He passed her a square of sandpaper.

"I dunno, it just said that was the best way to do it. I'm planning to do this job the best way, start to finish."

"Good-o," Sammy said. "If you show me, I could sand where you've already scraped. I could be careful."

"Yes, I think you could," Dicey said. His eyes had colors shooting out of them again, yellow flecks and green, that made up the hazel color when they mixed in with the brown. He hadn't grown so tall after all, she noticed, measuring him against her body. Not up to her shoulders yet. They settled down to work.

Sammy worked like Dicey did, without hurrying, without dawdling. They got into a kind of rhythm, working together. Dicey told herself, I should have remembered this about Sammy.

"I like these new jeans," she remarked. "Don't you?"

"Umhnm," he said. "I guess you and Gram had a good time. Do you think she'd take me for a bus ride and out to lunch? Ever?"

"I don't see why not. But she tells you what to order."

"Did she tell you what to order?"

"Yup."

"What did you do?"

"I ordered it. What do you think I'd do?"

Sammy laughed, a round, tumbling sound. "I think you'd refuse to get it. Because she told you."

"Gram said you're being an angel at school. Except you don't fly."

Sammy nodded, looking at Dicey's eyes. "It's all I *can* do, being good. Nobody there's even yelled at me, all this year so far. That's pretty good, wouldn't you say?"

"Are you sure you can't fly?" Dicey teased him. Then she said yes, it was very good, it was better than she had managed. "Do you like any of the kids in your class?" she asked.

Sammy shrugged, his eyes watching where the sandpaper rubbed at the wood. "The guys—well, you know, Dicey, they don't like goody-goodies. It doesn't matter." He shrugged again. "It's okay with me."

Dicey looked hard at him. His eyes were flat again. She wondered if that flat, holding-in expression was the one he wore all day long. "Is there anything you like about school?"

"Phys ed, because we play games. You know, baseball and kickball."

"Don't you play those at recess too?"

"Not me."

"Why not?"

"If I did—I'd get angry, and—if I exploded—you see, Dicey, when I get angry I don't know what I'll do. So I watch, and that's okay. Another thing I like."

"What's that?"

"I like being good. Because Gram will like it. Sometimes, I wish I'd been better, when Momma wanted me to."

Alarm bells were clanging in Dicey's head. "Sammy Tillerman," she said, shaking her scraper at him. "You don't think it's your fault, do you? About Momma?"

He didn't answer.

"But that wasn't anybody's fault, not even Momma's. It was just the way things happened."

"But I didn't help," he said. "And Dicey—you know what they say about Gram."

"But we know that's not true," Dicey said.

"But if Gram—" Sammy said. He stopped himself. "And I like Gram," he added. "It's not so much trouble to be good in school, if I keep remembering."

"*Are* you good, Sammy? I mean—you know what I mean. Are you?"

"No a'course not, you know that. But that's okay. If I had a job—but I'm too young, it'll be years before I can help out with a job."

Dicey thought for a minute. "Cripes," she finally said, "you've given yourself a pretty hard job as it is, as far as I can see. And you're doing pretty good work at it."

He nodded, pleased.

"But then, that shouldn't surprise me, because I know how hard you can work," Dicey said.

"Yeah I can, can't I?"

"Maybe you've outgrown fighting," she suggested.

He shook his head.

"I used to get in fights," Dicey told him.

"You never said that," he protested.

"You never asked me," Dicey countered. "I used to fight with girls and boys, and just about anyone. I can't even remember how many fights I was in. But I used to win a lot."

"Of course," Sammy said.

"And I'll tell you something funny. Not ha-ha funny, but queer. You want to hear it?"

"Okay."

"I used to feel good, after. Even if I lost. As if—I don't know—as if I'd exploded and that was over now."

He stared up at her. "You never get in trouble," he told her.

Dicey laughed. "I'm in trouble right now," she told him, feeling not at all upset about home ec and her apron. "I'm in trouble and I don't even care. Because"—she hadn't thought of this before—"it's my own trouble I made myself."

Sammy just stared at her. Then he turned back to his work and Dicey went back to hers. They worked without talking for an hour or more. Then Dicey felt a rubbing on her back, going around and around. Sammy was sanding her back. She turned and scraped down the leg of his jeans, but she had to bend over to do that and he started sanding her fanny. He was giggling. Dicey dropped the scraper and grabbed hold of his ankles. Sammy toppled over into the dirt beside her.

Before he could scramble up again, she started to tickle him under the arms. He squirmed and twisted under her hands hammering on the ground with his fists.

Then Sammy twisted around underneath her and wriggled free. He ran over to the workbench, and stood there, poised to fight her if she came near him. Dicey made a growling noise, on her knees like a tiger. She leaped at him. Sammy turned and ran to the dark side of the barn. He scrambled over the doorway into an empty stall.

"Hey, Dicey," his voice made little echoes from within the darkness.

"You okay?"

"You could keep chickens in one of these, they're huge. Look."

Dicey came over and unbolted the door. She stepped into the stall. Sammy heaved an armload of dry hay over her head.

Dicey puffed and sneezed and brushed the brittle hay from her face and hair and shoulders. "Just you wait until I get my hands on you, Sammy Tillerman," she said, trying to keep laughter out of her voice. He dashed past her, through the barn, out into the sunshine.

"Can't catch me!" he called.

"Gram doesn't like chickens anyway," she answered to his disappearing back.

Dicey wore her new jumper to school, and the bra of course, but she almost didn't notice that any more. You could get used to just about anything, she thought. Nobody noticed her new clothes, but then nobody noticed her much anyway, so she wasn't surprised. When she left English class to go to home ec, she saw Mina hanging around by the door. "Hey, Dicey," Mina greeted her.

"Hey," Dicey answered, walking right on past Mina and her friends. Mina got the message all right. Dicey heard one of the other voices talk as the girls followed her down the hall, falling behind because she was hurrying: "I don't know why you're looking for honky friends," the voice complained.

Dicey was hurrying to home ec class to get her seat in the back, at a table by herself, and to get her face all set and ready. They were starting a new unit today.

Miss Eversleigh stood in front of the class wearing her usual dark suit and usual nylon blouse with her usual pin on the lapel of her jacket. Nutrition was the new unit. Dicey kept herself from groaning out loud. She could peel potatoes and fry an egg, and that was about it, and she didn't want to learn more. She could also, she reminded herself, figure out things to eat and cook them over an open fire. But still, she wished Maybeth could be here instead of her. Maybeth would like it and be good at it. She hoped Maybeth could get this far in school.

Miss Eversleigh began to lecture about nutrition and food groups. Dicey sighed, opened her notebook, and began drawing a picture. In her picture, there was a little boat on an ocean, without any land around. The boat's sails puffed out. Dicey put some high-headed clouds in the sky. She grinned and put a crab at the bottom, under the water. The crab was staring up at the boat. Dicey decided not to put in anybody steering the boat; she knew who it was anyway. Miss Eversleigh's voice droned on.

Later, Jeff was waiting by the bicycle rack. Dicey thought he noticed her jumper, but he didn't say anything. He had a song for her, he said. Dicey stood in front of him, holding her books. He looked quizzically at her, as if there was something he wanted her to say, but when she didn't he began to sing right away. The song he had that day was called "Pretty Polly." Dicey had heard this cruel song, once before.

"Polly, pretty Polly, won't you come and go with me," he sang. His hands brought music out of the guitar. The story went on, and the man—Handsome Willy—killed Polly and rode away, "over mountains so steep and the valleys so wide."

Jeff looked at Dicey, waiting. Finally, he asked, pushing his dark hair from his forehead: "What do you think?"

Dicey shrugged.

"But don't you wonder? Why he killed her? What happened to him?" Jeff asked.

"Yeah, I do," Dicey admitted.

"So what do you think?" Jeff asked again.

"I gotta go," Dicey said.

Jeff shrugged. He was wearing a brown sweater with the kind of softly mixed greens and whites that was in the wool Gram bought for Dicey. Heather. "See you tomorrow, maybe." His gray eyes were concentrating on the face of his guitar.

"Sure," Dicey said.

Millie noticed her jumper and liked it and made a kind of fuss about it. Dicey thought, after all, she'd rather not be noticed. That afternoon there was another letter for Gram from the doctors in Boston, but this one was thin. Dicey wondered if Gram wrote answers to these letters. She wished she could read them, but she figured, if it was anything important—especially good news—Gram would tell them about it.

Sammy came out to sand with her while she scraped. He told her about a couple of boys in his class who had to stay in the principal's office almost all afternoon. They had tried to walk tightrope over the top of the swings, he reported. Everyone, he said (meaning all the teachers), got angry and scared. His own opinion was that since they had talked so much about it before they tried and had gathered a huge audience before they started shinnying up the tall poles, they planned to get caught.

"I wonder if I could do it," he wondered. "I've got pretty good balance. Don't you think I do?"

"I think," Dicey said, picturing the fifteen-foot metal swing sets, "that if you ever talk like that again I'll have a heart attack." She could see how it would look, Sammy's sturdy body and his head of yellow hair, with his arms out to keep his balance. And falling onto the packed dirt. "Seriously."

"Okay, Dicey," he said, with a smile in his voice. "We had a math test this afternoon," he added.

Dicey took in the information. "They didn't do it on purpose, did they? To get out of the test?"

"I think so," Sammy answered. "They're pretty tricky."

"Did you ask them?"

"Yep. After school. Ernie—he's the one who has all the ideas—didn't say yes. But he didn't say no either. He's bigger than the rest of us. Miss Tieds never even caught on," Sammy said.

"How was the test?"

"Easy," Sammy reported.

Just before supper, Dicey asked James when he was going to begin working with Maybeth. James pulled his eyes up from a book he was reading, as if he couldn't remember what she was talking about.

"James," Dicey said.

"I'll do it," he said. "Cripes, Dicey, give me a chance. I've got the paper route and school and all. There's no hurry."

The phone rang during dinner—in the middle of a big conversation about chickens. Sammy was trying to persuade Gram that they would be smart to get some chickens. "I'd feed them and everything. I'd collect the eggs," he promised. "They could stay in one of those empty stalls. The chickens, not the eggs."

Gram teased Sammy. "You'd give them names," she told him, "and then when it came time to eat one you'd say, 'We can't eat Hercules!'"

Sammy laughed. "I wouldn't name a chicken Hercules," he said. "I'd name it—Miss Tieds. I wouldn't mind eating that chicken."

"I couldn't ever eat any creature named Miss anything. Or Mister. You can't give chickens titles, boy. It's like—naming one Queen Elizabeth, or President Johnson."

"Johnson's not president any more, Gram," James informed her. She fixed him with a beady glance, and her mouth twitched. Before he could say anything, the phone rang and he ran to answer it. When he returned, he was running. "It's Toby, and he wants me to spend the night on Friday, and can I?"

Gram asked him if he wanted to, and he said yes. She asked him where Toby lived, and he lived downtown. She asked him about what time, and he told her after school on Friday and Toby's mother would bring him home Saturday afternoon. All the time, he was almost jumping with excitement. Gram asked him about his paper route. "Sammy'll do it, won't you, Sammy?"

"Sure," Sammy said.

"Sammy's too little," Dicey protested.

Both James and Sammy protested that. Dicey looked at Gram for advice.

Gram apparently agreed with the boys, and she gave James permission. He ran back down the hall to tell Toby, and then ran back to the table, full of plans for what he'd take and what they might do. Dicey looked at him and couldn't tell what to think. She was glad he had a friend, but she had the feeling that he wasn't going to do much to help Maybeth, feeling the way he did.

Her foreboding was correct. Dicey knew she was impatient for Maybeth. She tried not to nag at James. But she couldn't help asking him, about every time she saw him, whether he had figured out how to teach Maybeth. "What's the big hurry?" he asked her.

"The year's a quarter through," Dicey said. Their report cards were due out next week. They would get them handed out in a special homeroom at the end of the day next Tuesday.

"So what else is new?" James asked. His question was impatient, but his eyes shone with an excitement inside him, as if nothing could really disturb him, not even Dicey's nagging.

"But even if you can find a way to teach her, she'll go slowly. You know that, James. There's no time to waste."

"I'm not wasting time. I'm thinking," he told her.

"Yeah, but what are you thinking about?" Dicey snapped and walked away before he could answer. She knew what he was thinking about that made him so happy, and she was glad for him. But.

This holding on that Gram had talked about was more complicated than she'd thought. She had to hold on to James, for what he wanted, and hold on to Maybeth for what she needed. That was fine, except for when the wants and needs were at cross purposes. At least Sammy seemed more cheerful and was talking more and more about the kids in his class, as if he had time to notice them now.

When Dicey returned from work on Thursday, her whole

family except for James was in the kitchen. A thick silence lay all over the room. Gram sat quietly at the end of the big wooden table, her hands busy with yellow wool. She was rolling it up into balls, and Sammy was helping her by holding the wool. Maybeth had her head down and her shoulders were shaking. Dicey dumped her books and asked, "What's the matter?"

Maybeth kept her head down. Gram looked at Dicey and said, "She won't say." Sammy answered at the same time, "I dunno, she started crying when we got off the bus."

Dicey went to kneel before Maybeth. "Maybeth? What's the matter? Whatever it is, it's all right."

Maybeth raised her face. Her hair hung down wet at the side of her face. Her eyes were red and swollen, her cheeks were wet, her mouth quivered. She threw herself into Dicey's arms and kept on crying.

Dicey patted her shoulder and rumpled the hair at the top of her round little head. "I promise, it's okay, whatever. I promise, Maybeth," she said. "You believe me, don't you? You know you can believe me."

Maybeth's head nodded. She took a big, shuddering breath and got up. She went to stand beside Gram, where she could look at all of them. She twisted her hands in front of her.

"They all—" she said in a voice so low and little Dicey almost couldn't hear. "I didn't want—to have to tell twice," she wailed. Her voice got stronger, but her words came out choked and uneven. She was crying so hard, she gulped in air and gulped out words that shuddered with her breath. "When I read, they all, everyone, they laughed at me. And Mrs. Jackson couldn't make them stop. And I forgot everything. And she said they were unkind. And I couldn't make any words come out. And it was horrible, I don't know what to do—I don't ever want to go back there."

In the middle of this, James came bursting into the doorway. His cheeks were red from the long ride in the cool air, his eyes shone. As he listened, his face got quiet, thoughtful.

"They were all—all laughing—whenever I made a mistake—and I kept making mistakes. I couldn't help it."

James met Dicey's eyes. Dicey expected him to stick out his lower lip and look away. But he didn't. He nodded at her, just once. She could see him thinking. She could see him beginning to understand how it was for Maybeth and how she had to feel. She could see him being angry at himself for thinking it wasn't important. She could see him wondering what to say, to Maybeth.

"Because I can't," Maybeth wailed. "I can't—read, and I—can't learn."

"Who says?" James's cool voice cut across her tears.

"Everyone," Maybeth told him. She stood there, her shoulders heaving. You could see her stomach going in and out. She looked so fragile Dicey was frightened and wanted to run out of the room. Gram and Sammy were sitting with frozen, unhappy faces. Only James looked unconcerned, but that was an act, Dicey knew.

"Who's smarter?" James demanded of Maybeth. "Everyone? Or me?"

"I don't know," Maybeth mumbled. At least her sobs were dying down. James had her attention.

"Well, I know. It's me. And do you know what I say?" James asked her.

Dicey wanted to hiss at James, *Get to the point.* But part of holding on was letting him do things his own way. Maybe, after all, he was right, because Maybeth looked up at him and shook her head, no. Tears had stopped oozing out of her eyes, too.

"I say—you *can* learn. I say, I can teach you. And you know what else?"

Maybeth shook her head again.

"I'm going to. Whether you want me to or not, so you better say yes."

A little smile lifted the corners of Maybeth's mouth, like a wave licking at the shore.

"Have you ever known me to be wrong?" James asked. He sounded so confident, Dicey almost believed him.

"Yes!" Sammy shrieked, unable to bear the tension any more. "Lots and lots!"

At that, James grinned and shrugged. He kept his eyes on Maybeth, and she smiled back at him.

"Dicey thinks I can," he said.

"Do you?" Maybeth asked. "Really?"

Dicey nodded.

"All right," Maybeth said, in a little voice.

"That's settled then," Gram announced. She began winding the wool again.

"Here's what we'll do," James told Maybeth. "On Saturday morning, because I'll be in town, or maybe tomorrow night—if I ask I bet Toby'll want to. We'll go to the library and I'll take out all their books on reading. Did you know there are dozens of different ways to teach it?"

Maybeth shook her head, no.

"I asked Mr. Thomas. The reason there are so many ways is because there are so many different kinds of brains, to learn. I think we'll have our first lesson on Monday, Monday after school."

"I have piano lesson Monday," Maybeth protested softly. But her hands had stopped twisting.

"Okay, Sunday afternoon. And Monday afternoon after piano," James agreed. He looked around at all of them and added: "Sammy will have to take over my paper route. He *can* do it, Dicey. Better than me, because he's more careful."

"That's true," Sammy told her. He turned his face back to look at Gram. "It is."

"Sounds all right to me. How's it sound to you, girl?" Gram asked.

"Fine," Dicey said. She hoped James would be able to do what he had said he could. She could tell, watching him, that he was having the same doubts, and the same hopes.

Holding on was time-consuming, Dicey discovered. *Well,* she said to herself—pedaling out behind Sammy on Friday afternoon, watching him carefully throw the carefully folded papers onto doorsteps, noticing how he talked to barking dogs and rode alertly, using his ears as well as his eyes to watch traffic—*you knew that.* It was, after all, only what she had been doing as long as she could remember. It was, also, what she wanted to do.

James returned late Saturday, with reports of what a good time he had had and how they wanted him to come back—and they said soon. After supper, he settled down to read through a huge pile of books he had taken out of the library. They had lit a fire again, as they did most evenings now. Gram had gone up to the attic and brought down piles of warm socks, half-a-dozen pairs of workboots and a pair of red rubber boots for Maybeth. There were also a couple of rough, heavy sweaters for the boys. Dicey decided she would be glad to wear one of the old boys' sweaters on cold mornings, so Gram was knitting Maybeth's yellow sweater first.

When Gram entered the living room with the armload of clothes, James lifted his head from the book and exchanged a glance with Dicey. She knew he was thinking about what else was up there, in the attic.

After the little kids had been put to bed, James insisted that Dicey confer with him. What he really meant was that she should listen to him, but that was okay with Dicey. He talked and talked, about the different ways of teaching and the theories behind them. He used words she'd never heard before: dyslexia, dysgraphia, remediation, word recognition, effective learning, affective learning. Dicey didn't bother to ask him what everything meant. She just listened and nodded her head whenever he seemed to want her to. Finally he told her, "There's a lot I can't understand yet. People have such different theories about education, and they've studied them."

Dicey nodded.

"And I haven't had very much experience myself. I never paid too much attention to what other people were doing in class. You know?"

Dicey nodded again. Now she really was listening, however, because she wondered what James was leading up to. It wasn't like him to talk about what he didn't understand. He preferred to talk about what he knew.

"But here's what I think. Gram? Are you listening? If you think I'm wrong, I want you to tell me. Because I just *don't* know enough. But I think—for years and years they taught using the phonic method. Remember, Dicey? Where you learn what the letters and phonemes and blends say, and you sound out words."

Dicey didn't remember, but that didn't matter.

"My guess is, that if they've used it for years—and it's the way we learned, and Massachusetts has one of the oldest public school systems in the country, and it's a good one too—that's the one I want to use with Maybeth. What do you think? Because if it wasn't good it wouldn't have lasted so long."

Gram answered. "It's sound reasoning. But you haven't read all those books, have you?"

"No, how could I? Some I just looked over to see what the chapters were about."

"But if it's the way Maybeth was taught in Provincetown,"

Dicey said—then she stopped, noticing that she didn't even think to say *back home.* James waited, so she went on. "Maybe it doesn't work for Maybeth."

James's face was serious, and it was almost as if he was looking inside of his own head for the words he was going to speak, even though his eyes rested on Dicey. "Yeah, but listen. There's what they call the emotional overlay, when someone has reading problems. Like—I dunno, maybe like layers of paint and you have to scrape it off before you can get to the real problem. Like a kid who always gets in trouble in class, so he's always being punished and never gets his work done. That way he avoids looking stupid. Because he'd rather be bad than stupid. And Maybeth is better here—we all know that, don't you, Gram? She's not nearly so scared of things. Of people. It's not so complicated for her here. Without Momma to worry about, and what people say. My theory is, all that stuff interfered with her before and it won't interfere now. What do you think?"

"You could be right," Gram said.

"What are you going to do next?" Dicey asked James.

"Tomorrow, I'll study this book on the phonics method and then we'll start."

"Is that enough time?" Gram asked.

"Sure. And if I'm wrong, I know what method to try next. It's interesting, you know?" James told them, his eyes bright. "I had no idea it was so interesting. It's made me curious about what Maybeth thinks. I mean, I don't think she's got a reading disorder, it's just slowness. But I wonder. . . ." His voice drifted off. Dicey looked at Gram and grinned. Gram smiled back and reversed her needles to begin another row.

Dicey hung around quietly in the background during Maybeth's first lesson with James. She had her own books open in front of her, and she was sort of doing her assignments, but mostly she listened to James and Maybeth working. The two heads bent together over a pad of paper on which James wrote letters. Then he asked Maybeth what the letters said. Maybeth understood this, and Dicey thought she did pretty well at it. James's brown hair looked darker next to Maybeth's yellow curls; and her hair seemed to shine brighter next to his dark head. Dicey listened hard, not to hear precisely what they were saying, but to hear what the two speakers were like. If she was going to hold on, then she wanted to have a clear idea of who she was holding on to. So she could get a good grip.

Besides, she admitted to herself, if she could learn how James did it, then she could help him out if he needed it. If it worked for Maybeth.

CHAPTER 6

Despite Dicey's firm intentions to concentrate on her family—and on Gram too, and she didn't know how Gram would feel if she knew Dicey was thinking *that*—during the third week in November, the outside world seemed determined to get her attention.

First it was the weather, which turned chilly, then cold. The sky hung gray and flat, day after day. This muted all the colors, except for the bare branches of the trees, which turned deep black against that sky. When the wind was from the west, off the Bay, it carried a dampness in it that penetrated through Dicey's clothing and wound around her bones. She couldn't work on the boat in that weather, not without the danger of chillblains.

"What *are* chillblains?" Dicey had asked Gram.

Gram had smiled. "You know, I don't know. All my life I've heard about them and tried not to get them—because they sound so awful. Chill-blains," she repeated, listening to the sound of it. "As if the little veins in your nose freeze individually. We'll ask James," Gram concluded, looking back to her knitting. She was halfway up the back of Maybeth's yellow sweater. She had already finished the front.

And then, Dicey got her report card. This school made a real ceremony of report cards. At the end of the school day everybody went to his homeroom. When your name was called out, you went up to the front of the room. The homeroom teacher studied your grades and then he would talk to you about your schoolwork. These conversations were kept to a low tone. Everybody in the front row pretended they couldn't hear and weren't listening.

There were forty kids in the homeroom, so it took a while for Dicey's name to come up. "Dicey Tillerman," he called. Dicey went to stand next to the big desk. She tried to see the card, but he held it so she couldn't. He had his attendance book spread out in front of him, and he was making checks by each student's name after the report card was given out.

He asked his questions without looking at her. She stared at his ear to answer.

"This is your first year here?"

"Yes."

"Where did you go to school before?"

"In Massachusetts."

"Hunh. How do you like home ec?"

Dicey shrugged. He waited, so she put the shrugs into words. "I dunno."

"You've got a good attendance record," he said, concluding their conversation. He uncapped his pen and marked down two zeros on the upper corner, where there were places for absences and tardinesses. Then he checked off her name in his attendance book. Finally, he gave Dicey her report card.

Dicey didn't even look at it until she had sat down. She scanned down the grades. Home Ec: F.

That letter, F, jumped out at her eyes. *What?* Dicey wasn't any brain like James, but she did all right in school. Anger warmed her blood. What right did Miss Eversleigh have flunking her. She had gone to all the classes, she had done everything she was told. She had done everything badly, she knew that; she had done everything with a minimum of effort and attention. But she *had* done it, and she hadn't ever made any trouble in class, unless you counted the time they all laughed, and that wasn't her fault.

Dicey bit at her lower lip. She went back up the list of grades and saw a C+ by English.

Now wait a minute, she thought. She'd been getting B's and A's in English. This one had to be a mistake. Mr. Chappelle must have copied somebody else's grade down, instead of hers. She wondered how she should get it corrected. She decided, the best thing was to wait until the essays were handed back at the beginning of next week, then she would ask Mr. Chappelle. She could ask him right away, she supposed, but the class had been pestering him so much about how long it took to get the essays back that Dicey was starting to feel sorry for him. She was as impatient as everyone else, but it didn't do any good nagging and complaining at him. He'd promised to get them back on Monday, and he'd apologized for taking so long and he'd made excuses. Dicey felt—well, she'd believe it when she actually had her paper in her hand again. She wasn't at all sure he'd keep his promise, but she hoped he would. And then she'd ask him about the grade. She bet he would be surprised that he'd given her a C+. She was about the smartest kid in the class, certainly one of the smartest.

But was that F in home ec going to get her in trouble? When the bell rang, Dicey hurried out to see if Jeff was there. "Hey, Jeff," she greeted him.

"Hey, Dicey. Think we'll ever see the sun again? How long's it been, eight days? Did you ever hear a song called 'Dark as the Dungeon'?"

Dicey shook her head impatiently. "What happens if you flunk your minor?" she demanded.

"Did you do that?" he asked. His face was only curious,

with maybe a little surprise, she decided. His eyes weren't smiling at all.

"Yeah," she said.

"Don't worry. Nobody cares about minors much anyway. And until you're in high school, it doesn't matter about credits for graduation. Pass English, and they pretty much have to pass you. You passing English?"

Dicey didn't even answer that. She just gave him a look that said, *Of course I'm passing it, what a stupid question.* Then he did smile at her. He asked her if she wanted to hear the song, "Dark as the Dungeon," and she said, no, thank you, she couldn't, she had to get going.

She waited until after supper to show Gram her report card. Gram had to sign it. There was a place on the back, a row of dotted lines, and underneath the words "parent or guardian."

Gram put her knitting aside and looked at the front of the card. Then she turned it over and signed it with the pen Dicey had ready for her. Then she turned it over and looked at the front again.

Momma never even looked at the front, Dicey remembered. Momma, those last couple of years. She would take the report cards, one at a time, and sign her name carefully, four times. She had to be careful, because the boards on their old table were coming unglued and might make ridges in your writing, and it might look like you didn't even know how to write your name. Momma's long hair fell forward when she bent her head down. Momma said her hair started out the color of Sammy's and Maybeth's, but got darker as she got older. Momma's hair rippled down her back, like sunlight, like music. Like the music Maybeth was playing then, on the piano.

"Well?" Gram said.

"It doesn't matter about home ec," Dicey assured her. "That's just a minor. It's okay to flunk it."

"Is it," Gram wondered. "Why are you failing?"

Dicey thought about that. "I don't like the class."

"I know, you wanted mechanical drawing, I remember."

"And—I'm not trying, but I go to every class and do everything she says. Sort of." Then she told Gram about her apron, about how she got around the rules. She even told Gram about how the rest of the class had laughed, because once she was started that was part of the story. Dicey found she didn't mind telling Gram; and when Gram laughed too, she joined in.

"You aren't making trouble in class?"

"Nope, I keep quiet."

"You're sure it's not going to—I don't know, they talk about school records."

"I asked someone," Dicey said.

Gram looked at her for a long minute, then accepted it. "The rest—except for English—are very good. All A's."

Dicey looked down. She hadn't even noticed those, not really. "The English is a mistake," she said to Gram.

"Are you sure?" Dicey was sure. "You're not just fooling yourself?" Dicey shook her head.

"I'm going to ask him about it on Monday. You'll see."

"I believe you," Gram said. And she did, Dicey could tell. Dicey liked that. That Gram really believed her, because she knew her, made Dicey's heart swell up warm. Dicey felt like putting her arms around Gram and hugging her, hard. But she didn't, of course. Gram wasn't the kind of person who wanted to be hugged.

So Dicey just smiled, and said, "Thanks." She drifted over to the piano. She sat down beside Maybeth on the bench. For a while, she watched Maybeth's fingers pushing down the keys, the white keys and the black ones. She noticed for the first time what pretty, delicate hands Maybeth had and the way her fingernails shone rosily. Then Dicey looked at the page of music. It was something called a minuet, by someone called Bach.

(How would you pronounce that? Dicey wondered idly, listening, remembering the phonemes James talked about with Maybeth. *Bahk? Batch? Bash?* She'd ask James, if he knew.)

There weren't that many notes on the page of music, it didn't look too hard; but the music that Maybeth made from it sounded too perfect for the score to be as simple as it seemed. The notes flowed out from under her fingers. The rhythm was steady, but the melody danced round it as if doing whatever it wanted, whenever it felt like it. It sounded like a dance, and when Maybeth finished, before she could turn to something else, Dicey asked her, "What does it mean?"

"Mean? I don't know."

"Then how do you decide what to play loud, or fast, or smoothed together?"

Maybeth looked at her with round eyes. "It's just the way it sounds, when it sounds right."

"Play it again?"

Maybeth did. Dicey listened, and she still couldn't understand how Maybeth knew what it was supposed to sound like, all together. "I really like hearing you play," she told Maybeth. Maybeth smiled, and her eyes shone at Dicey. She didn't say anything.

Then, while Dicey was washing down the floor at work on Wednesday, and Millie was leaning over the counter telling her about chickens, what the best breeds were, what were each breed's advantages and disadvantages, Jeff came in.

Dicey saw him before he saw her. He had gone over to the sugars and was looking at the boxes and bags. He carried his guitar slung over his back, like a minstrel out of Robin Hood. He wore a down vest and his cheeks shone pink. Millie went to help him, and he looked up. Then he saw Dicey. "Hey, Dicey," he said, surprised.

"Hey, Jeff." She was careful *not* to sound surprised. She pushed the mop down into the bucket of warm water and sloshed some onto the floor. She swirled the water around with the mop before getting down to real scrubbing.

He came to stand in front of her. She ignored him.

"You work here?" he asked.

"Yeah."

"Every day?"

"Pretty near." She still hadn't looked at him.

"I didn't know that," he said. That was nothing Dicey needed to answer. "I've only been in here a couple of times in the last year," he said. "To pick up odds and ends."

He waited. Dicey mopped. He moved his booted feet away from where she wanted to clean. Dicey mopped.

"Dicey?" She didn't look up. "See you." She nodded.

She heard him pay for the box of sugar, heard the door close, heard Millie go back to her position behind the meat counter. She could feel Millie staring at her. Finally, her employer spoke: "He your fellow?"

Dicey snorted. "Just someone I met at school."

"He's kinda cute," Millie said. "Does he play that guitar?"

No, Dicey thought of saying, he just carries it around. But instead, because it was Millie, she answered politely, "Yes."

"He looks so young," Millie said absently. "And so do you, but I'm used to you, I guess. I remember"—her voice drifted on behind Dicey's head— "when we were young. Ab and Herbie. John Tillerman. I can't remember me that young though—isn't that a funny thing?"

"You remember Gram? What was she like?" Dicey had

stopped working and was looking at Millie's face. Millie was staring somewhere into the front of the store.

"I guess we called her pert," she said, with a smile moving her thick features. "She had quite a tongue, did Ab, and she'd as soon bite your head off as smile at you. She kept things hopping, wherever she was. Some people didn't, but I liked her. I guess she used to make us laugh sometimes, the things she'd say, the things she'd do. Then after she married John, it wasn't the same. Well"—she shook her face to bring her attention back—"I guess it never is. I guess she was kept busy on the farm, and her children, and things the way John wanted them. But I can remember. . . ."

Dicey stayed still, not to interrupt, not to distract Millie.

"Once—oh years ago—I saw Ab downtown with her three children, the little girl about as pretty as your sister. They were having a race, down the sidewalk, all four of them running as fast as they could. Oh—they were having a good time."

Millie stopped talking, and didn't recommence, although Dicey waited a good while. Dicey tried to figure out a question to ask to get her reminiscing again. Then Millie started talking again, as if she had been thinking her own thoughts in the silence.

"I never saw her much all those years. John mostly did the shopping. I guess she kept pretty busy. And then, she got queer. They always have shopped in here, the Tillermans," Millie said proudly.

Dicey got back to her work, trying to see the picture Millie had been looking at: Gram a young woman, like Momma, and her three children. Momma and Bullet and John, all of them in a race. Bullet would have been last because he was smallest. Unless Momma hung back to let him beat her. That was the kind of thing Dicey thought Momma would have done. She wished she could ask Gram if that was the way it happened.

The trouble with holding on was Dicey only had two hands. She felt like she was always off balance, trying to hold on to everyone. What happened next to put Dicey off her stride was that Millie remembered a message from Gram. The message told Dicey to wait at work until Sammy showed up.

"I thought you-all didn't have a phone," Millie remarked.

"Gram decided we needed one," Dicey told her. Dicey had finished the floor and put away the mop and bucket. They sat side by side at the checkout counter. Millie told Dicey what to order from the distributor and how much. Dicey wrote the number in, then quickly did the multiplication to figure out the price. Working beside Millie, sitting beside her, made Dicey feel small and quick. She had to be careful not to let that feeling lead her to making mistakes in calculation.

"Ab always did make her mind up quick and stick to it," Millie commented.

"Did she?" Dicey asked. "What do you mean?"

"I dunno," Millie answered. "Like with Cilla, her sister. You ever know Cilla?"

Dicey shook her head.

"It's funny I remember this, because I was so young, maybe just six. Ab was even younger, but I remember her saying she'd never like her sister, because Cilla was plain-out silly."

Dicey tried to picture her grandmother at five years old, or even seven. She couldn't. All she could picture was a midget Gram, shortened and shrunken, and with those dark, impatient eyes.

"It surely is a blessing for Ab that you turned up," Millie said. "I guess no matter what your momma did, Ab is happy to have you."

"You think so?" Dicey asked.

"I guess she's more like her old self these days," Millie said. Dicey believed what Millie was saying because however stupid

Millie might be at reading and numbers she had known Gram all of her life. And she had liked Gram all those years.

So Dicey was feeling pretty good, until Sammy came slouching into the store. The minute Dicey saw his face, his jaw stubbornly stuck out and his eyes daring her, she started to worry. She talked to him as she rode him home on her bike. "Where were you?"

"Detention."

"What for?" she asked, trying to sound as if she didn't care much.

"We had a bet, me and Ernie and some guys, and anyone who lost had to kiss Margaret. In class."

Dicey pumped her legs down and up. Sammy sat on the seat, holding onto her waist with his arms. He stuck his legs out to help with the balance.

"What was the bet?"

"You had to do ten chin-ups. I only did six."

"What about the rest?"

"They've got a club, you know? Ernie's president and he has a gym in his basement—and barbells too, he says. They did ten easy."

Dicey nodded her head. She pumped. She didn't much like the sound of this bet. Or of this Ernie kid. Sammy had said he was bigger, older than the rest of the class.

"Dicey?" Sammy asked.

"Yeah?" She turned her head a little to hear him better.

"Do you think we could put an exercise bar in the barn? They said I did good for the first time trying."

"I dunno, Sammy," Dicey said. "We could try." The way it sounded to Dicey, the boys had set up a bet they knew only Sammy couldn't do. Dicey didn't mind bets and double dares, but this one didn't sound fair.

"When I kissed her, she screamed bloody murder. You should have heard her, Dicey, she scared Miss Tieds half out of her pants. I only pecked her once, on the cheek, and it wasn't any fun. But—it was fun when Margaret screamed." Dicey could hear giggles mounting in his voice. He couldn't see her face so she went ahead and grinned.

"Then what happened?"

"Miss Tieds yelled at me for a while."

"What about Ernie and the rest?"

"They didn't do nothing; why should they get in trouble?"

Dicey saw his point. "Is there anybody else besides Ernie and his friends, anyone else you like?"

Sammy thought about that. "There's a kid—Custer. He's named after a general. Do you know? He fought at the battle of Little Big Horn. But he's already got lots of best friends. Ernie calls him Custard. But he sure can play soccer."

Dicey thought she'd ask James about these kids, what they were like.

Gram rode with Sammy on his paper route that afternoon, because it was getting dark so early. She took Dicey's bike. Dicey and James and Maybeth worked together in the kitchen. A chicken was roasting in the oven, and Maybeth had to get up to baste it every now and then, which gave James a chance to report to Dicey. "I asked Mrs. Jackson, and she gave me some second grade readers," he told her.

"Good for you," Dicey said. "How's it going, do you think?

"Okay," James told her. Dicey wasn't sure she could believe him. James asked Maybeth to sit down and read out loud from a book he'd gotten from the school library. It was a silly little book, filled with rhymes and bright pictures. The story didn't make much sense, not real sense, just silly sense. It was about someone called Sam-I-Am, who kept trying to get his friend to eat green eggs and ham. Maybeth read it and giggled and kept reading. The way she read it, the poetry sounded like poetry, and she didn't make any mistakes. Dicey praised her.

"It's a baby book," she said.

Dicey looked at James. "Sure," he said, "But—" Dicey didn't know if he was talking to her or Maybeth. "Did you hear how well she read it? You had to understand everything to get the jokes. More than just the words. They said in my book that learning to read with phrasing and fluently, that was a sure sign."

"A sure sign of what?" Dicey wanted to know.

"Someone who can read," James answered. "It's not an easy book to someone who can't read. Is it?" he asked Maybeth.

She smiled and shook her head.

"And the books Mrs. Jackson gave me—" His whole face lit up. "She's sure gonna be surprised. She doesn't know me—she doesn't know what we're doing—I wish I could see her face when she figures out what's happening." He sounded so sure of himself.

"Is it happening?" Dicey asked.

James let Maybeth answer. "I think so. I didn't remember what the letters say—then when James wrote them down on the cards, I remembered from before. I remember most of them. I knew them. But I didn't know how to remember them."

"So now our real job is to build up your sight vocabulary," James said. Dicey almost asked him what that was, but she figured she could guess, and he was eagerly pulling out a pack of flash cards to drill Maybeth. Maybeth was just as eagerly giving him her attention.

If it wasn't one thing, it was sure going to be another, Dicey said to herself when Sammy came in from the paper route the next day. He had cuts and bruises on his face and on his knuckles too. When she saw him, she just stared. She looked at Gram.

Sammy didn't say anything. Gram said, "He looks better now than when he first got home. We cleaned him up some."

"It wasn't in school," Sammy assured Dicey.

"On the bus," Gram said dryly.

"Who'd you fight?" Dicey asked.

"Some kid," Sammy said. He thought for a minute and then told her, "He was bigger'n me and a good fighter."

"But why?" Dicey burst out.

Sammy shook his head, no. He wasn't going to tell her.

Dicey looked at Gram's worried face and knew the same expression was on her own. She could have laughed. Here they were, getting what they wanted for Sammy, and they began worrying right away.

"Was it worth fighting about?" Gram asked Sammy.

"Yes," he said, his voice fierce.

Dicey tried to figure out what could be so important to him. She wondered about it all that evening, not even listening to the arguments Sammy used to try to convince Gram that they should have some chickens. Until Sammy said something that caught her attention. "They're like watchdogs, Gram."

Dicey sputtered, trying to swallow back her laughter. She was picturing chickens attacking a thief. Everybody was smiling, all around the table, and Sammy smiled the happiest of all. What did it matter then if he was getting into fights, or Maybeth never learned to read, or James pretended to be less smart than he was? Nothing mattered nearly as much as sitting together around this table, in the warm yellow light, all of them together.

That was true, she knew, but still she worried at the question of why Sammy was fighting. It couldn't be because of Momma, could it? In Provincetown, that was why, because of what people said about Momma and them. About not having a father living in the house with them, about not having their father's name.

Nobody in Crisfield knew that, or even suspected, except maybe Millie. Then what would make Sammy fighting-angry?

She thought about it during school the next day. Maybe the kids were teasing Sammy about being a sissy, because he was so well-behaved in school. That would make him fight. Maybe something to do with Maybeth, so maybe Dicey should tell him about how James was teaching Maybeth and they thought James's way might be working.

When Miss Eversleigh gave them an in-class assignment, to take fifty dollars and plan meals for a family of four, Dicey didn't have to think twice about it. She remembered how they had eaten that summer, and how little money they had spent. Soup, peanut butter, bread, milk, bananas. She looked at her list and calculated expenses. Apples, she added. She still had almost thirty dollars left. She bet nobody else knew how to spend so little money and keep from starving. Around the edge of her paper she drew boxes of doughnuts, the kind of stale, half-price doughnuts they had bought over the summer. She drew a few clams and mussels. She didn't even notice Miss Eversleigh come to stand behind her and read what she had written, because she was trying to figure out how to draw chicken wings. They had had chicken wings once.

Dicey saw the arm come down over her shoulder and the red pen go to the top of her paper. The pen wrote: *F. Nobody could live for long on meals like this,* the pen wrote. The letters were straight and short, bright and thick and angry.

Dicey almost said, We did. But she stopped herself. She turned to look at the woman's face. Miss Eversleigh was certainly angry, and angry at Dicey. Neither of them said a word. Nobody else in the class even noticed.

Dicey didn't much care if Miss Eversleigh was angry. What more could she do than flunk Dicey, and she'd already done that.

It wasn't as if she was teaching anything Dicey needed to know, or wanted to know. Who wanted to memorize food groups or talk about seasonal buying or how to store food while conserving energy. Who needed to know? Not Dicey. Or about how to put buttons on or cut out a pattern. That was for people who—didn't have anything more interesting to do. Dicey had much more interesting, and more important, things to do.

Miss Eversleigh stared into Dicey's eyes for a long time, as if trying to figure out what was going on inside her head. Dicey just stared back. It took more than a home ec teacher to scare her.

Finally, Miss Eversleigh went away to look at somebody else's paper, and Dicey got back to her thinking. If Sammy kept on fighting, then she would have to find out why. If he didn't, then it wasn't important. How many more fights would be keeping on? One, two, seven?

Miss Eversleigh stood at the front of the class again and called everybody to attention. She was going to make a speech, you could tell by the way her face was set, and she waited until every girl raised her face to look at the front of the room. Dicey shifted in her seat.

"I wonder if you girls understand," Miss Eversleigh said, "the importance of this course. If it were not important, I would not waste my time teaching it."

Dicey could hear the unspoken question behind each politely listening face: What's set her off?

"The materials we cover in this course are skills. I have spent years protesting the exclusion of boys from my courses." She waited, then spoke again. "I have always believed that there is as great a disadvantage to not being able to perform domestic skills as to not being able to perform intellectual skills, or athletic, or social."

Again she stopped and waited. Dicey was watching her, but

Miss Eversleigh did not look at Dicey. "You owe it to yourselves to know how to prepare a meal, or sew a seam, or spend money wisely. You also owe it to yourselves to know how to hammer a nail straight or change a tire, to eat at table with appropriate manners, to plant tomatoes, to acquire information you have need of. If you do not understand that, your understanding is faulty."

That was the end. Miss Eversleigh just stood there until the bell rang, a long, uncomfortable five minutes. Nobody stirred. Nobody said anything.

Dicey used the time to review her thinking about Sammy, to wonder how much a small electric heater would cost and whether that would make it warm enough to get back to work on the boat. She sneaked glances at the clock. Next Monday they were getting their English essays back. Mr. Chappelle had promised. She concentrated on that, anticipating what he would say about hers, feeling proud and glad.

CHAPTER 7

Dicey looked out the window and made her legs stay still. Outside, wind blew the branches of the two big oaks, ripping off the last of the brown leaves and carrying them away. The sky was a bright blue, and the sun shone with a diamond hardness. The brightness of the sun and the coldness of the wind combined to mark out sharply the edges of her view. She could see each individual brick on the old building, as if the cold made each brick contract into itself. The angles of the main entranceway, the clear edge of the cement sidewalk, the flat lawn, bare and brown now, all looked as if they would be cold to touch.

Dicey crossed her ankles again, containing her impatience. She was wearing jeans and one of the rough old boys' sweaters, a bright red one that hung loose about her torso. She had chosen it because it seemed like the kind of color her momma's brother Bullet would have liked, if she was right about the kind of person he had been.

Mr. Chappelle was putting off returning their papers until he had told them about the mistakes most of them had made. They were supposed to be writing these things down, the list of misspelled words, the grammar errors, the kind of topic sentence every paragraph was supposed to have. He was explaining and explaining. Everybody was quiet, just waiting for him to get finished. The thing that got Dicey was that he pretended he was doing this stuff first because it was more important than the grades. That was what he said, that the papers were a learning situation, and the grades didn't matter.

But Dicey suspected that he was doing this dull stuff first because he knew that once he handed the papers back nobody would pay any attention to him. It wasn't his fault, it was just the way classes went. You worked hard (or not so hard) for something, and when you got the results that job was over. The teacher might not think it was over, but the students sure did. The grade told you how well you had done (or what you got away with). The grade was what you looked for—not the red circles around mistakes. Sometimes, a teacher wrote a comment, *good work* (or *bad work*), and you looked at that, too. But mostly, everything they had to say they said in the grade. If there was something more important than the grade, Dicey wanted to know why didn't teachers ever say anything about that, like write you a note about it on your paper. If it wasn't worth his time to write down, how could he say it was worth hers?

She sat forward and sat back and sat forward. She looked at the clock—only fifteen minutes left; he'd have to hand the papers back soon.

"Now," Mr. Chappelle said, "you may be interested in seeing your essays." He smiled at his own joke, so a few kids made little fake laughing noises.

"Before I hand them out, there are two I'd like to read aloud to you." Dicey made herself lean back in her chair. She jammed her hands down into her pockets and stretched her legs out in front of her. "To share with you," Mr. Chappelle said, and reached down into his briefcase. He took out the pile of papers. He ran his hand through his red hair and looked around at everyone, his eyes sliding along the rows. He tried another joke. "Both of these essays were written by girls, but I don't want you boys to get discouraged. Everyone knows boys grow up more slowly."

Who *cares,* Dicey demanded silently.

He took up a paper and began to read.

There's this girl I know, you never know what she's thinking, even though everybody thinks they know this girl. You look at her face, but that doesn't tell you anything. Sometimes you know you don't know what's going on inside. Sometimes, you're not sure you don't know. I wonder about this girl. Here's what I've noticed.

Dicey thought this girl could be just about anyone, even Dicey. She could tell by the way the rest of the class was listening, they had the same feeling. The way it was written, it was just like somebody talking.

She's about the laughingest person you're liable to meet, if you live forever. Nothing but sets her off laughing. You could tell her you were flunking every course and about to be booted out of home and into the unemployment lines, and she'd laugh. She'd laugh until you might start laughing too. You could tell her you just got elected president of your class and captain of the football team and Prince Charming, all at once, and you know what she'd do—she'd laugh. Everywhere she goes it's nothing but laugh, laugh, until you feel like you're caught out in a rainstorm that won't never end. But I keep finding her crying when she thinks nobody's there to see. I catch her. And when I ask her, "Honey, why you crying so bad?" she never says one word to tell me. I stand there, passing out the Kleenex, and she's whooping and wailing and there's nothing can stop her once she's started.

By this time, Dicey thought she recognized who the person was describing: Mina. Because of the laughing. The crying wasn't anything Dicey had seen, but she guessed this was a pretty close friend of Mina's.

Another thing. She's always talking about you. Not behind your back, but right when you're having your conversation. "How are you, and what do you think, and what do you like?" She's mighty easy to talk with, this girl, because she's always interested in the other person. She listens and she remembers and she'll ask you, two years later, "Remember that fight you had with your father about your allowance? Do you still feel the same way?" I guess she's about the most unselfish person I know. But inside, she's always thinking about herself, patting herself on the back for being a caring, remembering person. She's got about the longest arms you'll ever see for patting herself on the back. So while you're telling her this sad, beautiful love story, and you're saying everything you feel—but everything—she's listening so hard you feel like she's curled up inside your own head and you think there never was such a person for listening to you. All the time, part of her's wondering if she's ever been in love or if she ever will be, and how it'll be for her, and she's thinking how great you think she is. This girl is just about something, and I sometimes wonder if even she knows what's going on.

But, Dicey thought, the only person who could know all that about Mina was Mina. Dicey sat forward in her chair. Was it Mina's paper? She slipped her eye over to where Mina was sitting. The smooth brown cheeks looked as if they'd never heard this before. Mina was looking down at her open notebook. But she wasn't smiling, the way the rest of the class was while they listened. The way Dicey started to smile, figuring out what Mina had done. Dicey was impressed by this paper, the way Mina wrote about herself. Boy was that an idea—that was an idea and a half.

To see her, she's got all the answers. Everybody else has trouble making up their minds. Should I do this? Do I want to wear that? Is it the right answer? Not this girl, she just knows the heart out of everything and everybody. She doesn't hesitate, she just puts her big feet out in front of her and gets going. And worry? That's a word this girl never heard of. It's not in her dictionary. She knows north from south, and she knows which way she wants to go. No regrets, not for her. If she makes a mistake—well she's made a mistake and so what? Confident, you'd call her, and for all you know you're one hundred percent right, there wasn't anybody since the Garden of Eden as confident.

But I've seen her do her hair one way then brush it out and do it another. I've seen her sit in one chair and then in another and then move to a bench and finally sit on the ground, until she hopped up to sit in the chair she tried first. I've seen her rip up ten starts on homework papers and only hand one in because she ran out of time to rip it up in.

By this time, the class had figured out that it was Mina the essay was about. They whispered it and looked at Mina. They wondered—interrupting Mr. Chappelle but he didn't seem to mind, he seemed to want them to guess—who'd written it. They asked one another, "Did you?" and answered, "No not me, did you?" Mina just kept staring down, but she was having a hard time not laughing out loud. Dicey was sure Mina had written it about herself, but she didn't know why she was so sure. She just knew it.

And all the time this girl's listening and laughing, all the same. I'm watching her and I don't know what she's thinking, and then I'm thinking, Maybe I do. I guess by now you know who I'm talking about, you know it's me, Wilhemina Smiths.

The class burst out laughing, and praised Mina. Mina looked around and pretended to take a bow. Mr. Chappelle told her to stand up. As she did, she caught Dicey's eye. Dicey pursed her lips into a mute whistle, to try to say how impressed she was. Mr. Chappelle stepped forward and gave Mina her paper. Mina didn't even unfold it to see the grade. She just sat down again.

After a minute, the noise in the room, and the occasional laugh, died away.

"Now for a horse of another color," Mr. Chappelle announced. He began to read.

At the first words, Dicey recognized it as hers. She stared at Mr. Chappelle's pale, impassive face as he read about Momma.

Mrs. Liza lived away up north, away out on Cape Cod, away in a town right at the end of the Cape. Her cabin was outside of town, right at the edge of the ocean. The ocean rolled up toward her rickety cabin, like it wanted to swallow it up; but it never did. Maybe it didn't even want to. The wind was always blowing around the cabin, like it too wanted to have that little building gone.

Mrs. Liza had children, but she never had been married, and the man who was her children's father had long ago gone and left her. She worked nights when the children were little, waiting tables in a restaurant, serving drinks in a bar, night-clerking in a motel. She always worked hard and was always willing to take days nobody else wanted, Christmas and Fourth of July, Easter. When the children got older, she switched to a daytime job, checkout in a supermarket. She hadn't had any training for the kind of job that paid well, so she was always thinking about money, hoping she would have enough. Every sweater she owned had holes in it.

She had reasons to turn into a mean woman, but Mrs. Liza just couldn't. She had a face made to smile, and her eyes always smiled with her mouth. She had long hair, the color of warm honey in the winter, the color of evening sunlight in the summer. She walked easy, high narrow shoulders, but loose, as if the joints of her body never got quite put together. She walked like a song sung without accompaniment.

Then slowly, so slowly she never really could find out the place where it began, life turned sour on Mrs. Liza. People said things. While she never heard them herself, her children heard them and got older and understood what people meant. Mrs. Liza loved her children, so that worried her. Money worried at her the way waves worry at the shoreline, always nibbling away at the soft sand. Her money seemed to run out earlier each week.

Mrs. Liza stood at the door of her cabin and looked out at the ocean. The ocean looked back at Mrs. Liza and rolled on toward her. She could see no end to the ocean. The wind that pulled at her hair was always blowing. She looked out at her children playing on the beach and reminded herself to get some tuna fish for supper; but she forgot.

Her eyes stopped smiling first, and then her mouth. The holes in her sweaters got bigger. Meanwhile, people talked and she didn't know what to say so they could understand. Meanwhile, quarters and dimes got lighter, smaller. Meanwhile, her children were growing bigger and they needed more food, more clothes. Meanwhile, nothing she did seemed to make any difference.

So Mrs. Liza did about the only thing left to her to do. She went away into the farthest place she could find. They cut her hair short. She didn't notice that, lying there, nor when they fed her or changed the sheets. Her eyes never moved, as if what she was looking at was so far away small that if she looked off for a second, it would be gone.

Mr. Chappelle put the paper down and looked up. Dicey felt proud: it was just about as good as she'd thought it was. It was really good. But everybody was absolutely quiet. Didn't they think it was good, too? She waited nervously. Maybe she just liked it because it was hers, the way you liked anything you had made yourself. Maybe Mr. Chappelle read it because it was so bad, to show the difference between hers and Mina's. Still nobody spoke. Mr. Chappelle was staring down at the paper. He was wearing a green tie.

Dicey didn't care if nobody liked it but her. She remembered how she had felt, writing it down. It was hard, and she kept scratching out sentences and beginning again. Yet it kind of came out, almost without her thinking of it, almost as if it had been already written inside her head, and she just had to find the door to open to let it out. She'd never felt that way about schoolwork before, and she wondered if she could do it again. She made her face quiet, not to show what she was thinking.

At last, Mina broke the silence. "That surely *is* a horse of another color," she said. There was laughter in her voice. "I guess it about beat me around the track—before I even left the starting gate." She looked around the class.

"Oh, yes, it's very well written," Mr. Chappelle agreed.

Dicey kept quiet.

"But who wrote it?" somebody asked, a boy. "And what happened at the end? It sounded like she died. But it didn't say she died."

The voices went on talking.

"It sounded like she was about to die."

"No, she was already dead."

"Where was she?"

"In jail? In a hospital? It said they fed her and changed the sheets."

"But what happened?"

"She couldn't support her family. She was poor, couldn't you tell? And it just got her down."

"Yeah, because she started out happy, didn't she?"

"Why didn't she get married?"

"The guy walked out, weren't you listening?"

"Maybe he didn't want to get married."

"Maybe he didn't want all those kids."

"But it takes two—you know what I mean. It wasn't just *her* fault."

"It wasn't fair what happened to her."

"Fair—what difference does fair make?"

"Did she go crazy? I would."

"And it's a mental hospital at the end? But it sounded like a jail picture, at the end."

"Who wrote it, Mr. Chappelle, tell us. You're the one who knows."

They stopped for his answer: "I do, and I don't," he said.

Dicey bit her lip. Now what did that mean?

"It's like one of the stories in our book," somebody said.

"What do you mean?" Mr. Chappelle asked quickly. "Did you read it in our text?"

How could she have? Dicey thought impatiently.

"No, I mean—it doesn't sound like one of us wrote it. It doesn't sound like anything I could write. I never knew anybody like Mrs. Liza. And even if I did, I couldn't—say it like that. Tell us, did *you* write it?"

Mr. Chappelle came around to the front of the desk. He leaned back against it, half-sitting on it. "No, I didn't. Dicey Tillerman did. Stand up, Dicey."

Dicey stood up. She stood up straight and didn't even lean her hand on her desk. Everybody stared at her. "I shoulda guessed," Mina said. She smiled across the room at Dicey, congratulating.

"What *did* happen to her at the end?" somebody asked, but Mr. Chappelle cut off the question.

"Do you have anything to say?" he asked Dicey. She kept her mouth shut, and her face closed off. She knew now what he was thinking.

"No? But I'm afraid I do. I'm very much afraid I have a great deal to say. I'm not one of your great brains, but I've taught this course long enough to be able to tell the kind of work students can do."

Dicey felt frozen. He wasn't looking at her, but she was looking at him, at his pale, flabby mouth out of which words marched slowly.

"Now I can't say what book this came out of—if it came out of a book. I can't even say for sure that it did come out of a book. Maybe somebody else helped Dicey write it."

He gave her time to say something there, but he didn't look at her. Dicey didn't say a word. In the first place, her tongue felt like it was frozen solid, and her head was a block of ice, and all the blood in her body had chilled and congealed. In the second place, he had more to say. She could guess what that was.

"But even if I can't prove plagiarism, I can still smell it. Besides, there was a restriction on this assignment. It was supposed to be about someone you knew. A real person. On those grounds alone, the essay fails."

Dicey should have known. She should have known this would happen, and everyone would believe him. The silence in the room told her what everyone was thinking. She was the only one standing up, for everyone to look at.

"What I primarily resent is the deceitfulness of it, the cheap trickery, the lies," Mr. Chappelle declared.

"That's not true."

Dicey turned to see who had spoken. She thought she could hear her neck bones crackling, like ice, when she turned her head.

Mina was standing up. She looked around the room, her eyes dark as coffee and puzzled. "How can you believe that?" she demanded of Mr. Chappelle.

"Come now, Wilhemina," he said.

"*I* don't believe it," she declared. Her voice sounded certain.

Mr. Chappelle looked around the classroom. Dicey could have laughed. He didn't quite dare order Mina to sit down, because people listened to her and liked her.

"Dicey wouldn't do that," Mina went on. "She doesn't care enough about what we think to cheat on something."

How did Mina know that? Dicey wondered. She wondered it deep behind her icy face.

"Someone like Dicey—she's too smart to worry about her grades; she doesn't have to worry. And if she cared what we thought"—her hand sketched a circle including all the students—"she'd act different. Don't you think?"

People rustled in their seats. They could think whatever they wanted. Now Dicey understood the C+ in English.

The bell rang, ending class, but Mina spoke before anybody could move to leave. "Stay here, I'll prove it."

"How can you prove it?" Mr. Chappelle asked. He had moved back behind his desk. "I've got these essays to hand out."

"Wait," Mina said.

They could stay or go for all Dicey cared.

"I can prove it," Mina repeated. "Dicey?" She looked across the room at Dicey. Her eyes were filled with sympathy. Dicey didn't need anybody's pity. But behind the liquid darkness of Mina's eyes, Dicey saw mischief. Mina knew she was right, and she was enjoying herself.

"Dicey? Is this someone you know?"

"Yes," Dicey said. She was talking just to Mina.

"Did you write it yourself?"

"Yes," Dicey said.

"What does that prove?" Mr. Chappelle muttered.

"Do you want to hear Dicey lie?" Mina asked him. "Dicey, is this someone you're related to?"

Dicey lifted her chin. She didn't answer. There was no way anybody could make her answer. In her mind, she made a picture: the little boat, she'd have painted it white by then, or maybe yellow—it was out on the Bay beyond Gram's dock and the wind pulled at the sails. Dicey could feel the smooth tiller under her hand, she could feel the way the wooden hull flowed through the water.

"Dicey," Mina asked, with no expression in her voice, "what are you thinking about?"

"About sailing," Dicey answered. "About a boat and how it feels when you're sailing it." Those might be the last words she spoke in that class, and why should she bother to make them a lie.

Then people did get up and go. They didn't look at Dicey, but they looked at Mr. Chappelle as they walked past his desk and picked out their papers.

Dicey was almost at the door when he stopped her and gave the paper to her. "I'm sorry," he said. "I'll change the grade—to an A+—and I'll change the mid-semester grade too, of course."

Dicey didn't say anything. She didn't care what he said.

"It's my mistake and I'm really very sorry," he said again. "I'm giving you an A for the marking period, of course."

It didn't make any difference to Dicey what he said.

She sat through horrible home ec without any trouble at all. On the outside, she was paring carrots and slicing them thin to boil them at the stoves. She didn't eat any, just scraped them into the garbage. She went to work, without even noticing if Jeff was outside playing his guitar. She did her work hard and fast and answered Millie's questions without thinking. She rode home through a wind like a knife blade, but it didn't make her cold. She put her bike in the barn and leaned her free hand against the boat for a minute before going on into the house. Gram was in the kitchen. Maybeth and James worked in the living room by the fire. Dicey put her books up in her bedroom and then came back downstairs. She peeled some potatoes for Gram, then cut them up into chunks for hash browns. Sammy came through, rubbing his hands and puffing out cold air. Dicey stood at the wooden countertop, slicing the potatoes first, then cutting across the slices, then cutting again perpendicularly. Slice after slice.

Gram was shaking chicken pieces in a brown paper bag. Dicey could hear the sound it made, like somebody brushing out a rhythm on drums. "How was school today?" Gram asked.

"Fine," Dicey said. She cut slowly, carefully, making her squares as even as possible.

"How's Millie?" Gram asked. There was a kind of sharpness in her voice, and alertness, but Dicey didn't turn around to read the expression on her face. She heard the chicken pieces shaking, in flour, salt, and pepper.

"Fine."

Gram was staring at her. She could feel it.

"You never said," Gram said without breaking the rhythm of the shaking, "if you got your English grade changed."

"Well," Dicey said. Then she couldn't think of how to finish the sentence.

"Well?" Gram asked after a while. "Was it a mistake? Were you right?"

Dicey picked up the last potato. She cut it into neat slices. She lay the slices down flat in front of her. "Yeah, it was a mistake. Boy was it a mistake." She felt pretty calm again, cold and still.

"What happened?" Gram asked. For a second, Dicey was irritated. It wasn't like Gram to insist on a subject Dicey didn't want to talk about. Usually, Gram understood and stopped asking questions.

"We had an essay to write," Dicey explained. She felt like she was talking to the potato, because that was what she looked at. Behind her, Gram moved around the kitchen, getting things ready. "A character sketch, about a real person and conflict. I wrote one, and thought it was pretty good. He handed them back today. He thought I'd copied mine. Or something. He thought the person wasn't real. He thought I'd taken it out of a book." She slowed her hands down. When she finished with this potato, what was she going to do about what to look at?

Gram's voice came from behind her. "It must have been pretty good, if he thought it came out of a book."

Dicey turned around. Gram was looking at her. "Yeah," Dicey said, hearing how fierce her own voice sounded, "it was."

"Did you tell him?" Gram asked.

Dicey shook her head.

"You mean he thinks you cheated?"

Dicey shook her head again.

"Exactly what happened?" Gram asked, sounding ready to get angry.

"He read a couple of the papers out loud, to everyone. Mine was one. Then he said, he thought I'd cheated but he couldn't prove it. But he said I hadn't done the assignment, because it was supposed to be a real person. So he was flunking it."

"In front of the whole class?" Gram demanded.

"Yeah."

Gram's mouth moved and her eyes burned. That made Dicey feel warm, down deep in her stomach. Gram was angry for Dicey's sake. "Can I read it?" Gram asked.

"Sure."

"Now?"

"Okay."

"Will you get it, girl? I've got fat heating."

So Dicey went upstairs to get her essay. She started the potatoes while Gram sat at the table and read. She placed the cubes of potato neatly in the hot bacon fat and turned the gas down to medium once she heard the fat start to sizzle under the layer of potatoes. She checked the lard in the other frying pan, to see if it was smoking hot yet. She got down a jar of tomatoes that Gram had put up that summer. Every now and then she glanced over to see what Gram was doing. Gram read the essay through once, and then again, and then again.

"Well," Gram said at last, "I can see why he thought it came out of a book. I like it, Dicey. I like it very much. Your poor momma. He couldn't know she was real. It *is* hard to believe. Are you going to tell him?"

Dicey shook her head. "Anyway, he knows," she told Gram. "He said he'll change the grade—as if that mattered—and on the report card too."

"Tell me what happened, Dicey," Gram said.

"Well, there's this girl in our class—we worked together on a science project, and she's about the most popular girl I guess. Mina. He was yelling at me for cheating, and she said she didn't believe it." As she recalled it, Dicey saw the picture she and Mina must have made and she started to smile. "I was standing up, I was the only one. And she stood up too, and she's—she's tall and strong-looking. And her voice—I don't know how to tell you, like an actress."

Gram nodded, listening.

"She said she didn't think I'd cheat or lie. Because I didn't care enough about what people thought. Well, she's right." Dicey grinned now. "Then she said she could prove it. So she asked me a couple of questions—she ought to be a lawyer, really. The bell rang and she told everybody to stay put and they did. Anyway, she proved it, I guess, because before I left he told me about the grades and he said he was sorry."

Gram was laughing. "I wish I'd been there," she said. "I wish I'd seen this. I like the sound of this girl. She your friend?"

"No, not really. I mean—no, not really."

"Hunh," Gram said, getting up from the table and going to the stove. She started putting pieces of chicken into the fat. Dicey stepped back. "Must have been hard on you, though," Gram remarked.

"It doesn't matter," Dicey said.

Then Gram started laughing again. "That teacher sure had his hands full, didn't he, between you and this Mina character. I bet he was sorry the day he assigned that essay." And Dicey joined in now that she could see the scene as if it was part of a movie. "Serves him right," Gram added, "and will you put those tomatoes into a saucepan?"

When James read her essay about Momma, he was impressed. He didn't say so, but Dicey could tell. He asked her why she had left things out, about what their house was like, or Momma losing her job. He asked why she hadn't told about Momma's kids more. "That's not the way it really was," he protested. "I mean—it is, it's what it felt like. But there was a whole lot more, wasn't there?"

"Yes," Dicey agreed. She thought Gram might bring up the subject of Mr. Chappelle's accusation, but Gram just sat there, knitting away on the start of Sammy's blue sweater. She had finished Maybeth's and then dampened it down and laid it on towels on the dining room table to block it into shape. When it dried, Maybeth could wear it. James went up to bed, and Dicey started to follow him, but Gram asked her to stay awhile.

"I've got some reading to do," Dicey protested.

"It won't be long," Gram said. "Sit down, girl."

Dicey sat down cross-legged in front of the fire. Gram sat in an armchair a little farther back from the flames. She was knitting the ribbing, purl two, knit two. Her quick hands moved the yarn back and forth over the needles. Her eyes were dark and her hair, at the end of the day, curled around her head as if nobody ever had combed it.

"I've made a lot of mistakes in my life," Gram began.

"I don't believe it," Dicey answered.

Gram looked up briefly at her and smiled. "Well, I do, and I was there," she said. "After my husband died, I had a lot of time for thinking. And then you-all arrived, and if you think that hasn't added things to think about you're not as smart as I take you for. But especially after he died and I was alone."

She looked up sharply to say, "Don't think I minded being alone."

"I don't," Dicey said, the smile she kept from her face showing in her voice and eyes.

"Good. I didn't mind being alone, and I don't mind you living here. But that's not what I'm trying to say. I'm trying to say—I married John, and that wasn't a mistake. But the way we stayed married, the way we lived, there were lots of mistakes. He was a stiff and proud man, John—a hard man."

Dicey nodded, because Gram had said this once before.

"I stuck by him. But I got to thinking, after he died—whether there weren't things I should have done. He wasn't happy, not a happy man. I knew that, I got to know it. He wasn't happy to be himself. And I just let him be, let him sit there, high and proud, in his life. I let the children go away from him. And from me. I got to thinking—when it was too late—you have to reach out to people. To your family too. You can't just let them sit there, you should put your hand out. If they slap it back, well you reach out again if you care enough. If you don't care enough, you forget about them, if you can. I don't know, girl."

Dicey watched into the fire, where blue-edged flames leaped up toward the chimney.

"I can't say any more that Millie Tydings is stupid," Gram said.

What did she mean by that? Dicey wondered. How did she get to Millie?

"Because Millie is always reaching out. She always had a hand out for me, not that I've taken it much. She's got one out for you, hasn't she, girl. I'm not saying that Millie's thought this out, but she didn't need to. Because there's wisdom in her."

Dicey didn't say anything.

"And I see this paper of yours as a kind of reaching out," Gram said. She stopped then, as if she was finished.

"What do you mean?" Dicey demanded. She wasn't going to let Gram stop there, not until she understood.

"Think about it," Gram said.

"No, you tell me. Reaching out? But for what?"

"I don't know," Gram said. "If I was sure, I'd say. For your momma, maybe. For all of us, maybe, but I don't think so. I think, maybe, it's reaching out for that school. Somehow. I'm not saying that's what you thought you were doing or what you even wanted to do. But it's how it turned out. And I'm sorry, the way it turned out. Because somebody's slapped your hand back good and hard. But I don't want you to stop reaching, just because it didn't come out the way it should have."

Dicey stared at her grandmother. Her mind was whirling. "That's why Mr. Lingerle—" she began.

Gram's smile flashed across her face, under the golden color the fire painted there. "He's met us halfway, hasn't he?" she observed. "I took him—in the nature of an experiment. You know? I wondered if I could. I like him, don't you?"

"Sure," Dicey said. "We all do. But that's why you told him how poor we are."

"You don't go reaching out with your hand closed up," Gram said. "It worked out all right this time."

Dicey thought.

"It took me so long to learn," Gram explained. "I'd like you to have more of a head start."

Dicey threw back her head and laughed. She didn't know why, except the feelings inside her needed some expression. If she grabbed Gram's hands and started dancing around the room, Gram would think she was crazy, for one, and she'd drop those stitches, for another. She was laughing because she couldn't hug her grandmother, and because she'd figured out something else right then: that Gram was reaching out for her, Dicey. And Dicey was laughing for another reason, because she had a phone call to make.

She found the address and number in the directory they kept beside the phone. Gram was curious, but didn't ask questions. Dicey knew Gram was curious so she didn't wait to keep her phone call private.

A man answered the phone. "Is Wilhemina there, please?" Dicey asked.

"Do you know what time it is?" the man answered.

"No," Dicey said. "I don't. I'm sorry, is it too late to call?"

"When I was a boy, my mother told me you shouldn't ever call after ten," the voice instructed her.

"I'm sorry," Dicey said again. She bit her lip to keep from giggling. He had a voice like Mina's, just as rich, only deeper. "I didn't know it was after ten."

"It's not exactly, not yet," the voice told her, "but it will be in seven minutes. I'll get Mina, but don't be long."

"Thank you," Dicey said.

"Who shall I say is calling?"

"Dicey Tillerman."

There was a short silence. "Ah," he said. She heard the phone at his end clatter down onto a table.

"Dicey?" Mina's voice came. "I won't, Dad," she called over her shoulder.

"I just wanted to say thank you," Dicey said. "For helping out today."

She could hear the smile in Mina's voice as she answered. "That was some fun, wasn't it?"

"Yes and no," Dicey said.

"I can understand that," Mina agreed. "I was thinking I ought to thank *you* for giving me such a good chance to show off. So I guess we're about even. Talk to you tomorrow, okay?"

"Okay," Dicey said. "I really liked yours, you know."

"We'll form a mutual admiration society," Mina answered. "See you."

"See you," Dicey answered. She turned back to meet Gram's eyes. "Wilhemina Smiths," she explained.

"Her father's the preacher, isn't he?" Gram asked.

"She's the one who—"

"I figured that out. I don't know, Dicey—" Gram didn't finish the sentence.

"You'll like Mina, you'll see," Dicey reassured her.

"Of course I will; I already do. But I'm a crazy old bat and my opinion's not worth a flea bite. I'm just wondering what her people will think. What they already think. About me."

"Who says you're a crazy old bat?" Dicey demanded. "James said you're crazy like a fox, he said that right away. You can't fool us, Gram."

"Good," Gram answered. "Are you going to bed or not? I thought you had reading to do."

CHAPTER 8

Mina and Dicey walked down the hall together at the end of the school day. A few people greeted Dicey, who hurried to keep up with Mina. "Hey, Dicey," they said. "Hey," she answered. "Hey, Mina," they said, passing by.

As they stepped out into the biting air, Mina asked, "How's it feel to be a folk hero?"

Dicey stopped and stared up at her companion. She didn't answer, except to say, "Most of them I don't even know their names."

"Hey, Dicey," Jeff called. He had a case for his guitar, probably to protect the wood from the cold air. Dicey was kind of sorry. She had gotten used to hearing a song or two at the end of the day. "I hear you put Chappelle into his place."

"That wasn't me, that was Mina," Dicey told him. "Do you know Mina?"

"Everybody knows Mina," Jeff said.

"Yeah," Mina answered. "Everybody knows you, too, friend."

"That's what they think," Jeff said. Mina chuckled.

"So, was this essay as good as everybody says?" Jeff asked Dicey. He sat on the wall, squinting up at her.

Now how was Dicey supposed to answer that? "No, of course not," she said. That was probably the truth. "But it was pretty good," she admitted.

Dicey went over to her bike. "Where are you going now?" Mina asked. She put her books down to wrap a long scarf around her head and tuck it inside her coat.

"To work," Dicey said.

"You've got a job? Where? Doing what?"

"At Millie Tydings's store," Dicey said. "I clean the place."

Mina bent over to pick up her armload of books. "Okay if I walk with you? I live downtown."

"Sure," Dicey said.

They went down the winding road that led from the school and out onto the main road into town. "How did you get work papers?" Mina asked. "You're not older than we are, are you? If you are," she said, "you sure don't look it."

"Millie never asked about them," Dicey said. "I guess she doesn't know about them. And she's known my grandmother all her life, so I guess she was doing Gram a favor."

"I never met your grandmother. I heard about her," Mina said.

Cars hurried past them. Dicey considered what to say.

"What you heard probably isn't true," she finally said.

"How come you live with her? And there are more of you, aren't there? Somebody told me—maybe my little brother. How come—" She stopped talking and stopped walking. "Dicey, was that your *mother* you were writing about?" Dicey looked up into Mina's face. She felt her mouth trying to find out what to answer. "No, I'm sorry, I shouldn't ask, I shouldn't say. Me and my big mouth. Pretend I never said that, will you? Let's forget it. Let's talk about the weather. Cold, isn't it?"

Dicey grinned. You didn't hold your hand out with it clenched up. Gram had said. "No, it's okay. It was Momma." She started walking again, and Mina walked with her. A fuel truck roared past them, heading east, inland. "That's how come we're here with Gram. There are four of us, I'm the oldest."

"I'm the second youngest," Mina said. She was offering Dicey a way out, but Dicey declined to take it.

"The funny thing is, we didn't know until this summer we even had a grandmother. Momma never said. And Gram didn't know about us, either, until just before we all showed up."

"Really?" Mina thought. "Do you get along okay? Are you going to stay long with her?"

"She's going to adopt us."

"But what about your mother?"

"The doctors don't think she'll ever get better." They were at the store by then, to Dicey's relief. "Come on in and get warm," Dicey said.

Inside, Sammy waited for her. He waited right by the door, watching. He was watching for her to come, but he didn't say anything when she said hello. Dicey introduced him to Mina. Sammy's forehead had a cut on it, and his cheek had been scraped. Somebody had painted his face with Mercurochrome. Millie started to come out from behind the meat counter.

"Sammy?" Dicey asked him.

"Did you ever play marbles?" he asked. Dicey shook her head. She guessed he didn't want to talk to her. But she wanted to know what happened.

"What are you doing here?" she asked.

He shrugged. "I can't ride the bus for a week. That's two days next week too."

"Why?"

"It's Thanksgiving this week," he told her. Dicey had forgotten.

"I forgot," she said. She introduced Mina to Millie. They shook hands and Millie told Mina to call her Millie, not Mrs. Tydings.

"Do *you* play marbles?" Sammy asked Mina.

"I used to," Millie said. "We all did, marbles and jacks. Jacks for the girls and marbles for the boys. Only the girls all wanted to play marbles too. I guess to show we could. I don't remember the boys ever wanting to play jacks with us. Kids still play jacks, don't they?"

Dicey never had.

"I did," Mina said. "Remember pig-in-a-poke?" she asked Millie.

"I sure do," Millie said.

"Everybody has them now," Sammy said. "I got some last week. I've lost about half of them," he said. "I'm coming home with you after work," he told Dicey. "I called Gram so she won't worry."

"Sammy, could you show me how to shoot marbles?" Mina asked. "Dicey's got to work, but I always wondered."

"In here?"

"No, outside—unless it's too cold for you."

"It's not cold around here," Sammy said. They went outside.

Dicey got to work. She was checking the sale dates on the canned and boxed goods. She did this once a month. Millie kept an eye on the dairy products and bread, but she forgot that other things also had limited shelf life.

"You won't be working on Thursday," Millie observed. "I had to remind Ab to get herself a turkey."

"We don't need a turkey," Dicey said. They hadn't celebrated Thanksgiving in Provincetown, except for the days off from school. "I could come in on Friday, if you wanted."

"I guess that's all right. I go up to Salisbury. I know a widow lady up there, she makes the dinner and I bring the turkey."

"I could come in Friday morning, if you'd rather," Dicey offered.

"Doesn't matter to me, the afternoon is fine. He looks like he was in a fight."

Dicey nodded agreement, but didn't say anything.

She tried, without success, to get Sammy to tell her what he'd fought about. All he would say was that Millie had washed him off. "She knew Gram when Gram was little. Do you think Gram knows how to shoot marbles?"

"Why would she know that?" Dicey asked.

"She might," Sammy insisted. "I gotta learn how or I'll lose them all and it's a dollar a bag."

"What about the bus?" Dicey demanded. It was hard trying to talk to him with the cold wind and without being able to see his face.

"It's my punishment for fighting on the bus," Sammy said. "It's okay. Do you mind?"

"I suppose I'm going to be riding you in, too," Dicey realized.

"If it stays cold, we'll have to put off playing until spring, and I'll have time to practice. The barn would be a good place," Sammy said.

Dicey gave up.

Gram grilled Sammy when they got home, but learned nothing. She didn't seem to mind the punishment of not being able to ride the school bus for a week; she agreed with Sammy that that was fair. "Except to Dicey," she added.

"It's okay," Dicey said quickly.

Gram dropped the subject until they had finished dinner and were loitering around the table. All during dinner they had talked about the Thanksgiving meal, and what they would eat, and whether they would ask Mr. Lingerle. Gram said she'd call him that evening, to see if he'd like to come out and eat with them. "But why none of you told me Thanksgiving was coming—what's the good of having children around if they don't keep you up to date?" she'd asked. But she was teasing them, so nobody answered.

Then, "What about these fights?" she asked. Sammy wouldn't meet her eyes. James looked a question at Dicey, and she shook her head to say she didn't know any more than he did.

When it became clear that Sammy wasn't about to say anything, Gram looked at Dicey and James for help.

"Who'd you fight with?" James asked. He got up to clear their plates away. Dicey realized he'd done that so Sammy would think he didn't care much about the answer. She thought that was pretty smart.

"Ernie," Sammy said.

"He that big kid?" James asked.

"Yeah. You never played marbles, did you?"

"I don't like him," Maybeth volunteered.

"Why not?" asked Gram.

"He picks on kids," she said.

"Does he pick on you?" Gram asked. Dicey knew what she was thinking.

"No. I keep away from him. He picks on them—in a mean way," Maybeth said.

"What did you and Ernie fight about?" Gram asked.

"Nothing," Sammy said. "Hey, Gram, did you used to play marbles when you were little? Millie said she did. So maybe you did. Could you play with me sometime, if you did? I bet you were good at it. So you could help me practice."

"Stick to the point," Gram said. "You fought with Ernie. Is he in your class?"

Sammy nodded.

"Do you like him?"

"I dunno," Sammy said. "He's my only friend."

"Was it just Ernie you fought with?"

Sammy shook his head.

"So you fought with Ernie and some of his friends," Gram asked. She sounded like she would never run out of patience. Sammy looked around the room.

"Yeah," he said. "They don't ride the bus."

"Was there anybody on your side?" Gram asked.

Sammy shook his head. "Custer tried to stop us. We weren't on school grounds," he pointed out. "And anyway, if I could get enough to win all Ernie's marbles, that would show him."

"Show him what?" Gram demanded.

Sammy looked around at all their faces. He was wondering if he had fallen into a trap, Dicey knew.

"Show him I'm better at marbles than he is," Sammy announced triumphantly.

"But Sammy, you ought to tell us what you're fighting about," Gram said.

Sammy shook his head. Dicey had to admire the way he stuck to himself. "It doesn't matter."

"If it doesn't matter, then why are you fighting?"

"It doesn't matter to you. It just matters to me." His jaw was thrust out and he changed the subject again. "You didn't answer if you'll play marbles with me."

"Oh, I don't know, I can't even remember—" Gram started. Then she smiled at Sammy, smiled slow. "I will, if you'll tell me what you're fighting about. And I was pretty good when I was a girl. Not even the boys could beat me."

Sammy was tempted. He wriggled in his chair and refused to smile back at Gram.

"Got you now," Gram said.

"No, you don't," Sammy told her, but smiling himself now.

"Okay. I give up. I'll play with you anyway, and I'll teach you everything I know, if I remember any of it. But I surely wish you'd tell us."

Sammy shook his head apologetically.

"Then I wish you'd stop."

"I try. I'll try harder," Sammy said. "Honest."

"All right. You're excused," Gram said. He burst out of the room. She sat looking after him.

"He wouldn't say anything to me, either," Dicey said, before Gram could ask.

"Well, I don't know," Gram said.

Neither did anyone else.

"It might snow!" Sammy greeted Dicey as she walked into Millie's the next afternoon. Certainly the sky had that heavy, leaden look to it.

"Not before we get home, I hope," Dicey answered. "I hope Gram can find us coats in the attic. Think we'll ever be allowed up in that attic?"

"Sure," Sammy said. "James said maybe there's a dead body up there. But I don't believe him."

"Neither do I," Dicey agreed. Although the old clothes, the old toys, the past, that might be kind of like a dead body to Gram. "How was your day?"

"I didn't fight," Sammy announced. Dicey stood in front of him, rubbing her hands to warm them, studying his round face. He looked up at her. His eyes were set far apart, the way Momma's and Maybeth's were, and his yellow hair straggled over onto his forehead. In his jeans and the big, old baggy sweater, he looked comical, and Dicey smiled at him. "Good for you," she said, suspecting that it wasn't for lack of temptation that he hadn't fought. "Ernie again?"

Sammy nodded and pushed his hands down into his pocket. He squared his shoulders.

"You need a haircut. I'll give you one tonight, a Dicey

special. Why don't you play with Custer, he sounds okay."

Sammy shrugged. "He's got lots of people who want to play with him. You ought to get to work, Dicey. Gram said we have stuff to do when we get home, for tomorrow. What do you think Mr. Lingerle will bring for dessert?"

"Something sweet and gooey," Dicey guessed.

"Maybe chocolate?" Sammy asked hopefully. "Can I help you?"

"Better not," Dicey said.

She had washed the inside of the windows and the whole meat case (moving meat and chicken and fish away from each section before she cleaned it) before Jeff appeared. Millie was at the front with Sammy, talking about something. They had just the ordering left to do before Dicey was through.

Jeff had come in, he said, to try out Millie's beef. Millie came back to serve him. He picked out a steak and pot roast and then added a couple of pounds of ground chuck.

"What do you want the chuck for?" Millie asked.

"Spaghetti sauce," he told her. She advised him to get regular ground beef for that. Hers had better flavor and less fat than the supermarket ground beef, she told him; it was just as good as chuck for spaghetti. He went along with her suggestion.

Dicey stood back watching him. He made his choices as if he knew what he was doing, pointing out the pieces of meat he wanted, selecting them from the display. He bent down to peer into the display counter, then studied what Millie brought up. He was really too thin, Dicey decided, seeing him clearly for what felt like the first time. His face was oval and tapered down to a small chin. He had a nose that was perfectly straight and eyebrows with almost no arch in them. His skin was pale, as if he didn't get outside much. His hair had as much black as brown in it, and his hands looked too big for his arms.

Dicey thought he was concentrating on his purchases, but he

turned to her and said, "I wish you'd stop staring at me. It makes me nervous."

Dicey was embarrassed. "I'm sorry." Then she laughed and went down to the front of the store where Sammy waited patiently. She set out the distributor's order sheets and sharpened two pencils. "It won't be long now," she told Sammy.

Jeff paid for his purchases, then lingered awkwardly. "I wondered if you'd like a lift home. I've got the car, and we could put your bike in the back. It's pretty cold."

"I've still got work to do," Dicey said. "But thanks, anyway."

"I'm going home with Dicey," Sammy announced.

"Are you? Who are you?"

"I'm her brother."

"Meet Sammy," Dicey said. "Sammy, meet Jeff."

"We could fit you in the car," Jeff told Sammy. "You don't take up much room."

Jeff was teasing, but Sammy wasn't in the mood to be teased. "I don't want to," he told Jeff. "I'd rather ride on your bike," he said to Dicey.

"You don't look much alike," Jeff remarked.

"So what?" Sammy said.

Sammy's unfriendliness was making Jeff uncomfortable, and Dicey—reaching out again—wanted to make him feel better. "I'd like a ride, if you don't mind waiting. Jeff plays the guitar," she told Sammy.

"So what?"

"So maybe you can get him to play for you while you wait," she said. "So maybe you could be polite when somebody offers to save me six miles of toting your great hulking body around." This made Sammy smile.

"I'm not hulking," he answered. "Okay."

Jeff and Sammy settled down on the seat made by the long

window. Jeff fetched his guitar and showed some chords to Sammy. Millie and Dicey worked at the counter. Out of the side of her ears, Dicey heard Jeff singing a long, repetitious song. Sammy watched Jeff's hands.

Waiting for Millie to decide whether she needed another carton of frozen peas yet, Dicey looked up to catch her employer watching the two boys. She suddenly realized that Millie might not like having them singing like that in her store. "Do you mind?" she asked Millie. "We didn't ask you if it was all right; do you want them to stop?"

"Why should I?" She turned to Dicey. "It's pretty," she added. "Supermarkets have music piped in. But do you think we should order the peas? Or wait for next week?"

At Jeff's car, Sammy argued about being asked to sit in the backseat of the station wagon. Jeff answered briefly that his father insisted that kids sit in the back, where it was safer for them.

"I'm not a kid," Sammy said. He was jammed in with grocery bags that had been moved onto the seat to make room for Dicey's bike in the rear.

"Yeah?" Jeff answered.

"Yeah," Sammy answered. "Kids are goats," he declared.

"I know that," Jeff said.

"So what?" Sammy said. "I don't care," he said in response to the expression on Dicey's face.

Dicey gave Jeff directions. When they got to the mailbox, Sammy said they could walk in from there, because they had to get the mail. Dicey looked at Jeff and shrugged. She and Sammy pulled the bike out of the back of the car. "Thanks for the ride," Dicey said.

"Any time," Jeff answered. "That is, any time I do the shopping, because that's the only time I get the car. I was hoping to meet your sister who sings."

"We're in a hurry for dinner tomorrow," Sammy said. "Because it's Thanksgiving. Thank you for the ride home." He handed the mail to Dicey, who noticed another thin envelope from Boston.

"Maybe another day," Dicey said.

"You mean that?" he asked. He had rolled down the window and was looking seriously at her.

"Sure," she said.

"Because I will," he warned her.

"Good," she answered, puzzled and amused.

She and Sammy walked up the rutted driveway together. "I don't know what you were so unfriendly about," she said to Sammy. He just shrugged. "It's cold today," Dicey said, to emphasize her point.

"It's not bad," Sammy said. "I can't smell snow."

"Not down south here. I don't know if it every really snows here. What did he sing?"

"Something about a man and a lady. It only had three chords, the same three, over and over. But they didn't sound boring. Do you think he'll really come to see Maybeth?"

"No," Dicey said. "Or maybe yes. I don't know. I don't know him very well."

"I liked him okay," Sammy told her.

"Did you? You could have fooled me."

Sammy turned before going into the barn to take out his bike. "I can't fool you," he assured Dicey. "I'm going to have to hurry, aren't I?"

"Burn up the roads," Dicey advised him. "You've got enough time before dark."

"I wonder how fast I can make it, if I really ride fast," Sammy said.

Dicey found Gram and Maybeth in the kitchen, surrounded

by different foods at different stages of preparation. James was busy carrying in logs for the fireplaces. He clattered through the kitchen, his forehead red and flushed, a heavy pea jacket buttoned up around his throat. "You like the coat?" he asked Dicey, puffing under the weight of an armload of logs. "There's one for each of us. They're old. They really made good jackets then."

A fire burned in the unused dining room, to take the chill off the air. Maybeth had pleaded with Gram to serve the Thanksgiving meal in there, and Gram decided to go along with her wishes. Maybeth wanted that room because she said it was prettier than the kitchen. Gram wanted it because it meant she could spread out her preparations. "It's been years since I put together a meal like this," she announced. Dicey couldn't tell whether she was wishing she wasn't doing it now.

There surely was a lot of work that went into it. Dicey put her books away and came downstairs to help Maybeth patiently rip a couple of loaves of bread up into small pieces for stuffing. Gram chopped onions and celery. She had a pan of chestnuts roasting in the oven. "And we'll all do them tonight after supper's cleared away," Gram announced. "There's no reason one person should be stuck with that job."

"Are they worth the trouble?" James asked.

"Tell me what you think tomorrow," Gram answered.

What Dicey thought, leaning back against her chair, her stomach stretched taut, was that the chestnuts were worth the trouble, the whole meal was worth the trouble. They sat around the dark dining room table, the five Tillermans and Mr. Lingerle. Outside, gray clouds crowded down on the land. Inside, the yellow firelight and the small electric lights on the walls made it feel like evening, instead of midafternoon.

James and Mr. Lingerle ate on, and the big bowls of sweet

potatoes and mashed potatoes, of beans and corn and tomatoes, all were half-empty. The turkey, which Mr. Lingerle had carved with unexpected skill, was almost half-eaten. Dicey thought about asking for another piece of the crisp skin, but decided that if she did she wouldn't be able to force down even a polite bite of the two pies Mr. Lingerle had waiting for them. Sammy sat beside her, moaning with contentment. Gram leaned forward, her elbows beside her plate, her curly hair brushed into order, her face—thoughtful and quiet. Maybeth's round eyes kept looking around the table, and her hands were quiet in her lap.

Maybe it was because they never had celebrated Thanksgiving before. For a piercing instant, Dicey longed for Momma to be with them, sitting on the other side of Sammy, to complete the picture. That was the trouble with being happy, it made you remember other things. Dicey looked at Gram and wondered what Gram was thinking of. She wondered if Gram was remembering other Thanksgivings, and other faces at her table. Momma was one of those, too.

"I wish we hadn't started yet," Dicey said. "I wish I wasn't full."

Mr. Lingerle lifted his face and halted his laden fork at mid-journey to his mouth. Each of the many ounces of flesh that made up his body seemed to emanate comfort, contentment, good will. Dicey couldn't stop herself from smiling at him: he was like Thanksgiving made into a single body.

"What we used to do, when I was a boy, was wait until later in the day to have dessert. We always made plenty of dessert, even though we knew we'd never be able to eat it. Then, at suppertime, instead of any normal meal, we would have the pies."

"But—" James said. "What if you still had room, at dinner. Now."

Mr. Lingerle chuckled. "You didn't *have* to wait."

"I've never had a chocolate pie," James mumbled. "I was saving room for some."

Sammy groaned quietly. Maybeth got up to clear the table. Dicey picked up the heavy platter that held the turkey, the carving tools, and a large, long-handled silver spoon that Gram called the stuffing spoon. She had pulled it out from a back drawer in the chest in the dining room.

"You know," Mr. Lingerle remarked, reaching out to take the spoon from the platter and holding it up, "this is probably valuable. It's old, I'd guess, and heavy."

"I know," Gram said. "So's the one in the cranberry sauce. I've thought of selling that one, if I had to. The stuffing spoon belonged to my mother. Those were good times for Crisfield, for the bootleggers, at least."

"You never said people in your family were bootleggers," James protested.

"Our family," Gram corrected him.

"Did they bootleg whiskey?"

"What else?" Gram said. "I never said so, but they were. This was way back. That other spoon now, that was left to me by my husband's aunt. In her will. She'd have had it buried with her if she could have. She hated to give anything away. I never did like it."

"There's beautiful workmanship on it," Mr. Lingerle told her, inspecting it.

Gram shrugged. "You'd know how to go about selling it," she asked.

"I've got a friend in Easton who has an antique store. Up in Talbot County where the money is— But Mrs. Tillerman, you don't need money, do you? I mean"—he became flustered and embarrassed—"I should have brought the turkey, I'm sorry. I never even thought, I was so pleased to be asked."

Dicey cleared away plates and watched Gram enjoying Mr. Lingerle's discomfort.

"Call me Ab," Gram finally said, putting a stop to his apologies. "We don't need money, but if we did it's good to know."

"That's a relief," he said. "Where'd my plate get to?"

Only Mr. Lingerle and James ate dessert. The phone rang and Maybeth answered it. It was for Sammy, who came back into the dining room to ask Gram if he could go play at Ernie's house.

"No," Gram said.

"Why not?" Sammy demanded.

"It's Thanksgiving," James reminded him. James had finished a thin slice of lattice-topped cherry pie and was about to begin on the dark chocolate sliver. "On Thanksgiving, families stay at home."

"Aren't they having a dinner?" Dicey asked.

"I said, no," Gram repeated.

"I could ride my bike. If they were having a dinner he wouldn't ask me," Sammy said.

"I said no and that's an end of it," Gram said.

"But then—I won't have *any* friends," Sammy told her.

But Gram shook her head firmly.

Sammy turned abruptly and left the room. When he returned, he was smiling and didn't mention it again. Mr. Lingerle said he would help with the washing up before he left. Gram said she had expected him to stay into the evening, if he would like to. He said he would like to and that only part of his reason was that he could have a real helping of the pies for supper. Gram snorted. He nominated James as his helper in the kitchen. The rest of the family he sent to lie down in the living room. To gather their energies for the walk, he said, the After-Thanksgiving-Dinner walk.

Late in the afternoon, everybody wrapped up in coats and walked down to the Bay. A film of ice lay over the water, going out about a hundred yards from shore. Gram recalled the times when the Bay had frozen so hard that you could walk out on it. Dicey thought of the oystermen working in this bitter weather and thought that the gray clouds reflected the gray of the water. She turned around to look back over the muted winter browns of the marsh to where the house stood, if you could see it.

As if it had been waiting to catch her full attention, the sky loosed a flurry of snowflakes. This wasn't a real snow, but swirled down lightly, like a rain shower. It came down so few and so slowly, you could watch the descent of an individual snowflake.

The children, led by Sammy, ran back up the path to the house. Once they'd arrived there, however, there was nothing to do. So they dashed back down the path, to join the two adults, who moved more sedately.

"It's snowing!" Sammy cried. "I don't have mittens!"

"I'll find some," Gram said. "I always wondered if it was worth hoarding all those old clothes away, but now I guess it was," she said to Mr. Lingerle.

"Makes me feel like running too," he remarked. He had a plaid wool scarf wrapped up tight around his neck. Snowflakes lay scattered on his thin hair.

"You should," Gram said. "You should take *some* exercise."

"I know, but I don't. I can't really," he told her.

"It's not good for you," she said. "All that extra weight."

He agreed, but didn't say anything. However, as they entered the warm kitchen, Dicey heard him say quietly: "If you really thought that, you'd not have invited me to dinner."

"You know better than that, young man," Gram snapped. Dicey grinned. Gram's way of reaching out was sure original.

Dicey herself was thinking about several things at once, about what that last letter from Boston might have said, about why Sammy wasn't angry at being refused permission to go to Ernie's, about James's friend Toby, who was going to spend the night with them on Saturday for James's birthday present. ("That's all I want," he'd told Gram. "Just that. And a chocolate cake, like Sammy's. And if you'd make a crab imperial? For supper. And—" "I have just been struck deaf," Gram announced. "I cannot hear another word you are going to say on the subject.") And Dicey was thinking about how the ocean never froze but always smashed up the little ridges of ice that dared to form at its edge at a quiet low tide.

By the time they went to bed, a light dusting of snow glittered over everything, glistening white in the dark air. But when Dicey emerged from Millie's the next afternoon, there was no sign of it. The cold weather had been nudged aside by an unexpectedly balmy day. Sunlight poured warm out of a cloudless sky; the breeze blew gently, wafting the warm air around. The temperature, Millie told her, had reached the sixties at midday. Dicey peeled her sweater over her head and saw Mina walking toward her, wheeling a bike.

"I brought my bike," Mina said unnecessarily. "I thought I'd walk out with you a ways. I've had enough family to last me a year, and it's gonna happen all over again at Christmas. Can you believe that?"

Dicey didn't know what she was supposed to say. She didn't say anything.

"So can I?" Mina asked.

"Can you what?"

"Walk with you."

"Sure," Dicey said. They were silent for a block, until Mina asked if Dicey had a nice Thanksgiving, and Dicey said she had.

They were silent again. After a while, Mina asked, "Was it awfully different from your other Thanksgivings?"

Dicey was watching a bright red cardinal fly across the road into an empty field. He flew with a queer, swooping motion, low to the land. He flashed red ahead of them and at eye level.

"They don't fly high, like other birds," Dicey observed to Mina.

"We get a lot of cardinals around here, all winter long," Mina told her.

"We never had Thanksgiving before, with Momma," Dicey said. She couldn't seem to keep her mind on the conversation; she couldn't seem to pay attention. It felt like spring fever. "We were too poor," she explained.

"That's no sin," Mina declared.

"I never said it was."

Mina turned her head and looked at Dicey. "I never said you did. I was just trying to tell you—where I stand. Your brother's a lot like you."

"Did you meet James?"

"Sammy."

"Sammy isn't. He looks like Momma."

"That's not what I meant."

"Then what did you mean?" And suddenly Dicey's mind was clear again, like a sudden cure from spring fever when an icy rain surprises you.

"What's got you jumping down my throat?" Mina demanded.

Dicey looked up at her, struck by a sudden thought: "Or is this the way you talk about the other person?"

Mina chuckled. "I should have known better than to write that where you'd hear it. I should have known you'd understand it and remember."

"Yeah, but is it?" Dicey insisted.

"Yes and no," Mina told her. The road was almost untraveled, and they walked slowly, in no hurry to get anywhere. "Look Dicey. See, I've got these problems."

That surprised Dicey.

"I mean, I'm pretty smart, and certainly smarter than most of the kids around here. I'm black. I'm a black female. Oh and—well, look at me. Tell the truth, I could be thirty years old and have kids of my own, couldn't I? Big as I am. If you just look. See what I mean?"

Dicey grinned, and nodded.

"And I began getting these—bosoms—when I was ten; I started bleeding when I was eleven—I ask you, what are people going to think?"

"What does that matter?" Dicey asked.

"So here I am, this giant oddball—and with more personality than anybody needs—and along comes a scrawny little kid who's at least as smart as I am and nobody's doormat. So I said to myself, Mina Smiths, you get to know that girl. I mean, I've known you for two months, and you never got close to asking me if anybody ever French-kissed me."

"Cripes," Dicey said, "why should I want to know that?"

"That's what I mean."

Dicey thought about it. "It could be, I'm just immature," she said.

"I thought of that, but that's not the feeling I get. So I'm really interested in you, because you're interesting. Get me?"

"Yeah," Dicey said.

"So what is it about your brother that makes you jump down my throat?"

And Dicey told her about the fights he'd been in recently, and the fights he'd been in before, in Provincetown and in Bridgeport. "He won't tell us why," Dicey said. "That's why we're worried."

"Who's we?"

"Me and Gram," Dicey said.

"Did he tell you before?"

"No, but I could figure it out." Dicey told Mina about what it was like for them all in Provincetown and about how she had finally understood this summer how scared and angry Sammy got. "But it's not the same here," Dicey argued, although Mina hadn't said anything. "It's not at all the same for us. Even Maybeth—shows the difference."

"Lemme think a minute," Mina said. Dicey waited, feeling how warm the lowering sun was on the side of her face. It wasn't as warm as a fire, but it warmed her in a deeper way. Then Mina threw her arms up into the air and clapped her hands together over her head. Her bike clattered onto the ground. She ignored it and turned a bright face to Dicey. "It's gotta be your grandmother," Mina declared.

"Hunh?"

"Maybe you don't know this," Mina continued, talking fast and eagerly, "but your grandmother's—people around here have considered her—" As she realized what she was saying, her voice slowed down. "I mean—she's got a reputation for weird chess. As long as I can remember."

Dicey could feel anger mounting. "You never even met her. You don't know anything about her, and she isn't." She bit at her lip.

"See what I mean?" Mina asked, ignoring Dicey's anger. "You're like him, you flare up—don't try to deny it—as soon as I brought your grandmother into it. I bet you did some fighting too, when you were younger. I bet. Did you? Come on, tell me. Did you?"

Dicey had to smile, Mina was so pleased with herself. "Yes, of course, and about Momma. So you think the kids might be saying things about Gram?"

"Don't you? Doesn't that sound like what kids would do?"

It did. "But what can we do about it?" Dicey asked.

"I dunno. How could I know that?" Mina asked.

"What would you do?"

"Me? I'd probably go down to school and bash in a few faces. I've always been so big, nobody fought back against me much. But that'd be the wrong thing to do."

"Yeah," Dicey agreed. She could see a picture of Mina descending on Sammy's second-grade classroom. "You wouldn't really," she said.

"I'm not sure," Mina said. "What's your grandmother like?"

Mina didn't give you a minute to catch your breath, Dicey thought. Conversations with her were like running, running along the ocean. "Come and meet her and see for yourself."

"Another time. Today, I've got to get back home. I'm only loose for a couple of hours, under strict orders to get back to help with supper. There are fifteen people eating at our house."

"Who are they all?" Dicey asked.

"They are all—every one of them—immediate family. My parents and brothers and sisters, a couple of husbands, a couple of wives, a couple of little kids. It's a circus, I can tell you that." She looked west to where the sun was and said, "And now is the time for me to pedal back to it."

"Come meet Gram sometime," Dicey asked.

"Wild horses couldn't keep me away," Mina said. "See you."

"See you." Dicey mounted her own bike and rode off in the opposite direction.

She found Gram sitting on the back steps. Gram wasn't doing anything, for a change, just sitting in the sunlight. Dicey sat down beside her. She didn't know how to say what she was going to say.

"What if Sammy's fighting about you?" she asked Gram.

Gram's face swiveled around to look at Dicey. Gram's hazel

eyes were set deep into her face. Her nose was straight and proud. "Don't be stupid," she said. Her skin in this light showed fine lines under the fading tan.

"I'm not," Dicey answered. Anger tightened Gram's mouth, but Dicey sat it out.

Gram just stared at Dicey for a minute. She was sitting about where she had been sitting when Dicey first saw her, ever. She was dressed as she had been then, too, long overblouse, a long full skirt and bare feet. Then Gram stood up. "It's too cold for bare feet anyway," she said.

"But Gram—"

Gram turned around.

"What about it?" Dicey asked.

Gram just turned away and went back inside. Dicey followed her into the kitchen. "It's what you told me," she insisted to Gram's back. "It's what you said, about reaching out."

"And even if it's true, what am I supposed to do?" Gram asked. "It's too stupid."

"I think you ought to find out," Dicey said. "You could talk to Sammy."

"It's not as if I haven't already done enough," Gram declared. Her chin was high and stiff.

Well, that was true. Dicey knew that.

"It's nobody's business how I live my life," Gram announced.

Dicey left the room. She went out to the barn and worked on the boat. She finished the side she had started in September. In the failing light, she saw Sammy ride his bike up to the big doors. The dim light disguised his individual features, so he could have been any seven-year-old, home and tired. He dismounted, holding the bike upright with his hands and landing lightly on his feet. He could have been a picture of his uncle, the other Samuel—Bullet—Dicey thought. She had always assumed from Gram's reaction to Sammy that he looked like Bullet. But she didn't know, she didn't know anything about Gram's children. Except Momma. She wished Gram would talk about them, so she could understand— Understand what? she asked herself. Understand why Gram wouldn't even think about if Sammy was fighting over what people said about her, wouldn't even talk about it. The figure in the doorway wheeled its bike inside and became Sammy himself.

"You finished one side," he announced.

"Looks good, doesn't it?" Dicey said. He came to stand beside her, and she put her hand on his shoulder.

"Are you going to work tomorrow morning?" he asked.

"Sure, it's Saturday."

"Would it be all right if I sanded it, even if you weren't here?" Sammy asked. "I'd do a good job."

"I know you would," Dicey told him. "That would be okay with me, if you wanted to."

"Good-o," he said. He looked earnestly at her. "I won't try to share the boat with you, Dicey. Honest."

Dicey looked back down at him. "You're a goof," she told him. Her arms slipped down behind his back until her fingers could dig into his rib cage. "A genuine goof and I'm going to call you Goofy."

He laughed, twisted away, and ran out of the barn. Dicey followed him, crying out that she was going to get him, and tickle him until he wet his pants. Sammy laughed so hard he fell over onto the ground. Dicey pounded on him.

Saturday was as warm as Friday, and Dicey changed into her shorts and a T-shirt after lunch, to work on the boat. She preferred wearing the boys' shirts, but they had to be ironed. She ran her hand carefully over the area Sammy had finished that morning when she had been washing down shelves at Millie's. The wood was silky smooth under her fingers. The air was silky smooth around her body. James and Maybeth were working in the kitchen. Gram sat knitting and listening. Sammy was off delivering papers. Dicey scraped at the second side, puzzled by this strange warm weather but pleased by the chance to spend an afternoon alone with the boat.

When someone spoke her name from behind her, she swung around, startled. Jeff stood in the doorway. He had a bike, and his guitar was slung over his back. "Whatcha doing?"

"I'm the one to ask that," Dicey snapped. What was he doing there anyway?

He stepped back and moved his head confusedly. Dicey just about decided she didn't think much of him when he spoke again.

"Look," he said. "I thought I'd come out and see you, and I want to meet this sister of yours. If you're busy, I'll go. If you don't like the idea of me being here—you just have to say so."

Dicey was already sorry for her anger. "No," she said quickly. "It's not that. Come on in. I've only got a little more to do here. I was just surprised to see someone. You surprised me."

He leaned his bike against a post and came closer. She thought he might be laughing. "If that's the way you react to surprises, I'll be careful not to surprise you again. What *are* you doing?"

"Scraping it down."

"That looks hand-made. Do you sail?"

"I have. Just once. My grandmother's going to teach me. I like it," she added.

"Want to hear a song while you work?"

"What about the one you played for Sammy." That way, he'd know she was really trying to make peace.

"Ah, my twenty-minute number." He seemed to understand

that Dicey didn't want to fight with him. He sat down on the ground and ran fingers over the strings. He adjusted the tuning of two, then ran his fingers along the chord again. For a minute, Dicey watched him. Then she went back to work.

The song was about a man and a lady, just like Sammy said. It told him about the wife of a rich man who fell in love with somebody else and took him home with her while her husband was away. The husband came back and caught them together. He challenged the other man to a fight and killed him. Then he made up to the lady, sitting her on his knee, asking her which man she preferred. But she told him she preferred the other man, even though he was dead, preferred him "to you and all your kin." Dicey liked that. She liked the spirit of it. So the rich man took the lady where everybody could see, and he cut her throat.

Dicey had finished what she planned to get done that day, but she worked until the song was done. "But why are they all like that?" she asked Jeff. "Why are they all unhappy endings?"

He shrugged. Dicey cleaned off the scraper and put it away.

"Do you know any happy songs?"

"A couple. Not many. Tolstoy says happy marriages are all the same, but unhappy ones are each different. Maybe that's why, maybe being unhappy is more interesting."

"Tolstoy? Who's that?"

"A writer. A Russian. My father told me about it."

"Why would he tell you a thing like that?"

Jeff shrugged. He didn't want to talk about it. Dicey rubbed her hands clean on her shorts. "Well, come on in and meet people. James's friend Toby's coming over this afternoon too, so there'll be lots of people around."

"What's your sister's name?"

"Maybeth. She's gonna like hearing you play."

By the time introductions were made and questions were answered, Toby had arrived. And Sammy had returned, and a whole new set of introductions and questions had to be covered. Toby was about James's size, with light brown hair and big glasses that magnified his eyes. At first, they all stood around in the kitchen, then Gram moved them into the living room. Jeff went right to the point with Maybeth. "Dicey says you sing."

Maybeth gripped her hands together and looked big-eyed around the room. She didn't say anything.

"So do I," Sammy declared.

"I wasn't thinking of this much audience," Dicey added.

"As a fact," Gram announced from the doorway, "they all sing. I don't. Not where anybody can hear me, that is. You wouldn't either."

James and Toby were standing awkwardly in the middle of the room. Sammy stood with them, studying Toby. "You wanna go down to the dock?" he offered. Toby looked at James; they didn't seem to know what they wanted to do. "We could ride bikes," Sammy suggested.

Jeff sat down on the floor by the empty fireplace and spoke to Maybeth. "Dicey did tell me you could sing well," he repeated, looking across the room at the little girl. "Actually, what happened, I told Dicey I thought she had a pretty good voice and she boasted about you." He played a couple of chords.

James and Toby went over to look at the bookcases.

"Gram, could you make cookies?" Sammy asked.

"I think I know how," Gram said.

"Chocolate chip?" he insisted.

"Maybe," she agreed.

"Now?" he said. "Please?"

"In a minute," she said, looking at him sternly.

Jeff began to sing, accompanying himself. "When first unto this country, a stranger I came—" He stopped. "Dicey?"

"Okay," she agreed.

Dicey sang with him, and after a couple of verses, Maybeth joined in. Her voice was stronger than either Dicey's or Jeff's, and after a bit they tapered off singing and just listened. Once she was singing, watching Jeff play the guitar, Maybeth forgot to be shy.

At the end he said, "Dicey was right," at the same time Maybeth moved to sit in front of him and say, "I like that song."

"But it's wrong," James said. "Jacob doesn't have the coat of many colors, it's Joseph."

"Because that's the one his brother put blood on," Toby added, standing beside James. The two earnest, intelligent faces looked at Jeff. "Jacob's the one with Esau, remember?" Toby asked.

"And the birthright and the blessing," James said. Dicey thought there was no need for him to show off that way.

"And Joseph goes into Egypt," Toby said, matching James. "And his brothers do all bow down to him, just like in his dream."

Jeff's gray eyes were dancing, Dicey saw, and he was having a hard time not smiling. "I know," he told the two boys. James's eyes lit up, and he glanced quickly at Dicey, and nodded at her. The two boys sat down on the floor. "I wondered about that," Jeff went on, talking seriously to them. "If it's Jacob because he's a thief, the man in the song. And it can't be Joseph—only, the man in the song is part Joseph, part Jacob, isn't he? I mean, Joseph was a stranger in Egypt, and Jacob stole."

James looked impressed, and if anyone had asked Dicey she would have admitted that she was, too. She didn't know what they were talking about, except it was probably from the Bible. But everybody had relaxed and she knew that when she suggested another song, Maybeth would join in eagerly. She tried to think of all the songs she wanted to sing. They had the whole warm afternoon before them.

"You said you'd make cookies," Sammy repeated to Gram. "I could help you," he added, going to stand beside her.

"All right," Gram said. They left the room. James and Toby took out the checkers set. Dicey looked at the gleaming guitar on Jeff's lap and asked him if he'd ever heard "Who Will Sing for Me?" He hadn't, so Dicey and Maybeth sang it. He asked them to teach it to him. He had a light, rhythmical way of playing his guitar, picking at it with his finger, not strumming it.

They were perfecting their version of "Amazing Grace," in three-part harmony, when Gram came back into the room. Mina entered behind her, smiling broadly. "Brought you an alto," Gram announced.

Jeff flashed a smile up at Gram. Dicey got up to say hello. "I didn't hear you knock," she said.

"She didn't. Came right in the back door. Like certain other people," Gram said, looking at Dicey who had done just that, that first day they came. "Not what you're thinking," Gram said quickly to Mina.

"I didn't think it was," Mina answered just as quickly. "It looked like—I thought, Dicey's family weren't the kind to use the front door and scrape shoes—so I thought I'd just be one of the gang. It is a gang here, isn't it?"

Gram surveyed the room. She didn't say a word, and they waited for her to say something. Sammy ran in to fetch her, because the cookies were ready to come out of the oven.

They went through "Amazing Grace" again, and Mina's voice *was* a full alto. Dicey wondered how Gram knew that. "I hope you're not sung out," Mina said, settling into a chair. "I could spend the afternoon singing, and that's the truth."

"You choose the next one," Jeff told her.

"You won't know it," she countered.

"I can pick up almost anything," he said. "Can't I, Maybeth? You tell her—you've been watching close enough."

Maybeth just smiled, and said, "I think he can."

Mina, curling her legs up under her denim skirt, challenged Jeff. "It's a gospel tune." She started to sing, a kind of prayer song, about a man whose only friend was God. By the time she got to the third line, Jeff had joined in, to show Mina he already knew it. They sang together: "Someone beckons me from heaven's open door, and I can't feel at home in this world, any mo-ore."

Maybeth looked at Dicey. "That's like Stewart's songs," she said.

"Who's Stewart?" Jeff asked. He was playing softly now, as if he didn't want ever to stop.

"Somebody we met last summer," Dicey answered. She pushed her lips together, because she wasn't going to say any more about it.

"Because of the way you say the words," Maybeth explained.

Mina looked at Jeff and shrugged. "Whatever they say, right?"

"Let's do it again," he suggested. "Maybeth, can you? Dicey?"

Maybeth could, but Dicey didn't remember the words yet, so she hummed along. Gram brought in a plate of warm cookies and sat down to join them, listening. Sammy perched himself on the arm of Gram's chair, like a pet watchdog, Dicey thought.

CHAPTER 9

Sammy ran up the street to meet Dicey as she rode to work the next Monday. It had rained the night before and he splashed in the puddles. The arms on his sweater flapped and his gait was awkward, as if his knees might at any time give out. It wasn't until he was close to her that Dicey saw why: he was laughing.

"You know what she did? She came to school. She beat—"

"Who?" Dicey interrupted. She gave him about half of her attention, glad that he was glad. The rest of her mind was trying to remember something about Miss Eversleigh, something that had begun to tickle at the edge of her memory while she was separating eggs today in home ec. But it had nothing to do with eggs, and how to beat the whites stiff, and how the yolks were rich in iron.

"Gram. Dicey, are you listening?"

Then Dicey did listen. "Gram? What about her?"

"I told you, she came to school. She had a bag of marbles, and they weren't new ones either. They were old. She said she found them in her attic and they must have belonged to one of her sons. She gave them to me!" he cried. "I left them safe with Millie, but she gave them to me. You can see them."

"So she brought you some marbles at school?" This was strange behavior.

"No, that's not what I said." Laughter poured out of Sammy's face, like lights from a firecracker. "It was at recess, lunch recess. And she played marbles with us. She won all of them, everybody's, even mine."

Dicey stopped walking and waited to hear the rest of this story. A couple of firecrackers were going off inside her head, too.

"She made us let some girls play too. And that got Ernie mad, but Gram said if he was going to play he was going to play fair or she wasn't going to be in any game with him. She was kneeling down, and her skirt got in a puddle."

"How did—did everyone play?"

"Everyone wanted to. They asked her to come back tomorrow, but she said she was the Lone Marble Ranger and only came once. So we better learn all we can." Dicey could picture her grandmother crouching down among the second graders, concentrating on the marbles.

"The Lone Marble Ranger." Sammy giggled. "So we did. And then she gave everybody back the marbles she won. Because she said she had so much more practice. Except me," he said, "she gave me her old ones."

"Good-o," Dicey said, that being about the only thing she could think of to say.

"Yeah," Sammy agreed. "And Custer said he wished he had a grandmother like that, and Ernie said he was glad he didn't have a crazy grandmother."

"And what did you say?" Dicey asked.

"Nothing. Why should I say something?" Sammy asked. "It was fun; I wish she would come back. They asked me, would she, and I said, 'No, Gram does just what she says she will.' But wasn't that a crazy thing for her to do?" he asked happily.

Crazy like a fox, Dicey thought, but did not say.

Gram had also been in to see Millie, and Millie had something to say about "Ab when she's up to something."

"What was she up to?"

"Dunno," Millie said. "But she made me laugh, I guess. She had that devilment look in her eye, and I guess I've seen it often enough to know what it means."

"What does it mean?" Dicey asked. But Millie couldn't tell her.

Dicey was washing the outside of the front windows, taking it slowly because the sun on her shoulders felt so good, when she felt somebody come stand beside her. Miss Eversleigh, in her same suit and pin, with her same teacher face. Dicey smiled at her. She couldn't help it: her mind was still on Gram beating all the second-graders at marbles.

"I didn't know you could smile," Miss Eversleigh remarked. Something about her tone of voice and her glance made Dicey remember.

"Miss Eversleigh." She dropped the squeegee into the bucket and dried her hands on her jeans. "I wanted to ask you. You were talking to us, but I wasn't listening. Last week? But I think I'd like to know what you said."

"I was talking to you," Miss Eversleigh said. "Mostly to you. I was talking about you."

"But what did you say?"

"Why do you ask?"

"Because I have a feeling I should have paid attention." That was as far as Dicey was willing to go. Miss Eversleigh pursed her lips.

"I said that it was important to learn the things we are doing in the class."

Then Dicey found she could remember. "Because they take skill. That's what you said, isn't it? You said it takes as much skill as building something."

Miss Eversleigh nodded. She was looking at Dicey as if she couldn't understand what Dicey was up to.

"Okay," Dicey said. "Thank you. I remember now. I never meant to be—disrespectful to you."

"And?" Miss Eversleigh insisted.

"And?" Dicey asked. She knew, though, what Miss Eversleigh wanted her to say. Instead she said, "I guess I think it's interesting to say that, and I'll think about it."

"But you won't try harder and care more?" Miss Eversleigh inquired.

"How can I say that? I haven't even thought about it yet."

"You're a strange child," Miss Eversleigh said. She was holding a purse in her two hands, right in front of her stomach.

"I guess so," Dicey agreed.

"Well. It was nice running into you," Miss Eversleigh said. She didn't sound like she thought it was nice.

Miss Eversleigh walked on down the street. Dicey forgot about her and turned back to her work. Maybe it *was* important to know how to do those things. If Gram didn't know them, where would the Tillermans be? Maybe Dicey ought to try to learn them. If you learned something, that didn't mean you had to do it. Just because you knew how to do it. All it meant was, if you had to, or if you wanted to, then you could.

When Gram put a tall apple pie down on the table for dessert, Dicey knew she was up to something. When Gram brought out a quart of ice cream to serve with the pie, Dicey was sure of it. Dicey sat quiet while the pie was cut and scoops of ice cream put on top of the flaky brown crust. The pie was still warm. You could tell because the ice cream slipped off the top and nestled down against the side of the slice. The apples inside smelled tart and sweet and had been cooked to a deep honey-brown color. Dicey put her nose over it and inhaled the aroma: apple, cinnamon, nutmeg.

"What did you do today?" she asked Gram. As if she didn't know.

Gram fixed her with a mischievous eye. "Not much. I changed the sheets and did a wash. I made a pie. I played a game or two of marbles—and won." She waited. Dicey didn't say a word, didn't let her face show any emotion. "As you undoubtedly heard," Gram said at last. Dicey grinned. "Then I picked up a few things at Millie's."

Dicey just waited. She was sure there was something more.

"And I had an appointment at the lawyers," Gram announced. "At which I was told that you are now, legally and officially and permanently—and any other lee they could think of—my responsibility."

"We're adopted?" James asked.

"That's what I said."

"No, it's not," he pointed out.

"Well it's what I meant and since you understood me it must be what I said."

The children looked at one another around the table. Gram looked at the pie she was eating.

"Good-o," Sammy said. "Good-o," he repeated.

"And we'll always live here?" Maybeth asked.

"You are my heirs and assigns," Gram said. "I thought it was good news," she declared.

"It is," Dicey said. That explained Gram's mood. Dicey herself had felt pretty good after hearing about the marble game. She felt pretty terrific now, knowing they were adopted. If this was really their home now—and it was—she could understand why she felt safe now, but why was she also feeling excited?

"I'm glad to hear that," Gram said to her, "because I also made a call today, since I was downtown and the weather was fair. I called to meet the family of your friend Mina."

"What?" Dicey said. Her fork clattered down onto the floor. She bent to pick it up.

"For the same reason that I took on the second grade at marbles," Gram pointed out.

Dicey didn't know what to think. She wondered what Mina's parents had made of Gram's visit. She couldn't think what Mina would have to report about the call.

As it turned out, Mina didn't have much to report. She told Dicey about it during lunch. "I don't know, Dicey, I don't know what got into her. What gets into her?"

"I don't know," Dicey said. Although she had some idea.

"They were confused," Mina told her. "They didn't know what to think. Do you know what she said to my father, first thing?"

"She didn't tell me anything," Dicey said. She wasn't sure whether she wanted to know or not.

"She said: 'I've come to put a face on the bogeyman.' What was Dad supposed to answer to that?"

"I dunno," Dicey mumbled. Gram certainly didn't beat around any bushes. Then laughter escaped her, even though she tried to hold it in. "I wish I'd been there."

"It went all right, I think," Mina admitted. "My mother said she's a lady, no question. Mom only says that about any white woman who doesn't ask if she does daily cleaning."

"Gram wouldn't do that," Dicey protested.

"She's a minority."

Dicey looked at her friend with an idea of the difficulties this girl might face; and she knew she had only the vaguest idea of them. Mina must know much, much more. "What are you going to do? What do you want to do?"

"When I grow up?" Mina asked, laughing. "Who knows? My mom's an RN, and there's always work. But I don't know—I'd rather be a doctor than a nurse, if I was going into medicine. I think I'm smart enough. What I want is—not to do something just because it's available to me because I'm black and female.

You know? I want to really choose. What about you?"

Dicey was surprised. "I've always been so busy trying to keep things together until tomorrow, I never thought about much else. I just do what needs to be done."

"I'm pretty sure I want to go to college," Mina continued. "What about you?"

"I told you, I never thought more than a day ahead."

They looked at each other with curiosity, with interest.

The world was full of surprises; and, Dicey began to believe, interesting surprises. It was mostly the people who made it surprising. Jeff—who waited for her after school and made it clear he intended to walk with her to work—reinforced that opinion.

Jeff carried his guitar slung over his back again. He put his books on top of Dicey's in the basket of her bicycle. He took her bicycle from her and wheeled it for her. It felt strange to Dicey to walk without anything to carry, without anything to push; with just the walking to do.

Jeff talked about how he had a good time at Dicey's house. He talked about the weather. He told her his father was a college professor and was gone three days a week, up to Baltimore to teach.

"Why do you live way down here?" Dicey asked.

Jeff shrugged. Something he didn't want to talk about.

Dicey changed the subject back to the singing they had done. "Maybeth liked it," she told him. "She liked you," she added, because it was the truth.

"Well," Jeff said. He looked at her with glances out of the side of his eyes, as if he was nervous.

"What's the matter with you?" Dicey finally demanded. They were standing beside the porch of Millie's store, and he wouldn't give her the bicycle so he could take his books out and let her get to work. She saw Sammy watching through the window.

"There's something I want to ask you—" he began.

Dicey knew what it was. "I said she likes you, and that means that any time you want to come back and sing with her it'll be fine. I didn't mean to be so—unfriendly. When you first got there. But she has to work hard at school, and she's taking piano lessons, so only on weekends. Okay?"

"But—" Jeff said. He swallowed and tried again. "There's a dance at school." Dicey nodded; she had seen the posters. "Will you go with me?"

Dicey's mouth opened. It opened and it stayed open. She grabbed for the handles of her bike. Jeff didn't look at her, just reached in for his books. What was she supposed to say?

"You haven't said," he prodded her.

"But I can't do that," Dicey told him.

"I didn't think so."

"Then why did you ask?" Dicey demanded.

"Because I want you to," he snapped back at her. "There's no crime in that," he pointed out.

Dicey liked the way he got angry when she was unfriendly. She didn't know why she liked it, but it made her willing to explain. "I'm—too young for dances. I'm only in eighth grade. I don't want to go to dances. And all. Besides," she added desperately, "high school boys don't take out eighth-graders."

"Who cares?" he asked.

Dicey couldn't answer that. Certainly she didn't. "I really am too young," she assured him. "Really."

At that, he smiled again. Good, Dicey thought, we can continue to be friends.

"But next year you'll be in ninth grade," he said.

"I think so."

"And I'll be in eleventh."

"You'd know more about that than I would."

"Ninth-graders are much older than eighth-graders."

"Are they?" Dicey asked. This was a pretty stupid conversation, but she was enjoying it.

"I'm going to ask you again next year," he said.

"Okay," Dicey answered. She leaned her bike against the window and went inside without looking back.

She didn't care if he asked her again next year, just as long as he didn't ask her again tomorrow. The last thing Dicey wanted to do was to go to a dance and jump and jiggle around, getting hot and sweaty. She was bored just thinking about it. On the other hand, she admitted to herself, it was nice he wanted to ask her, it was flattering. She was singing when she pulled the big broom out of the closet. "When first unto this country, a stranger I came."

"You're certainly cheerful today," Millie observed.

Mina, walking part of the way home with Dicey, said the same thing. Dicey was watching Sammy ride on ahead on her bike and circle back, then ride off ahead again. Mina said, "You haven't said anything sharp or cross for half a mile. Did Jeff ask you to the dance?"

"What do you know about that?" Dicey demanded.

Mina laughed. "That's more like it. I know I'll be going to it. I know Jeff asked me if I thought you'd go with him. I said probably not. He said he didn't think so either, but he thought he'd ask. Were we right?"

"Yeah," Dicey said. "Why should he ask you first?"

Mina shrugged. "He's smart enough—you're not an easy person, Dicey."

Well, that was no surprise, although it surprised Dicey that Mina thought so.

"I think he only asked you this time because he was afraid you'd get popular and he wanted you to know—"

"Never mind," Dicey said.

"But I don't think he needs to worry about that. I told him you're pretty strong meat."

"What does that mean?"

"You know perfectly well what it means, Dicey Tillerman."

Dicey guessed she did. And she guessed she liked that. "So are you," she pointed out.

"Yeah, but I've got charisma," Mina argued. "And I'm a clown. I'm much easier to take."

"If you think about it, everybody has something—wrong about them," Dicey said, following her own thoughts. "I mean, some flaw, or something you just don't like. But some people, it doesn't seem to matter so much. You know there're things wrong, but it's just part of them and you like them. And other people—no matter what, you won't like them. Take Millie. I started out disrespecting her, because she's not smart, not at all. But she's been a good friend to my grandmother—all her life, without changing—and she never asks anything much from anybody and—I don't know, now I think she's pretty unusual. Or Mr. Chappelle—especially these days—I mean, he acts like I can't do anything wrong. And that's not right, Mina. And the way he pussyfoots around me, it makes me sick. But I never liked him before and I never will."

"Or like blood relations, you always like them no matter how much you don't," Mina observed.

Dicey nodded enthusiastically. "But with other people, not family, you choose," she said. "What do you think? Do you think we choose people by what's important to us? Like whether someone's brave or not."

"So bravery is one of the things you choose by?" Mina asked.

"Sure," Dicey said. "And music."

"Music's not a quality," Mina protested.

Dicey noticed that Mina had them talking about Dicey again. She made a mental note to ask Mina what *she* chose by, but was too interested in her own ideas to do that right then. "It is too," Dicey insisted.

"You can't *be* music," Mina argued.

"But you have it, don't you?" Dicey asked. "Don't you?"

Mina started laughing instead of saying anything. "That's what I like about you, Dicey. With everybody else, they want to talk about boys, or clothes, having babies. You know?" Dicey didn't know. "But with you—"

"I don't know anything about boys, or clothes, or having babies," Dicey pointed out.

"But if you did you wouldn't talk about them the same way. I bet," Mina said.

Afterward, Dicey couldn't remember if it was that same afternoon, or another one, that she got home to find Gram slamming around the kitchen. When she tried to remember, she only knew that it came between Thanksgiving and Christmas, that day. If she could have, she would have thanked Momma for waiting so long, to give them time to get used to each other.

When she found Gram crashing piles of dinner plates down onto the counter and then angrily scrubbing out the cupboard with a sponge, Dicey figured the welfare check had arrived again. Whenever it came, Gram was in a bad mood for at least a day.

"I've been thinking," Dicey said to the stiff back. "It's only four and a half years before I can get a full-time job. Then we won't need any extra help from anyone."

Gram slammed the plates back in place and began pulling out glasses. When a glass shattered, she seemed satisfied rather than angry. "No, you won't. You're going to college, girl. Whether you like it or not."

"But—" Dicey said.

"I didn't, and your grandfather didn't. So you are. And James and probably Sammy too. There's to be no more talk about quitting school."

She jammed the broom into the closet and got back to the shelves.

"Did any of your children?" Dicey asked. She was playing for time, fishing around in her mind for some understanding of why her grandmother seemed so particularly het up.

"John did. Last I saw of him. He was gone and gone."

"Ah," Dicey said. Her grandmother's hair was slicked down, as if she had combed it with a wet comb.

"Now go get together some clothes," Gram said. She still didn't look at Dicey. "There's a suitcase in your room, I already put my stuff in it."

"But why?"

"We're going to Boston."

"To see Momma? But why? I'll miss school and work, and who'll take care of the little kids? Is something wrong?"

But Gram wouldn't answer her. She wouldn't answer any of them when they asked. Dicey thought it must be bad news and probably that Momma was worse (but how could she be worse?) or dead (but why would Gram take Dicey and go up to Boston if that was the case?). Sammy thought maybe Momma was better. Maybe coming home with them. James didn't say a word, but he agreed with Dicey, she could tell. Maybeth just sat quiet at the table. She had her hands clasped together in front of her, clasped tight.

Mr. Lingerle was going to drive Gram and Dicey to the airport in Salisbury, where they would take a plane to the airport in Baltimore, where they would try to get a plane to Boston. "We can't afford that," Dicey said.

"We're selling that wretched cranberry spoon," Gram told her. "It's not a vacation." She glared at Dicey.

Dicey packed underwear and her brown dress and a couple of blouses. She wore her jumper for traveling in. She put the few dollars she'd saved from her wages in the pocket of her jumper, just in case. She wished she knew what to expect, so she could begin getting ready; but Gram wouldn't say anything.

It was deep, hazy twilight when Mr. Lingerle drove them up in front of the little airport building. Gram had sat silent and hunched forward all the way up there. Neither Dicey nor Mr. Lingerle could think of anything to say, except when Mr. Lingerle looked at Dicey in the rear-view mirror and told her, "I'll call your school to tell them where you are."

At the airport, Gram burst out of the car and into the one-room building. Dicey and Mr. Lingerle hurried after her, not even bothering to park the car properly. Dicey carried the suitcase. The plane they were going to take was already outside, its two engines grinding, its two propellers turning. Mr. Lingerle came with them as far as a tall cyclone fence. "Mrs. Tillerman—Ab—" he said, awkward. "I just want to say, I'll take care of the kids. Don't worry on that score."

Gram turned a stony face to him. "I know that or I wouldn't have asked you."

She didn't say it very nicely, Dicey thought, but the effect on Mr. Lingerle was as if she had paid him a big compliment. He stood up a little straighter. He pulled an envelope out of his pocket.

"Here," he said. "Just in case."

"What is it?" Gram demanded.

"Some money," he told her. "You might need it if you're there long."

Dicey stood, biting her lip. The little windows in the plane shone yellow, and the air was filled with the noise of the engines. Purple twilight crowded down around them.

"I thank you," Gram said. She took the envelope and, without looking at it, put it into her purse. Then she wheeled around. "Come along, girl," she said. Dicey picked up their suitcase and followed her onto the plane.

There were only a couple of other people riding on that flight, two men in business suits who had papers spread in front of them. They drank something from short glasses and talked. Gram took a seat by the window. "You sit ahead of me, if you want to look out," she instructed.

A man in only the trousers and hat of a uniform, his plaid shirt unbuttoned at the neck and the sleeves rolled up, leaned over to tell them to strap themselves in. Dicey shifted the suitcase to the floor in front of the empty seat beside her and obeyed him. She'd never ridden in a plane before. She didn't know anything about what to do.

Nothing was what to do, apparently. The plane rocked along the ground for a while, then struggled up into the air. Below, looking out the window, Dicey could see scattered lights. Some of them were still, and those would be houses. Some of them moved, and those would be cars. After a few minutes, they were over the Bay. Night darkened around the humming plane.

The same man offered her coffee or tea, but she shook her head. She wasn't hungry or thirsty. She wasn't anything clear. She felt her grandmother's silent stony presence behind her, and Dicey wished she knew whatever it was Gram knew. She felt like she shouldn't be excited about flying, but her heart lifted with the plane, and her nose was pressed against the thick glass. She felt worried and depressed about this hasty journey, because it had to mean something bad. Something bad for Momma.

Unless Sammy was right, but then why was Gram so—angry? If Momma was going to come home, it would mean more expenses, and a lot more work for Gram. Until Momma could help. If it was good news, and Gram was trying not to be optimistic so she wouldn't be disappointed, she might act this way. You never could tell with Gram. You could trust her, but you couldn't tell.

Dicey turned her head to look at Gram through the narrow slot where her seat didn't meet the curved wall of the plane. Gram was staring out the window. She hadn't unbuckled her seat belt, she hadn't taken off her coat, she hadn't moved her purse off her lap. Her face was turned out the window, but Dicey bet she wasn't looking outside at anything. Every now and then, Gram blinked.

Dicey looked back out her own window. Below her, more lights, clustered together (towns or cities, she thought) and the long, snaky stream of red and white lights that marked highways. She smiled down at the moving picture, like some kind of Christmas display. She shouldn't be smiling, she thought, but it was so new a way of seeing things, and beautiful; she couldn't really help herself.

The airport at Baltimore was a huge, sprawling building. Gram and Dicey threaded their way through throngs of people. Dicey followed Gram, saying nothing. She stopped when Gram stopped, standing just behind her. Gram stopped first at an information booth to ask about flights to Boston, then hurried down a long hallway to the counter of an airlines. She bought two tickets for the 8:45 flight to Boston. One-way tickets. She checked in their suitcase. Then she led Dicey to a coffee shop and instructed her to order something to eat. "You've got to eat," she said.

Dicey asked for a hamburger and french fries. Gram asked for a pot of tea.

"And something to eat," Dicey told her. Gram snorted, looked at Dicey, and ordered an English muffin.

The plane to Boston was a large, a turbo-prop, Dicey read in the information folder. She settled herself into the seat by the window, with Gram beside her now. This plane had two propellers and two jet engines. Dicey watched the activity on the ground around them as they waited for take-off. Gram sat stiff beside her.

Dicey didn't know what she, Dicey, was doing here. She turned in the soft seat to ask her grandmother. They were rushing ahead, into the night, and Dicey really wanted to be back home, back in her own room with nothing more to think about than whether she had done her homework well enough. She felt like asking Gram to help her.

But help her with what?

"Gram?" Dicey said. Her voice croaked a little.

"They just called me this morning," Gram announced. Her mouth moved but none of the rest of her face did, and neither did her hands clasping the purse, nor her feet in stockings and loafers. Gram had placed her feet neatly side by side, like empty shoes in a closet.

Dicey wanted to say to Gram, Can I help you? But she couldn't do that; Gram wouldn't tell her. She sighed and put her nose back against the window.

The plane finally moved, taxied out of its parking slot and down to the end of a long runway marked by lights. When the big machine started down the runway, Dicey was pushed back in her seat by the speed. As it lifted off the ground, she could feel how it turned from heavy to light. She had a sensation of free flight. The plane soared up, and Dicey soared up with it.

"Can you *feel* that?" she said, without turning her head. Gram didn't answer.

A stewardess, with her face painted on and her hair painted down neat and her uniform as perfect as if it had been shellacked into position, brought them each a little plastic tray of juice and one pastry sealed into plastic. Gram also got a cup of tea.

Dicey ate the pastry, even though she wasn't hungry. She ate Gram's pastry too and drank both their glasses of oversweet juice. When the stewardess at last came back to take the trays, Dicey turned her attention back to the window.

If she had a map, she would know what those cities below were. If she had a map, she could trace their journey northward. If she had a map, then she would ask Gram about where they were, and the two of them could talk instead of each sitting there, locked into her own silence.

In Boston, Gram waited by the baggage claim, pointed out their suitcase to Dicey without a word, then strode out the exit to find a cab. She gave the driver an address. By that time, Dicey was getting sleepy, but she still wondered how Gram knew where she was going.

City streets passed by the cab windows, most of them empty of people but marked by the lit signs of stores and the illuminated plate glass display windows. Dicey felt the cold on the outside of the tightly closed car windows. Their driver was a dark shape at the front of the car. Gram was a dark shape beside her.

Gram took them to a motel, two stories high and with some cars parked in front of it. The motel faced onto a busy street. Gram went into the office, where she filled out a form and took a key. She led Dicey, whose hands felt too cold to retain their grip on the suitcase, up some stairs, and down an open walkway to a door. She opened the door.

The room was square and green. It had a huge TV set

attached by a chain to the wall, two beds, each covered by a green bedspread, and a table between them upon which a black telephone sat under a lamp.

Dicey put the suitcase down on the top of a low bureau. She caught sight of their reflection in the mirror over the bureau, both of them pale and stony-faced. Gram sat down on the bed, her purse still in her lap, her feet close together. She seemed to be thinking.

Dicey found the bathroom and used it. She thought about taking a shower, but decided she didn't want to. She returned to see Gram standing in a long flannel nightgown, about to get into bed. Gram had folded back the spread on Dicey's bed. Gram went into the bathroom.

Dicey stripped down to her underpants. For a top, she wore one of her shirts. Gram didn't say anything. When Dicey was settled in the strange bed, Gram reached over to turn out the lamp.

The room wasn't quite dark, because the light from the motel's fluorescent sign slipped in through a crack in the curtains. The noise from the highway outside pushed in too. Dicey lay on her back and looked up at the ceiling. "What about Momma?" she demanded harshly, across the darkness.

No sound marked her grandmother in her bed, as if Gram was lying like Dicey and staring at the ceiling.

"Gram?"

"Tomorrow," her grandmother said.

Gram woke Dicey the next morning. Dicey changed into clean underwear and a fresh blouse. She pulled on her high socks and tied her sneakers. She washed her face and brushed her teeth before putting on her jumper. Gram was entirely dressed by the time she had finished, dressed and standing by the door. Dicey grabbed her jacket. Gram wore an old blue wool coat, with big round buttons up the front, which hung tired from her shoulders.

They had a quick breakfast in a coffee shop just down the street. Then Gram headed up past the motel, walking so fast Dicey had no time to notice what they were walking past. "How do you know where you're going?" she panted. Her breath came out of her mouth like smoke. She jammed her hands into her pockets and noticed how white and cold Gram's fingers looked on the hand holding the purse.

"He gave me directions."

"Who?"

"The doctor."

Two blocks up from the motel and one block off the busy street, Gram mounted cement steps to a square brick building. She entered through the heavy wooden doors that swung out into the cold. Each door had a green wreath on it.

Dicey scurried after her. Why had Gram told her to come along, she wondered angrily. She might as well not be there, for all the attention her grandmother paid to her.

The building looked like it had once been a school. It had a broad central corridor. A woman sat at a long desk in the middle of this, with chairs lined up in rows on either side of her. All of the chairs were empty. Gram marched up to the woman. "I'm Abigail Tillerman," she said.

The woman's face registered no expression. She was a soft-looking woman, with her hair in white waves and a light sweater over her creamy blouse. Her nails gleamed pink. "Yes?" she asked politely.

"My daughter—" Gram began.

Understanding flashed across the woman's face. She put one hand on the phone beside her. "Yes, of course, Mrs. Tillerman. Dr. Epstein is expecting you. You'll want to go down the hall, take the second door on your left, and the fourth door on your right after that."

"I want to see my daughter," Gram said.

"But Dr. Epstein—and it's not visiting hours—" the woman mumbled. She still had her hand on the phone. Then she said, "All right. The little girl can wait down here. It's the fourth floor, the ward on your left. I'll call up to tell them to expect you. The elevators are back by the entrance, you can't miss them."

"The little girl," Gram said, "will come with me."

Dicey almost smiled in her relief at Gram acting normal again.

"If you insist," the woman said. Her worried eyes went from Gram to Dicey and back to Gram.

Gram didn't say anything.

"They're self-service elevators," the woman said weakly.

It was a large elevator, about as big as Dicey's bedroom at home. Two young men in white pants and doctors' shirts were on it, but they didn't say a word and got off at the third floor. Dicey and Gram got off at the top and walked down a central hallway that matched the one downstairs. The linoleum had been laid on in blocks and worn down colorless. The place smelled of cleansing liquid and the empty hall reverberated with muffled sounds.

As they came to a set of glass-topped swinging doors, a nurse came through them. She stepped out into the hallway. Her uniform was crisp, and she wore a white cap on top of her brown hair. She had a heavy, strong face. "Mrs. Tillerman? I'm Preston, the floor nurse." Her voice was soft and sweet, like a summer breeze. As soon as she heard the nurse's voice, Dicey felt better, as if things couldn't be so bad after all. Preston's voice didn't match at all with her face or her mottled red hands. It would be soothing to hear her voice, Dicey thought. If you were sick.

"And you must be the oldest girl, Dicey, wasn't it?" Preston asked. Dicey looked up, and then looked down again. Her tongue was twisted in her mouth, but she couldn't answer.

"Just come with me then," Preston said.

It was a big room, where the light was tinged with yellow from the yellow shades halfway down over the windows. After the nurses' desk, with a counter and a phone, with cabinets filled with bottles, the room was filled with beds in rows. Each bed was surrounded on three sides by curtains.

Some of the beds had people lying flat in them. Some had people drawn up, knees drawn up, hands drawn up around knees, bodies drawn up back against the headboards. One of the figures, which Dicey saw out of the corner of her eye as they walked past, was so small she couldn't help staring at it. It was a kid, a little kid about as big as Sammy. The little figure curled back against the pillows, staring blankly ahead. Dicey had never seen anybody so still, not even Sammy deep asleep.

"Here we are," Preston said. She stood aside.

Gram went to one side of the bed. Dicey stood at the foot. Inside her, her heart was squeezed tight against her chest. She stood and stared. Her heart was squeezed so tight it broke into pieces, sharp pieces that cut against her lungs and throat and stomach.

Momma.

CHAPTER 10

Momma lay absolutely still, with her arms down beside her body. The veins along the back of her hands stood out blue. The sheets were pulled up over her chest. Her neck looked small, too small to ever have held up her round head. Her head lay back on the pillow, surrounded by an aureole of honey-colored hair. The bones in her cheeks and her forehead and along her jaw were covered by such thin skin that it looked like a pale veil fitted around her, not like skin at all. She lay still, absolutely still.

Dicey could see the fresh white sheets rise and fall, just slightly, as Momma breathed.

Well, Dicey said to herself, she'd known it was bad news. She could see what was happening, and she knew why Gram had rushed up here. Momma was dying.

Dicey felt herself begin to shake, inside where it didn't show to anyone. Gram stood at the side of Momma's bed, looking down at her, as motionless as her daughter. Dicey stood at the foot of the bed, shaking so hard the pieces of her heart almost made a noise she could hear. Nobody moved. Nobody said anything. Dicey stared at the blank face, willing Momma to open her eyes and look at them.

Gram didn't say a word, but when Dicey looked back at her she had tears coming out of her eyes and sliding down her cheeks. Dicey wanted to say something to her, but she couldn't think of what to say. It wasn't like Gram to cry.

You don't know anything about her, really, Dicey shouted to herself inside her head. *You don't know what she expected to find up here, yet you don't know what she's thinking about.*

Preston came to put a chair down beside Gram. She handed Gram a tissue. Gram wiped her eyes and blew her nose. She took off her coat and put her purse on the floor. She sat down on the chair. Preston put another chair on the other side of Momma, and Dicey moved stiffly over to sit on it. After that, they were alone in the thick silence of the ward, Gram and Dicey, and Momma.

Gram reached out for one of the still hands. She held it in both of hers. "Oh Liza," she said. Dicey had never heard anything sadder than her grandmother's voice.

"I have them with me, Liza," Gram said, in the same voice. "They're all home with me. Dicey and James, Maybeth and Sammy. I'll take care of them, I promise you. I wish you had come with them. I wish you had come home years ago. I miss you. I missed you the day you left, and every day since then."

She stopped, took a breath, then started talking again. "I've got Dicey here with me now," she said. She talked and talked, about the children and what they looked like. She told about how they had arrived. She talked about what they were doing in school, at home. Dicey watched Momma's unresponding face and did not listen.

Dicey felt as if she was broken into pieces and didn't know how to gather herself together again. She was angry at herself about this. It wasn't as if she hadn't expected bad news. It wasn't as if she had ever expected to see Momma again, not after the way Momma had wandered off and forgotten them. There was no reason for Dicey to feel so sad and hurt.

Dicey unbuttoned her jacket. She was too cold to take it off, but the air in this room was close and stale and choking. The curtains that separated their narrow cubicle from all the other narrow cubicles were white, faded to pale yellow.

Momma's eyelids never moved. Her pale eyelashes rested on her cheeks. Maybe, Dicey thought to herself, while Gram's voice talked on, maybe it was so hard because this was really Momma, not some idea of her. All the time Momma had been gone, Dicey had carried around an idea of her. The idea was of Momma sleeping, and behind that were all the ideas of Momma that Dicey had saved up over her life. But idea wasn't the same as real, and real hurt.

Because she remembered Momma moving around. She remembered Momma's voice singing. She remembered Momma's eyes looking glad or worried, or laughing. She remembered Momma bringing Sammy home from the hospital. Momma was tired, then, and worried about how to take care of them; but she was still glad to have Sammy, and James and Maybeth and Dicey too. Momma loved her children. You could tell in the way her hands rested on their heads. (Dicey could still recall the feeling of Momma's hand resting on her head.) And in her voice when she talked to them. You could tell in how long she tried, how hard she worked.

Dicey wondered if Momma had known that she was worked out, and tired out. If she had felt herself crumbling at the edges and that was why she had started them on the road to Bridgeport. Trying to get them to a safe place before she crumbled away.

A hot flame of anger shot through her: Momma was good, and she didn't deserve to be dying here. She deserved to be with her family, at Gram's house, seeing how things were working out all right. There was no call for Momma to die, no reason for it, no good to come of it.

". . . paper mulberry tree," Gram was saying. Dicey caught the words. "You remember that, surely. Where John built you the platform so you could get away when they got too rough for you. Your brothers, your father, your mother, too. I remember that. That was a fine thing John did, I thought. And telling Bullet never to go up there, because it was your place. He stood up to your father, too, and made him give the lumber.

"Your father is dead. He's buried next to Granny—you remember, in the cemetery by the Methodist church where we used to take flowers. It was a heart attack. Quick, and that's good. Bullet too—he's dead too. In Vietnam. They said, should they send him home, and I said, 'Why bother now. What difference would it make.' John was gone by then. After he took that job in California he just stayed out there. I guess. He sent me an announcement, about getting married—oh, years ago, and we didn't answer. I have it somewhere. There have been sad times, Liza."

The body on the bed made no response.

"But good times too. Then, and now again, with your children. I was alone for a long time, and there were good times in that, too. I keep thinking."

Preston's voice interrupted Gram. "Dr. Epstein's here. Mrs. Tillerman?"

Gram lifted her head. "I don't want to leave her alone."

"It doesn't matter to her," Preston said. Her voice made the words gentle.

"It does to me. Stay with your momma, girl," Gram said to Dicey.

Dicey nodded. Gram let go of the hand she had been holding. She put the arm down flat and got up. Dicey reached out to take the hand on her side of the bed. It was cool, unresponsive. She leaned over toward her mother's still face and began to talk. "Momma? We're fine, really. We're going to live with Gram."

Somehow holding onto the hand, she had the same impulse Gram had had, to talk. Talk was reaching out to the form on the bed, even though you knew it couldn't be called back. Dicey began to tell her mother what had happened to them, after the last time they had seen her.

After a while, Gram came back and sat down again. She looked at Dicey across the bed. "You might want a word with him yourself," she said. "She's dying."

"I can see that," Dicey snapped.

Gram just nodded, and that made Dicey sorry she'd snapped. But she didn't know how to say so to Gram. Gram opened her purse and took out her wallet. She gave Dicey five twenty-dollar bills and the key to the motel room. Dicey took them in her hand.

"It's almost Christmas," Gram said. "See if you can find something for your brothers and sister." She looked down at Momma's face. "Have a good walk. If you find something for yourself . . ." Her voice drifted away. She reached out and took up Momma's hand again. She glanced at Dicey. "I knew this was going to happen. But still . . ."

Dicey sat, her hand clutching the money and key.

"Get off now, girl. There's nothing to be done here. Nothing but wait."

Dicey fled. Outside, in the corridor, a doctor stood. He was smoking on a thin cigar. He wore a white coat and was a slim, mouse-faced man. Dicey was about to turn down the hall to the elevator when he said her name. "Dicey Tillerman?"

She went over to him. All she really wanted was to get away and walk fast. There was pain in her that needed walking out, or burning out. Because it was Momma lying there in that bed, far away and going farther.

"Did your grandmother tell you?"

Dicey nodded, biting her lip.

"We did everything that could be done with the resources we have. She never really responded. She was undernourished, too, when she arrived here. Maybe she'd starved herself. She never *tried.* Never responded to any treatment, medical or psychiatric. We're surprised she even held on this long." He sighed. He seemed to want to say something that would comfort. Or something that would explain. "Maybe it's better this way," he said lamely.

Dicey could feel her eyes burning up at him. She wanted to ask, *Why? How?* How could someone die of just being crazy, the kind of sad, faraway craziness that Momma had?

But he didn't seem to know what else he wanted to say. He drew back, away from her, as if he was afraid she might hurt him. Dicey almost told him not to worry, the only person she was hurting was herself. But she didn't feel like bothering.

"I don't know why your grandmother insisted on coming up," he complained.

Dicey waited.

"Believe me," he said, almost pleading. "It *is* better this way."

Dicey just stared at him; and then she walked away.

She burst out of the building. She hadn't buttoned her coat and the air was freezing cold. At the sidewalk, she stopped to push the big buttons through their holes and to look around her. Her fingers were numbed by the air, and she noticed a rim of dirty gray snow by the side of the road. Pieces of paper blew around on the sidewalk until they came to the edges of the buildings. There they nestled up forlornly.

Dicey didn't have a hat or mittens, she didn't have shoes that kept the cold from coming up through the soles of her feet. The icy wind stung at her cheeks. That was all right with her. She had an angry fire now, inside of her. She didn't know who she was angry at, that doctor, or the whole hospital, or even Momma. She had trouble breathing deeply as she strode along, with her head down against the wind. And she was angry at herself too: because it wasn't as if she hadn't guessed this, it wasn't as if she'd ever thought Momma would come back. So why should it bother her so much? She was being stupid. She didn't believe that Momma had meant to go away like this, she didn't think that Momma wanted to.

But just the same, she had.

Dicey wasn't hungry so she turned down a street that had a lot of stores on it. She had a pocketful of money. She didn't know why Gram had given her so much. Probably it was a mistake.

Dicey walked down the street, fast, looking in the windows. Then she walked up the street. People jostled past her, but she couldn't be bothered to get out of their way. If someone shoved her she shoved back, not looking.

This street had small stores. Dicey went into a toy store, where Christmas carols filled the air inside. It had dolls and games, stuffed animals and building sets and airplanes, toys that little children could pull, and wooden trucks painted in bright colors. She thought Maybeth might like a fancy doll, but she couldn't find one that didn't have an empty, simpering face. Some of the dresses the dolls wore were beautiful and fancy, but all of their faces had blinking round eyes and little turned-up noses, and if they were real faces you wouldn't ever like those people. Dicey couldn't buy something like that. She thought James might like a game, but she didn't know what except maybe chess. Chess was for smart people. But the chess sets had lightweight plastic pieces, and she didn't like that. She thought Sammy might like a teddy bear, but she thought he wouldn't like to be given one.

How was she supposed to buy these things? Dicey demanded, her anger spreading to include Gram. And they should be buying something they needed.

They were always buying things they needed, Dicey thought angrily to herself, leaving the toy store abruptly.

She looked in the window of a store that sold things made out of wood. There was a huge toy train, with an engine and a coal car and a passenger car and a freight car and a caboose; it was big enough to let a little kid push it along with his feet as he rode on it. The grain in the wood swirled around. It reminded Dicey of the sailboat, and she knew that if she went inside and touched the sides of the train cars, they would have the same silky feel as the sides of the boat that Sammy had sanded down for her. Standing up on racks, a couple of wooden plates next to a wooden goblet caught her eye. It wouldn't be bad, Dicey thought, to eat off wooden plates. They were surely pretty, with a deep, polished gleam to them. She wondered what would happen if she didn't paint the sides of her boat. She had a glimpse of how it might look, bobbling beside the dock with the sails rolled up and the wooden hull shining. She guessed she would have to varnish it, and varnish cost more than paint.

The next store she went into was for ladies. She went in because her hands were cold and she saw gloves in the window. The pair she liked weren't fancy, just plain leather. Inside, when a woman with a doubting face approached her, Dicey asked to see them. She slipped her hands into them. The gloves were lined with something warm and woolly. On the outside, they were soft brown leather, and the thick seams looked strong. Dicey looked at her own hands and measured with her memory's eye. They would fit Gram.

The woman said they cost fourteen dollars. Dicey had eighteen dollars of her own money, back in the motel room. She wanted those gloves, and they were practical too. She wanted them for Gram's hands when her fingers turned white with cold.

She wanted to give something to Gram, not at Christmas but right away.

Somehow, carrying the bag holding the box with Gram's gloves, Dicey felt a little better. She began to think about the little kids and what they might like getting. When she saw a secondhand bookstore, she went in. James always liked books. If she could find something old and thick. Old books didn't cost as much as new books.

The air in the store was dusty and warm. A young man sat by a cash register at the front, his feet looped into the bars of a tall stool. He was wearing scuffed boots, and seeing them reminded Dicey of her own cold feet. She stamped on the floor and peered into the room. Rows and rows of bookcases made alleyways down the long room. The young man was reading. Dicey started down one row.

Paperbacks, regular hardbound books, fancy leather ones, one after the other, like stalks of corn in a field: how was she supposed to know what James would like? She had never heard of any of these stories, or any of these writers. She bet even James hadn't.

Dicey reached up and pulled down one book. She chose it because it was bound in red leather. When she looked inside, it was in a language she'd never seen before. Not English. She put it quickly back and moved on.

She would go up and down every row, she decided, and maybe something would catch her eye and if it did maybe she would buy it. But she wanted to be sure it was something James would like. It was warm and quiet in the store; nobody paid any attention to her. It was like Momma's hospital in a way, with the books lined up like patients. You didn't know what was inside them.

Dicey wondered if James knew how very many books there were in the world. She guessed maybe he did. Every now and then she pulled one down to just look at it. The only book that she could recognize as interesting was a big book of songs, with piano music. She studied that for a long time, turning the pages and looking at the pictures. She had heard of about half the songs. Some of the others had words she liked. But James wouldn't want a song book. She slipped it back into place, sighed, and went on down another aisle.

She was partway down the last aisle when she had a sudden idea. In the toy store, there were planes you shot from catapults with elastics. The planes had broad white wings and shiny red fuselages. She could see Sammy playing with one of those, out front by the paper mulberry, making the plane soar and swoop. She grabbed the bag that held Gram's gloves and hurried outside again. She hurried so fast she almost stepped into a puddle of ice-frosted water at the curb.

In the toy store, children and their mothers were crowding around the shelves. It was a tiny store, bright with the colors of the paints and bright with the music of Christmas carols. Most of the people in it were young. They talked and quarreled, they laughed when they found something they liked. Some of the women had long lists they would take out and study.

Dicey went back to where she had seen the planes on display. They were plastic, but not the same kind of light plastic as the chess game. If there was such a thing as fancy plastic, that was what these planes were. She picked one up and felt its balance in her hand. It had long tapering wings; probably so that it could sail out farther. She looked at the way the catapult worked, and that, too, seemed strong. Then she looked at the prices.

Thc littlest plane cost five dollars, the middle size cost ten, the large one cost fifteen. Fifteen dollars for a toy—you'd have to be pretty rich to be able to spend that much money on a toy. But in comparison, the littlest plane looked too small, meager. Dicey took the middle size.

The girl behind the counter gave her only one, harried, glance before she filled out the receipt and put the plane and catapult into a box. She put in a big elastic too, and took Dicey's money.

"What if the elastic breaks?" Dicey asked.

"It won't."

"How do you know?" Dicey asked.

Instead of getting angry, the girl smiled. She took the top off the box and put in two more elastics. She put the top back on and answered, "Because I have one myself, at home."

"Oh," Dicey said. "Thank you," she said.

"It'll last," the girl assured her.

Dicey nodded. After the warmth in there, maybe because they sold toys, the street seemed even dingier and colder. Dicey went down past the wood store again, and then back to the bookstore. There she bought the big songbook for Maybeth. She knew what James would say, that Maybeth couldn't read it. "So what?" Dicey answered inside her head. "She can read the music, and besides, I thought you said her reading was improving, and I bet she can, anyway." The book cost nine dollars, and Dicey was surely surprised by that, because, after all, it was old. But it was what she wanted to give Maybeth. It was what she was sure Maybeth would like.

Dicey felt as if she was a million miles away from the hospital. And that felt better.

The next store she went into was the wood store again. A man with a beard was reading a magazine behind a glass-topped counter. Dicey went right up and asked him, "Do you have chess games made out of wood?"

She was finished with her question before he had finished

lifting his face to look at her. He pushed his glasses up on top of his head. All he did was nod, yes.

Dicey was about to ask him how much they cost when he stood up straight and moved slowly to the opposite side of the store. He took down a box and opened it.

The top of the box slid back, in grooves. The box was roughly made. It hadn't been sanded smooth, or waxed. The chess pieces lay jumbled together inside. Dicey picked a couple out and looked at them. They weren't fancy, but they felt warm in her hand. Some were stained black, some were left a plain, pale white. A lot of them were little round-topped figures, just the right size to hold between your fingers. Some had been carved into rough statuettes. Dicey thought she recognized a tower for a castle and two tall figures, one a man, one a woman. He named them the king and queen; he named knights and bishops, pawns, rooks. The details weren't carefully cut, but you couldn't confuse the pieces. "I get these from Mexico," he explained.

"Are there any made here?" Dicey asked.

He tapped his finger on the top of the counter, pointing her attention below. There, a set of wooden chess pieces was arranged for play on a wooden board. These pieces had been carved, but not stained. One of the woods was a rich brown color, like tea. The other was a pale, shining gold. Dicey could see the points on the queen's crown and the flowered embroidery along the foot of her robe. The knights rode rearing horses, and on their shields Dicey could see dragons with long twisting tails.

"It's beautiful," she said, crouching down to see closer.

"Thank you," he answered, and she knew he had made it himself.

"How much is it?" she asked.

"Six hundred."

Dicey looked up, then asked how much the Mexican set was. "Fifteen," he told her.

She told him she'd take one, and said she wished she could buy the beautiful set.

"I'm not sure I want to sell it," he told her.

"You could make another," Dicey told him. "Couldn't you?" she asked.

"Of course, but each time—the wood is different. Look," he said. He pulled over a rack on which hung a dozen bracelets, each made out of a circle of wood. The man was right, each bracelet was entirely different, even though they were all exactly the same. On some of them the grain of the wood made designs that looked almost like carvings. Some of the woods were light and shone as if from inside; some glowed golden, as if late afternoon sunlight was shining on them; and some were dark and had a gleam like a field freshly turned over for planting. She reached out to touch them.

There was one she especially liked, a ring of golden wood with a dark grain. "Oak," he told her, before she asked. He took it off the rack and handed it to her.

Dicey held it in her fingers, feeling how smooth it was and studying the deep glow in the wood. She wondered if anyone ever made boats out of such wood as this.

"It's four dollars," he said. "Try it on."

"Oh, it's not for me," Dicey told him. She was thinking of Maybeth, and she didn't know why because she had already bought a present for Maybeth. But the wood seemed so beautiful to her that she knew Maybeth would like it. Then she recognized the similarity: the wood had the colors of Momma's hair. And if she was going to spend fifteen dollars on James, she should spend that much on Maybeth too, because that was fair. And she could feel how Maybeth would like the bracelet and would always keep it. She decided to buy it.

While he added up her bill, Dicey looked around the shop. He made boxes in all sizes, the way he made bracelets. They were simple boxes with lids that fit down over the tops. But all of them had been constructed out of a variety of woods, and the woods seemed to fit together as the pieces of a patchwork quilt do. The different woods talked together, Dicey thought, looking at them; only it was more like singing in harmony than conversation. The man also made little figures of raccoons and birds, rabbits and—something that had to be a chicken pecking at the ground for food.

"Wait," Dicey said, crouching down again. He came slowly back toward her. "Is that a chicken?"

He looked where she was looking. He took a maddeningly long time doing anything, answering any questions, Dicey thought. "Do you want to hold it?" Dicey nodded.

Dicey held the little carving in her hand. It made her smile, the busyness of that chicken, determined to eat and eat and do nothing else. The chicken looked cross, its feathers ruffled and fluffed out. It wouldn't be easy to live with that chicken.

He watched her studying it. "I meant to carve a jay," he said slowly, "but that piece of wood just wanted to be a chicken."

"I think," Dicey said, "that's the way with chickens."

"It's four dollars too," he said. "Do you want it?"

"Yes," Dicey said quickly, thinking of Sammy and how he would laugh. The man turned the carving over and pulled off a price tag. Dicey thought the price tag said something with two numbers, and she looked at his face. He was rolling the tiny square of paper in his hand. He knew she'd seen.

"You liked it, you saw right away what it is," he told her.

"My little brother keeps pestering us to get him some chickens," Dicey explained.

"Ah, then you don't live around here. In the city."

"No, in Maryland."

"Maryland? What are you doing up here?"

Dicey stared at him. "My momma's in the hospital," she said shortly.

"And you're doing some Christmas shopping while your father visits her."

"It's my grandmother," Dicey told him. She didn't have to tell him anything, and she didn't really want to. But it was so hard to say—she was talking about as slowly as he did. If it was so hard to say she thought she ought to say it. Because not saying it wasn't going to change anything.

"Everything going to be all right?" he inquired. He didn't ask to be nosy, but to tell her he sympathized with her. Dicey heard that in his voice.

"No," she answered, her throat tight and the pieces of her heart squeezing again.

He put down his sales pad and lay his pencil beside it. He folded his fingers together, and Dicey could see how they were covered with cuts. Old cuts and new ones. "I'm sorry to hear that," he said slowly. Dicey nodded and blinked her eyelids, fast. "I'm sorry the world is the way it is and always has been. It's not easy, is it?"

"How could it be?" Dicey snapped.

"I can imagine how it could. Can't you?" he asked her seriously.

And Dicey could, but it wasn't true, so that didn't make any difference.

"I tell myself," he said, "that it's like the wood. Sometimes, things just have to happen, it just has to be the way it turns out. Are you old enough to have something you tell yourself?"

That surprised Dicey. She swallowed, remembered, and nodded her head. "I saw a tombstone, once. It had—'Home is the hunter, home from the hill, and the sailor home from the sea.'"

He studied her face for a long time, and then didn't say any more, as if she had answered his question and he didn't have anything else to ask. Dicey didn't wonder about this, as she paid her bill and took the bag into her hand. She had just made up her mind about something.

Momma was going to come home with them. No matter what, she wouldn't leave Momma up here.

Dicey dropped the packages off at the motel and ate a quick supper in the coffee shop. Then she went back to the hospital. She didn't ask anybody permission, she just got right on the elevator and rode up to the fourth floor. She went right through the big doors and down the aisle to where Momma lay.

Gram sat in the same chair, holding onto the same hand. She was talking softly, but she stopped when Dicey stood at the foot of the bed.

"She's coming home with us," Dicey said.

"I know," Gram answered, tired. "I've promised her. I promise you."

Dicey sat down in her own chair. She unbuttoned her coat. "You should have something to eat," she told Gram. "It's getting dark. It's cold."

Gram stood up stiffly. Dicey took Momma's limp hand in her two chilly ones. She began to talk to Momma's empty moon face.

When Gram got back she told Dicey she was going to spend the night at the hospital. Preston would walk Dicey back to the motel, and she was waiting downstairs, and Dicey should hurry because the nurse had stayed late just to see Dicey safely back. Dicey didn't argue. Preston, hurrying beside her down the dark streets, asked if she'd be worried about staying alone in a motel room. Dicey wasn't worried, why should she be? She watched TV for a while, but it was stupid so she turned it off and got into her bed. Then she hopped out to put the box with Gram's gloves in it into the pocket of her jacket, so she wouldn't forget them in the morning. Back in bed, she turned out the light and slept.

When Dicey arrived back at the hospital the next morning, the receptionist hurried down the hall to meet her before she had a chance to get on the elevator. But all the woman said was, "Are you going up?"

Dicey didn't answer, just stepped into the machine.

Preston stood with Dr. Epstein when she got off, and they, too, seemed to be waiting for her. But they didn't say anything.

Gram sat by Momma's bed, her face gray with fatigue. But she wasn't holding Momma's hand and Momma wasn't breathing under the smooth sheets. "She's dead now," Gram said. "At about dawn. I wanted to wait until you could make your farewells."

Dicey nodded. She came up close to kiss Momma's cool forehead and to brush her sad, short hair. She felt Gram move out of the cubicle as she whispered good-bye from all of them. When Dicey was back in the pale yellow aisle with Gram, she saw that Gram was just standing there. As if Gram didn't know what to do.

"Oh Gram," Dicey said. Whatever Gram might think, Dicey went up and put her arms all the way around her. They were of a height, she noticed. They didn't cry, they just stood there, holding onto one another, holding close. Dicey could feel how strong Gram's arms were, and how strong were her own. Strong and warm.

"You have to let go," Gram said harshly, in Dicey's ear. But she didn't loosen her arms. "You have to and I have to."

Dicey understood. It was Momma they had to let go of.

"I don't want to," she answered softly.

Gram pulled her head back so she looked into Dicey's face. "Neither do I," she said. "But I will, and so will you. Because if you don't—let go—it can make you crazy." Dicey just stood there. "Are you listening to me, girl?" Gram demanded.

Dicey nodded. Gram's hand patted her back and that reminded Dicey. "I got you some gloves," she said. She took the box out of her pocket and handed it to Gram.

"Why'd you do a thing like that?" Gram demanded. "You don't know my size, and where'd you get the money?"

Dicey understood Gram's anger and let it wash over her. "Open it," she told Gram. They were standing in the watery light as if they were alone. Gram took the top off the box.

"Well," Gram said. She took the gloves gently out of the box and stroked the leather with her fingertips. Dicey watched. She knew now why she had wanted to give them to Gram right away: she wanted to give Gram some of the feelings of yesterday afternoon. Because yesterday afternoon, buying presents and thinking about her family, Dicey had felt better. She hadn't forgotten, but she had remembered other things as well.

"Yes, I like them, you know that," Gram snapped. She slipped one on, then pulled it off. She folded the gloves carefully and put them into her purse. Then she reached out to take Dicey's hand. "Let's finish this business and get home," she said.

CHAPTER 11

The four of them stood in the hallway, Gram and Dicey, Preston, Dr. Epstein. Nobody knew what to say.

"I'm sorry," Dr. Epstein said at last. His hands moved nervously, and Dicey bet he would have liked to light one of his little cigars. His eyes flickered away from theirs. "It's for the best. Some of our cases linger on for years."

Gram cut him off. "I appreciate all you've done," she said briskly. "And you, as well," she said to Preston.

"Now about the arrangements," Dr. Epstein began.

"We'd like to take her back with us," Gram said.

A frown crossed his face. "But I understood that she lived in Massachusetts. I understood when she was first identified . . ." His voice tapered off, then ceased. "Ordinarily, Mrs. Tillerman, the charity cases are given over to medical research when . . ."

Dicey felt the heat of Gram's anger and saw, out of the corner of her eye, Gram's chin lift.

"Yes?" Gram asked.

The doctor did not like this conversation.

"The expense," he said. "The undertaker, shipping the coffin—down to Maryland, isn't it? I don't think you can pay for it—unless, of course, our records are mistaken."

"How much would it be?" Gram asked.

"I don't think it could cost you less than seven hundred

dollars," Dr. Epstein answered. His mouth pursed, as if he didn't like to talk about money.

Dicey's heart fell. Seven hundred dollars. They would never have that much money, not for something that wasn't necessary. Then she noticed something: her heart was back in one piece. How had that happened? It wasn't that she didn't feel sad. She felt sad enough, and sad in a way she'd never felt before. Because now Momma was really gone for always. Dicey must have let go and never known it.

"Unless she were cremated," Preston said. She spoke to the doctor, as if she were suggesting that to him. He shrugged. "If you were to have her cremated and carried her with you," Preston said to Gram in her gentle voice.

"Not to mention burial expenses," Dr. Epstein remarked.

"In Maryland, a cremated body can be buried wherever you want," Gram announced. "Thank you," she said to Preston. "I wonder if you can recommend an undertaker."

"You'll see to all this?" Dr. Epstein asked the nurse. She nodded, not speaking. He shook hands with Gram. He nodded to Dicey and strode importantly off down the hall.

Preston gave them the name of an undertaker. She didn't say anything sympathetic, didn't apologize, didn't try to make them feel better. She just helped, as much as she could, telling them how to find the undertaker's, telling them that the undertaker would come to pick up Momma and thanking them for coming to be with Momma.

When they stepped out onto the sidewalk, Gram halted. She opened her purse, took out her new gloves, and put them on her hands. She breathed in deeply. "The air stinks," she remarked. They set off together.

The undertaker, who wore a dark suit and a solemn expression, received them in his office. He sat behind his desk and filled out forms while Gram gave him information. "I should tell you," he said, "that Miss Preston called. She thought you would want to expedite the cremation. I have already dispatched a vehicle to pick up the deceased."

"That's right," Gram said.

Dicey tried to think of Momma as the deceased and not as Momma. Gram reached out to take her hand and held onto it. Dicey held on back.

"What will the charge be," Gram asked.

"There is a minimum charge of three hundred and fifty dollars. Then the urn, of course."

Dicey looked up, surprised.

"In which to place the ashes," he explained to her. "We have a good selection. If you will choose the one you want, you can return to pick her up at"—he looked at his wristwatch and consulted a paper on his desk—"three o'clock."

But when they studied the urns, Dicey couldn't see any she wanted, not for Momma. Some were tall china ones with dark flowers on them. Some were cold metals, silver and brass. Some were plain white china and looked like vases. Dicey didn't say anything, however. It wasn't as if she could pay for any one of them. She stood back and waited.

"No," Gram muttered to herself. "No and no and no." She looked at Dicey and spoke grimly. "Not for Liza."

"But if we're supposed to let go," Dicey said, because it was what she had been thinking to herself.

"I'm willing to let go," Gram declared, "because I have to. But I am not going to lose my grip on—on what's right."

"That doesn't make sense," Dicey pointed out.

"I don't care. Haven't you got any ideas, girl?"

Well, of course, Dicey did. She had an idea of a box made from many different kinds of wood. She had an idea of the warm brown tones, of the careful workmanship, of the patient sanding smooth. She had an idea of something made by those slow hands, those hands marked by the work they did. But she had no idea of what such a box would cost.

"I was in a store yesterday," she said to Gram. She was going to say more, but Gram cut her off:

"Good. I'll have to explain the delay. We should hurry, I expect."

The wood store wasn't empty when they got there, so they waited for the man to slowly serve his other customers. One of the people was buying goblets, another was trying to decide about the big train in the window. Dicey was glad the store was busy.

While they waited, she showed Gram the boxes she'd been talking about. "You're right," Gram said. "I'm glad you were with me. I'm so defeated, I might just have taken one of those horrible things."

Dicey stared at Gram. Defeated? Well, she guessed she could understand that.

The man recognized Dicey and greeted Gram as if he recognized her, too.

"We are looking for a small box," Gram said.

The slow eyes moved between them and then up to the shelf Gram indicated. "I'm sorry to hear that," the man said.

Gram's eyes snapped at him.

"Your granddaughter was in yesterday," he said. "Let me show you."

He brought down three boxes, each about the size of a loaf of bread. They chose one where the band of black walnut ran like a ribbon, as if it were tying down the top of the box. "How much do we owe you?" Gram asked.

"Nothing," he said.

"Young man!" Gram snapped. "We are not asking for charity."

"It's okay, Gram," Dicey said. At the same time, the bearded man put his hands around the box they had chosen. The cuts on his hands were like the grains of the different woods.

"Yesterday, I thought to give her something," he said to Gram. "I don't know why—yes, I do know why, but I couldn't put words to it. But not out of pity. I would like to give this box to you. I'm honored, you see. You do see that, don't you? But I don't know if you would take it as a gift."

Gram stared at the hands around the box. Then she said, "Yes, I'll take it," in a low voice. "I'll take the gift and I'll thank you for it," she said, more briskly. Dicey could almost hear the creaking of Gram's fingers as she let go of her pride.

"Good," the man said.

They delivered the box to the undertaker, who told them to return at five. Then they had a late lunch and returned to the motel room to pack. They talked about ordinary things, about taking a train to Wilmington and a bus from there to Salisbury. Dicey changed into her brown dress and belted it at the waist. She and Gram weren't exactly going to make a march, but she wanted to mark the formality of the occasion, taking Momma home. They talked about the presents Dicey had bought, of which Gram approved. Then Gram asked, "Wasn't there change?"

Dicey had more than forty dollars left in her coat pocket and she gave that to Gram. Gram opened her purse to put the money in her wallet.

She looked across to Dicey sitting on the other bed. Gram's face looked frightened. Dicey caught part of the feeling.

"How are we going to pay him?" Gram asked. Her voice was whispery.

"Pay who?"

"That undertaker." Gram's hands fiddled around with the money in her wallet. Then her fingers explored her purse. "I never thought—about that expense. I thought about travel and room and meals and even the Christmas shopping. But not about the cost of an undertaker. How could I have been so stupid?"

"We can return what I bought," Dicey suggested. "We could, except the gloves, and I've got four dollars of my own money left."

Gram rustled desperately through her purse. Then she pulled out the envelope Mr. Lingerle had given her, looking at it as if she had forgotten what it was. She opened it and pulled out crisp money in fifty dollar bills. "Five hundred dollars," she said softly. "Five *hundred*—he must have gone to the bank. He must have guessed. I ask you, Dicey, isn't that something for him to do? How did he know?"

Dicey wasn't thinking about anything except that the color was coming back into Gram's cheeks.

"Did I look all that discombobulated when I left home?" Gram demanded.

"No," Dicey said. "You looked like you knew exactly what you were doing. I thought you did," she complained.

"Well, you were wrong," Gram snapped. "But that's all right now. Remind me to thank him."

Dicey snorted. Gram wouldn't need any reminding.

"We'd better call them, don't you think?" Gram told Dicey. "To tell them. And when we'll be back."

"Will they be home from school?"

"I believe in getting things over with," Gram said.

So they called the house in Crisfield. Gram placed the call, placed it collect. She spoke to Mr. Lingerle first, brushing aside his sympathy but making a point to tell him that without his money she would have been in real difficulty. She told him that they were taking a train that got into Wilmington at eight in the morning, and they would take buses down from there. Gram expected to see everybody at home, after school, she said. As far as Dicey could tell, Mr. Lingerle was saying *yes, ma'am* and *yes, ma'am* on the other end of the phone. Then Gram handed the phone to Dicey.

She told James first. "Momma died," she said.

"I figured that out," he told her. His voice sounded thin. "It's better this way, Dicey," he said in that same thin voice. "I read about it, at the library. Almost nobody recovers, when they're as far gone as Momma was."

"You didn't tell me that," Dicey said. "And I don't think it's better, no matter what you say."

"And it isn't as if . . . She really died last summer," James told her.

"That's not true," Dicey snapped, although she understood what he meant. The worst of the letting go had been the hope they'd still had, last summer.

"Yes, it is," James answered.

Dicey stopped arguing with him. She heard Sammy wrestle the phone from James with an angry demand.

"It's not true, is it, Dicey?"

"It's true, Sammy," she told him. "It's really true. She didn't want to."

"How do you know?"

"I don't know, how could I know?" Dicey admitted. "But I feel it. She didn't mind, she never even opened her eyes."

"But, Dicey, I wanted her to get better," Sammy said.

"I know," Dicey told him. "It'll be all right, Sammy, it will. We'll all be all right. Adopted means—somebody wants you to be her family."

"But I wanted Momma to be all right too," Sammy wailed.

"So did I," Dicey said. "But she wasn't." She thought for a minute, trying to see Sammy holding onto the phone, in the living room; trying to see his face and into his brain. "You know what I'd do if I were at home?" she asked.

"What?"

"I'd go out to the barn and sand down on the boat. Is it warm enough to work in the barn? That wouldn't make anything better, but it would make me feel better."

"I have to deliver papers."

"After the papers. Try it, Sammy. If you want to. Let me talk to Maybeth?"

"Dicey?" Maybeth's voice asked.

"We're going to be home tomorrow," Dicey told her sister.

"We're all right," Maybeth said. "Are you all right? Is Gram?"

"Everybody's all right," Dicey said. "Except Momma."

"I know," Maybeth said, her voice sad and musical. "I know." She didn't say anything more, so Dicey hung up.

"I hate the telephone," Dicey announced to Gram.

"You need to have one," Gram told her. "With children in the house. We'd better get going. We have to check out and go over to that undertaker's. Have you kept the box out?"

They had to wait, in a room so thick with the smell of flowers, so thick with slow heavy music, so thick with a soft carpet that soaked in any noises, that Dicey felt as if she was swimming underwater for too long. When the man came out to give back their box, Dicey reached out for it, and held it close against her chest. Gram paid the man silently.

They took a cab to the train station, bought tickets and sat waiting on hard wooden benches. They boarded the train as soon as it pulled into the station. Dicey lifted the suitcase up onto a rack overhead. She sat down by the window and held the box on her lap. After a while, the train started on its way.

It was snowing when they left Boston, in big flat flakes that shrouded the sky. The train rattled along.

Gram got them some supper and brought it back to the seats in a cardboard tray. The sandwiches were wrapped up in thin plastic, and still they were dried out, but the sodas were all right. When they had finished, Gram looked out the window.

"I can't see a blessed thing," she said. "I'm going to sleep." She spread her coat out over her legs, like a blanket. She leaned her head back and closed her eyes, but she continued talking. "It's funny, if you think about it. This is the only time I've traveled out of Maryland, and I can't see a thing."

"Gram," Dicey said, her voice so loud Gram's eyes popped open. "But you knew how to do everything."

"I knew how to do nothing," Gram told her. "I just did everything. There's a difference. You should know that."

"Cripes," Dicey said, remembering how she had followed her grandmother around, not having to worry about anything. "That's brave."

Gram closed her eyes again, and her sudden smile flashed across her tired face. She hadn't slept at all last night, Dicey guessed.

"Tillermans have that kind of courage," she told Dicey. "We have brave spirits. It's brave hearts we don't have. Think about it, girl. Except your momma, she had a brave heart, for trusting people, or loving them. For all the good it did her. I wish I knew." Then Gram's eyes flashed open again, and her face looked entirely awake:

"I have some hope for you, too. You, and all of you. But why they use hearts for love, I don't know."

"It's where you feel things," Dicey said, remembering, feeling. "But not valentine hearts."

Gram agreed and closed her eyes again. "Those bright red

hearts, perfectly symmetrical. And those overweight cupids they put with them, for Valentines, babies with rolls of fat on their legs and chipmunk cheeks. I never could like a fat baby. My babies were skinny and hairy. When she was born, your momma had a head of curly black hair—like a cocker spaniel. Can you imagine your momma like that? Of course, it all fell out within the week, but can you imagine?"

Dicey almost answered this, but she saw that Gram was asleep.

The train made frequent stops, and Dicey watched to see the names of the places. She knew she should put her head back, close her eyes and try to sleep; she knew she couldn't see anything much out of the windows, between the heavy snow and the speed of the train. But she shifted the box against her arm and peered out. Her seat swayed and jounced as the train rattled over the tracks.

After every stop the conductor came by. He looked at the two ticket stubs tucked into a hook above Gram's head. He glanced at Gram and then looked at Dicey. After two stops he finally asked her, "What is that box for?"

Dicey couldn't think of what to tell him.

He began a kind of game, guessing what might be in it. Love letters from her boyfriend, he guessed, and a stamp collection, a pet mouse, her jewelry, something to eat, sea shells, buttons. Dicey got so she was half-waiting for him, and she was ready to shake her head at him, no. The snow lightened as they traveled south. Once, looking out the windows on the other side of the car, Dicey thought she saw water. She was sure she saw a black field that glimmered like water and stretched out like water.

Dicey realized that the train was going the same way the children had, last summer.

For some reason, this disturbed her. She climbed out of her seat, holding the box carefully. It wouldn't pop open; she knew how tightly the lid fitted down. But still, she carried it gently. She found a bathroom at the end of the car and let herself in the door.

This bathroom was smaller than a closet, and somehow it seemed to lurch more than her seat did. She went to the bathroom, flushed, and ran some water in the sink to splash over her face. She caught a glimpse of her face in the mirror, pale above the dark brown of the dress. Her eyes looked wary. She wondered why. Once the box, which she had set on a counter just about big enough to hold a purse, started to slide off. Dicey caught it in damp hands.

Instead of going back to her seat, Dicey went through two cars to find the snack bar. There, she spent a long time looking at the menu. Finally she decided on another soda and a package of potato chips.

To reach her money in the pocket of her dress, Dicey had to rest the box on the countertop. The man working there stared at it. "That's a pretty thing," he said. "What's it for, school stuff?"

"School stuff?" Dicey asked.

"Pencils, erasers, paper clips?"

"Oh," she said. "Oh, no." She took up the little cardboard tray that held her purchases and fled.

Dicey stumbled past people sleeping in their seats. Because both of her hands were holding something, she couldn't grab at seat backs to keep her balance. She had never realized that trains were this hard to walk in.

Back in her own car, she sat down in empty seats across from Gram. Her grandmother was sleeping soundly, even though her head rolled with the swaying of the train. Dicey opened the can of soda to pour half a glass. More than that might spill. She tore the top off the potato chips. She settled the box in her lap.

She felt like she was running away again the way they had run away from Bridgeport, or even before that when Bridgeport was the place they were running to. To be awake in the deep dark of night; that might be what was causing the feeling. Then she could see, as if she held a map in her hand, the places the four of them had traveled over. The snow outside had faded away. Dicey watched out the window.

The train rattled over the Connecticut River, where they had taken a boat to row. She didn't know how she knew so surely that the broad black belt was that river. But she knew. She could remember how it felt to row across the black water and not know what waited on the opposite bank.

Twenty minutes later, the train pulled into the big railroad station at New Haven. Dicey peered out the dirty window, but she was looking at the pictures her memory made. The train pulled out of the station and back into darkness.

The pictures her memory made had songs in them, clearer than the noise of the train. All the songs seemed to be blending together, into music as complicated as some of Maybeth's piano pieces. But Dicey could pick them out, each one, each separate melody.

The people they had been last summer, the person she had been—Dicey guessed she'd never be afraid again, not the way she had been all summer. She had taken care of them all, sometimes well, sometimes badly. And they had covered the distances. For most of the summer, they had been unattached. Nobody knew who they were or what they were doing. It didn't matter what they did, as long as they all stayed together. Dicey remembered that feeling, of having things pretty much her own way. And she remembered the feelings of danger. It was a little bit like being a wild animal, she thought to herself.

Dicey missed that wildness. She knew she would never have it again.

And she missed the sense of Dicey Tillerman against the whole world and doing all right.

But had anything really changed? Dicey looked across to her sleeping grandmother, and she thought about her job and school, about James, Maybeth and Sammy, about Mina and Jeff. She thought about the little boat she was preparing for next spring. She thought about Gram's house, their house, about the fields folded around it and the Bay beyond. Whatever was outside the window flashed past so fast she couldn't really see it.

She thought to herself, she had to let go of what had gone before too, didn't she? The people of last summer. And who she had been.

Dicey felt as if she was standing in the wind and holding up her hands. She felt as if colored ribbons blew out of her hands and danced away on the wind. She felt as if, even if she wanted to, she couldn't close her fingers around those ribbons.

Dicey knew that she was sitting very still on a train, moving across the night. She knew her hands were wrapped around the wooden box that held the ashes of her momma. But she felt as if a wind blew through her hands and took even Momma away.

What did that leave her with? The wind and her empty hands. The wind and Dicey.

As if Dicey were a sailboat and the sails were furled up now, the mainsail wrapped up around the boom, and she was sitting at anchor. It felt good to come to rest, the way it felt walking up to their house on a cold evening, seeing the yellow light at the kitchen window and knowing you would be warm inside while the darkness drew in around the house. But a boat at anchor wasn't like a boat at sea.

Except, Dicey thought, a boat at anchor wasn't planted there, like a tree. Furled sails were just waiting to be raised, when the sailor chose to head out again. And even trees and houses weren't as planted as they seemed to be, and maybe nothing was.

How was Dicey supposed to understand?

Because if their friend Will kept his word and stopped by when his circus traveled north next spring, it wasn't all letting go.

How was Dicey supposed to know what to do?

At that, Dicey closed her eyes and slept.

When she opened them, Gram was leaning over her. "You look better," Dicey announced. The sun was trying to shine in through the dirty windows.

"You don't. Use the bathroom now, we're about to get there. I'll hold the box," Gram said.

Dicey shook her head. She went back to the bathroom, but there was a woman already waiting by the door. The woman looked at her without interest. Then she caught sight of the box. "Is it a present for someone?" she asked. "It would make a lovely planter."

Before Dicey could speak, the woman sidled past an emerging man to slip into the bathroom.

Dicey put the box on the floor this time and rubbed cold water over her face. She polished her teeth with her finger. Then she had to go to the bathroom again. All the time her mind was turning over a question.

She was still stepping over Gram's legs when she blurted it out: "You tell me to let go. But you told me to reach out, you told me to hold on. How can I do all those things together? Gram?"

Gram's eyes took a minute to really see Dicey, as if she had been thinking about other things. "It's nice to know you listen," she answered.

"It would be nicer if you explained," Dicey snapped.

"How can I explain?" Gram demanded. "How can I explain what I don't know?"

"Then why did you say?"

"Because it's what I learned," Gram told her. She reached over to where Dicey's hand was clenched on top of the box and wrapped her own hand around Dicey's. "If it were simple I could explain. But you never know what's the right thing to do. And even that's not entirely true: sometimes I've known. But most of the time—oh, I don't know, girl."

"But you have to know," Dicey said in a little voice.

Gram shook her head. "Don't know why I should. Nobody else ever has. Except maybe your grandfather, and he was always wrong."

Then Dicey smiled.

"And even he wasn't always wrong," Gram muttered. She tightened her hand around Dicey's for a minute before withdrawing it. She laughed briefly. "You couldn't even count on him to be wrong. I might have learned to enjoy him, if I'd tried. I thought I was trying, but maybe I wasn't. But I've let go of that grief and that anger."

"Was that the right thing to do?" Dicey asked.

"How should I know?" Gram answered. "It feels right, and that's about all I have to go by. Or any of us have. And we'd better get ourselves ready to get off this machine," she concluded.

"But Gram." Dicey stood beside Gram. Gram reached up to pull down their suitcase.

"What I mean, girl, is you keep trying. One thing after another. Sometimes just one, sometimes all three, but you have to keep trying. I don't have to tell you that, do I?"

"I guess not," Dicey said unhappily. Gram didn't look any happier than Dicey felt. They stood in the little metal platform-room, where two cars joined, waiting for the train to slow down and then stop.

Dicey tried to think about Gram. Gram had let go of everyone, everyone had gone. Then she and James and Maybeth and

Sammy had appeared. They had made her reach out and hold on. Or she made herself.

Not quite everyone had gone, Dicey realized, with a quick sideways glance at her grandmother's profile. Because there was this one son, John. At least, he was still alive, probably. The idea grew in Dicey like a bubble, swelling out. John had gone away years ago, and—Gram had told Momma that somewhere there was a wedding announcement. If Dicey could find it. If Dicey could write to the address, and even if he wasn't there somebody might forward it.

Dicey could guess what Gram would say about that idea. But, she thought, maybe Gram counted John as one of her mistakes, and maybe Dicey could do something about that. The place to begin looking was the attic. But they had given their word not to go up there.

Dicey chewed on her lip, thinking. There would be another way to start looking. She could think of it.

The train slowed down. They buttoned up their coats against the wind as the conductor came to open the door. Gram carried the suitcase, Dicey carried the box. "We'll get right into a cab, I have no idea when buses run," Gram said when Dicey joined her on the platform. "There's a lunch counter at the bus station," Dicey remembered.

But a small group of people hurtled down the platform toward them.

"We came to meet you!" Sammy called.

He threw himself at Dicey, and then burst away to throw himself at Gram. By that time, James and Maybeth came to stand close. Gram put down the suitcase and gave everyone a kiss on the cheek or forehead, depending on which was closest. She hugged each one of them tightly to her. James's surprised eyes turned to Dicey, but she couldn't begin to explain.

Mr. Lingerle drifted up. "I hope you don't mind?"

"We'll never all fit into your car," Gram declared. But she was smiling.

"What's that?" Sammy asked, reaching out for the box. "Is it for me?"

Dicey shook her head.

"We'll explain later," Gram said. "No questions. We haven't eaten," she said.

"I never rode on a plane," Sammy said to Dicey. "Or a train either."

Dicey sighed. What was she supposed to say to that? "Why aren't you in school?" she asked.

"It's Saturday," Sammy said. "We had to get up really early."

"Everything go all right?" Gram asked Mr. Lingerle.

"I think so," he told her. "I may never be the same," he added, with a little smile, "but that's an improvement."

"You think so?" Gram asked. "Well, you'd know best."

"Mrs. Jackson asked if you would talk to her," Maybeth said. She was walking between Dicey and Gram. James had taken the suitcase.

Gram's chin went up. "First thing," she said to Maybeth. "Don't worry."

"I think it's for something good," Maybeth told her.

Dicey looked around at all of them, and a lump formed in her throat. They were all here, and Momma too. Her hand tightened around the box. She didn't know if she was sad or glad. She couldn't sort out the sadness from the gladness.

Gram sat in the backseat, with Maybeth on her lap, because even Sammy had to admit he couldn't sit still, even for the short drive to a McDonald's. James was on one side of her, and Sammy on the other. Dicey sat in front.

"What is the box for?" James asked Dicey. "I've been trying to think."

Gram's eyes met Dicey's. Dicey nodded her head, to say she thought it was all right to tell, but she didn't think she could be the one to say it.

"For your momma," Gram announced.

"But Momma's dead," Sammy protested.

"You had her cremated?" James asked.

"So she could come home with us," Dicey told him. His face was stiff, but he nodded his head.

"But it's too small!" Sammy cried, and burst into tears.

"Poor Momma," Maybeth said.

Gram pulled Sammy's head onto her crowded shoulder and let him cry there.

CHAPTER 12

They buried Momma beneath the old paper mulberry tree at the front of the house. James and Sammy dug down into the earth at a place where two big roots forked apart. Gram, Dicey and Maybeth stood and watched. The boys took turns lifting shovelfuls of the dark, soft earth. All around, the ground was carpeted with yellow leaves. A cold wind blew at their backs, from the east. In the west, the sun was setting, behind long streamers of clouds that lay like bars along the line of its descent.

Nobody said anything. Dicey could hear the wind soughing in the distant pines and creaking through the paper mulberry. She looked up into its bare branches.

Clearly visible now were the thick wires that the leaves hid during the summer. The tree had four main trunks, growing out of one base, spreading apart as it grew taller. The clumsy wire ran like a fence between these branches, about fifteen yards up. If the wire weren't there, Gram had told Dicey, the tree would spread out and split, broken apart by the weight of its own growth. Gram told Dicey that the first day Dicey ever came to the farm. "That tree is like families," Gram had said, and Dicey, looking up now at its branches, wondered what, in that case, the wire was like.

Up beyond the branches and over the roof of the house, the sky was a pale, remote blue, across which long clouds drifted.

But on the ground, the sunlight still painted the bare trees and the dry grass with light. When she looked across to the west, she could see the splash of the sun's colors, pink and red, and the brightness that burned behind the long clouds and made them glow around the edges. Dicey knew how the surface of the Bay would look under this early winter sunset, like cloth-of-gold.

The last shovelful of dirt plopped onto the ground. James put the spade down. Gram took the wooden box out of Dicey's cold hands and knelt to place it in the hole. Then she stood up.

Dicey wondered if they should speak words or sing something. She looked at the faces of her family, trying to decide. Maybeth and Sammy stood shoulder to shoulder, with identical wide, hazel eyes, watching Gram. James, like Dicey, stood away. His eyes met Dicey's, as if he, too, was wondering if they should speak or sing.

But Gram, with her curly hair wild and her mouth stiff, bent over. She picked up a handful of dirt and dropped it back into the hole. It sounded almost like rain falling. James followed Gram's example, then Sammy, Maybeth, and at last Dicey.

It was Maybeth who took up the shovel to refill the hole. Dicey took the shovel from her when the job was about halfway done.

Dicey patted the last shovelfuls of dirt with the back of the spade. Then she picked up a few of the faded yellow mulberry leaves. She scattered them on top of the bare place, as if they were flowers. She stood there, in the cold shadowy wind, holding onto the shovel. The last light of the day flowed around them.

"She's really gone now," James said.

"You might say that," Gram answered slowly. "Or," she said, "you might say she's come home now. Maybe it's both. I don't know."

James took the shovel from Dicey and walked back toward the barn to put it away.

"I still love her," Sammy said.

"I should think so," Gram answered him briskly.

Maybeth moved over to stand beside Gram. She reached out to take her grandmother's hand. Gram reached out for Sammy, resting her free hand on his shoulder. They went slowly around behind the house, following the path that led to the back door, and inside.

Dicey stood alone and unmoving. But inside her head her own voice spoke clearly: "Gone and home." Those were all the words to speak over Momma, all the songs to sing.

Home and gone. It didn't seem possible that both of those words could be true, but they were. Dicey shivered in the wind and went inside.

She found the kitchen empty, but the sound of music from the piano drew her to the living room. James was poking at the fire with a long piece of kindling, stirring up the flames. Sammy lumbered into the room, staggering under an armload of logs. He and James put a couple onto the fire and piled the rest beside the hearth. The flames leaped up.

Dicey went to stand behind Maybeth. The music came out under Maybeth's fingers, strong and orderly, the notes mingling, the melodies winding together. It was that Bach again, Dicey saw. When Maybeth finished, she put her hands in her lap and turned around to look at Dicey. "I wanted to sing something, but I didn't know what."

"I know," Dicey said. "Where's Gram?"

"She went upstairs," Sammy said. "She said to wait here. I heard her pulling down the stairs to the attic," he announced. "James says it wasn't but it was."

James didn't look around to contradict this. He just shrugged his shoulders. James, Dicey thought, said it wasn't because he hoped it was.

They heard Gram's footsteps coming down the stairs. When

she entered the living room, she carried a pile of thick leather albums, a pile so tall she had to peer over the top to see where she was going. She put them down beside her usual chair.

Gram had taken off her stockings and loafers and was wearing a pair of heavy socks on her feet. Her cheeks were streaked with dust.

"I found these," she said, wiping her hands on her skirt. "I thought you might be interested."

"Pictures!" cried Sammy, jumping up.

"There's some other stuff up there—toys and I don't know what-all. You ought to take a look, someday when it's sunny. It's cold enough up there now to freeze off a mouse's ears. You hear me?" Gram demanded, as if they were all in trouble.

"I hear you," James answered. Dicey smiled.

"That's settled then," Gram said. "I thought you might like to look through these, while I get us some dinner. Won't be much. I haven't looked in the refrigerator."

"But Mr. Lingerle said he was going to get some pizza for us," James protested. "He's going to bring it by, in a little while."

"Why would he do a thing like that?" Gram asked.

"Because we never had it," Sammy said. "We told him and he was surprised. Did you ever?" he asked Gram.

"Never wanted to. Who could want to eat something that looks so oozy?"

"I could," Sammy told her.

"Because he's our friend," Maybeth answered Gram. Gram nodded.

"It's not oozy," Dicey argued.

Gram snorted.

"It's succulent," James suggested.

Gram snorted again.

"And he's going to have things on it," Sammy told her.

"Things on it?" Gram asked. "Things?" she repeated, as if the word squirmed in her mouth.

Dicey giggled.

"Pepperoni and sausages, he said, and mushrooms and onions," James told her. He was trying not to smile. "Smothered in melted cheese. Succulent," he said again, with satisfaction.

"Oozy," Gram repeated. "Oozy with *things* on it."

"Tell you what," Dicey offered. "I'll make you a couple of scrambled eggs, there must be eggs in the ice box. And a nice piece of toast."

Gram's mouth twitched.

"And there'll be more pizza for me to eat!" Sammy cried, clapping his hands.

At that, Gram laughed aloud. "Then let's look at these pictures. Where shall we start?"

"With the oldest," James suggested.

"With Momma," Sammy said.

"You choose," Maybeth said.

"The big brown one, second from the top," Gram said. Sammy rushed over to get it. He joined his brother and sisters on the floor. Gram sat behind them. They crowded their heads together, to see better. James opened the album.

The first photograph showed three children, dressed up for the picture. The girl was in the center, wearing a dress with a sailor top and a pleated skirt. Her yellow hair showed up pale in the black-and-white picture. She was a happy little girl, with round cheeks and a shy smile. On one side of her stood a boy who was wearing a suit. He looked about ten, and big for his age. He had short, light-colored hair, and his hands were held behind his back. His dark, angry eyes looked at the camera. On the other side of the girl was a boy younger than she was, dressed in a sailor suit that had short trousers. This boy was dark and slender, and he looked as if he had trouble standing still for the camera. His eyes had mischief in them.

"Where's Bullet?" Sammy asked.

"There," Dicey pointed to the little boy.

"But he's supposed to look like me," Sammy protested. "And he looks more like James."

"There are other kinds of resemblances," Gram said from behind them. "Like wanting to get his own way and not giving up, ever."

The children thought about this, studying the pictures. Dicey considered her uncle John. She wasn't sure, any more, about what she ought to do, if she ought to try to do anything, to find him. She wasn't even sure about what she *wanted* to do. She let her eyes fall from the page and rested them on her hands, as if—she was a boat and dropping anchor to let the storm blow itself out. The confusion was like a windy storm. And then she smiled to herself, because she had a suspicion that the confusion wasn't a storm that would blow itself out, it was going to be a permanent condition. Well, she guessed she could get used to it. She guessed she might even get to like it. She might as well try to like it, she thought, since it wasn't going to go away. About Uncle John, she would wait and see—wait a week, a month, a year, and see what she thought then.

It was Sammy who broke the silence and answered his grandmother's remark: "Does that mean," he asked solemnly, "that I'm going to get chickens?"

Gram snorted.

"Are they going to a party?" Maybeth asked. "Momma looks like she's going to a party."

"Yes, they were," Gram said. "Bullet—he didn't want to go. He wanted to do some fishing or crabbing or anything that would prevent him from spending the afternoon indoors being polite. Now I notice, John doesn't seem too happy about it either, does he? Did I ever tell you how Bullet didn't go to that party?" she asked.

Well, of course she hadn't, and she knew that as well as they did.

So Gram began the story.